DEATH NO STRANGER

REGAN BARRY

Our dead are never dead to us, until we have forgotten
them.

— GEORGE ELIOT

Every night it's the same.

I see through his eyes, hear through his ears, feel through his skin. It's a waking vision, a prophecy, fulfilment date unknown.

In the darkness, his shadow grows large and small as he steps through pools of light spilling from streetlamps. His breath rasps and his footfalls smack on wet pavement, loud in the quiet that falls between passing cars. Chilled air, humid from the day's rain, clings to his face and probes the collar of his coat.

He always approaches along Queen Edith's Way. The grandiose houses loom threateningly as he passes, as if outraged by this invader from a lower, lesser stratum of society.

He turns the corner, and my perspective shifts. He's in the street where I live. Here, it's quieter and darker than the main road. Not a soul is about. It's too late even for the London commuters to be on their way home; too late and too cold for dog walkers.

The exterior of my house glides into view and advances steadily, though I am *inside*.

The scene freezes.

He's halted.

I see my home: solid, square, respectable, expensive. Four

sets of windows surround a central front door. A child's idea of a house made real. The skeleton of a wisteria clutches the red-brick wall, and tough, evergreen shrubs dot the garden beds. Not a weed in sight. So very respectable.

Why does he pause? Is he checking he has the right place? Or is he figuring out the best way to break in? I cannot hear his thoughts.

The vision has replayed in my mind night after night, over and over, ending at this point and starting again. But this time it doesn't flip back to the beginning.

Tonight, he moves forward, closer to the house—

'Are you feeling all right?' Thomas asks.

My husband's words suck me back to the warmth and comfort of our living room. Thomas sits in his armchair watching a political debate programme on the television, idly holding a half-empty whisky tumbler, knees splayed. He's loosened his tie and unfastened the top button of his shirt.

I sit on the sofa. 'I'm fine. Why?'

'You gave a little gasp just now.'

The light cast by standard lamps in two corners of the room highlights the grey in his hair and deepens the lines on his face. He's aged a lot these last five years.

I attempt a smile. 'Did I? I-I just remembered something I've forgotten to do at work.'

He nods. 'The central's too high.'

'Sorry?'

'The central heating's set too high. It's the depths of winter and I'm sweating.'

'It'll turn itself off in a minute.'

'Hm. Don't worry about it.'

'What?'

'The thing you forgot. I'm sure it can wait until morning.'

'Yes, it can.'

'Are you sure everything's all right?' He turns towards me. 'You look pale.'

'Yes, I...' The vision flashes before me again, stronger than ever.

He's close to the house now.

He's standing outside the front door in the dark. Thinking? Waiting?

'Phillipa,' says Thomas. 'Phillipa. What's wrong?'

I'm back in the lounge. The room is solid, real. Not a waking nightmare. The only sounds are from the television—strident voices arguing punctuated by the calming tones of the host—not the crackling of car tyres over wet tarmac or the dripping of rain-sodden trees. The two lamps gifted by Thomas's father at our wedding provide illumination, not the overhead glare of sodium streetlights.

'Did you have a difficult day?' Thomas asks.

'Yes, I did,' I reply, glad of the excuse he's handed me, 'it was rather challenging.' He knows I cannot say more. Patient confidentiality regulations forbid me from mentioning anything about what I do, except in the vaguest terms.

He reaches across and squeezes my hand. 'I know I've said it before, and I know what your answer will be, but you *could* give it all up tomorrow if you wanted to. Lord knows we can afford it now.' He doesn't only mean his recent move to a new, more profitable practice. The inheritance from his father's estate has paid off the house and all our bills and still left a sum we could retire on comfortably.

'Will *you?*' It's my standard response, given reflexively. I'm convinced the final seconds of my life are ticking away.

'What? Resign?' Thomas snorts with derision at the idea. 'After all the work I've put in? You must be joking.'

It was not supposed to be like this. I've misjudged things. Misjudged *him*.

I could phone the police, but what would be the point? The station is halfway across the city, and our area is not the sort of place police cars patrol. They would never get here in time. Anyway, I cannot move.

I can only watch, with two sets of eyes. Part of me sees the jumble of colours and shapes on the television screen and, in my peripheral vision, Thomas.

Another part of me sees my home from the outside. The heavy living room curtains are closed and the lamps' light is too weak to penetrate them.

Perhaps he's wondering if we've already gone to bed. Or does he suspect we have an alarm?

We don't have an alarm.

Question Time is finishing. The host is telling the audience the location of the next show. I won't be seeing it.

Thomas presses the button on the remote to turn off the television and, with the effort of someone who has been sitting for a couple of hours, gets to his feet.

I don't move.

'Coming to bed?'

I stare at him.

'Phillipa...' He leans over me, peering into my face.

A tap sounds at the window.

'What was that?' He walks four steps towards the curtains, lifts one and pulls it back.

He gasps, a great whoop of indrawn air. The sound is so dramatic it's almost comical, like something out of a bad horror film.

His hand jerks backwards, dropping the curtain.

'Someone's there!'

He faces me for my reaction, but still I cannot move, cannot respond.

With horrified fascination, he lifts the curtain again and peers into the darkness. Several moments later he says, 'Whoever it was, he's gone. I didn't recognise him. Must have been some homeless person.' He releases the heavy fabric and the curtain closes once more. 'Should I call the police? Or maybe I'll just go out and take a look around.'

In high-stress situations, people get the urge to fight or run away. They can also freeze, especially when they feel threatened. In prey animals, freezing is common.

I am not prey.

I snap out of my fixed state and stand up. 'The police won't get here in time.'

I look around the room for something heavy or sharp.

'In time for what?' Thomas asks.

The sound of shattering glass explodes from somewhere in the house.

My husband makes the whooping noise again. He is bug-eyed.

The kitchen. The noise came from the kitchen.

I see the poker by the fire. It's not much of a weapon, but it's better than nothing. As I reach for it, the living room door slams open.

He's got a knife. My knife from my kitchen.

The three of us are frozen.

He looks different from how I remember him. His hair is slick from the damp night air and lies flat against his scalp. Sweat makes his skin glisten, and the light from the lamps throw shadows on his face. He looks older and, unsurprisingly, far more threatening. Or is it only that he's dropped the mask he always wore?

He doesn't speak, only looks from Thomas to me, grinning, deciding. I know his thought processes. He's pleased he got the right house, delighted as he anticipates fulfilling his most basic desire. It will give him a thrill, and afterwards he'll dwell on the memory, reliving the pleasure.

I hear choking. It's Thomas.

The intruder makes his decision. It is five strides of his long legs from the doorway to my husband, accomplished in a couple of heartbeats. The thrust of the cut is expert. Blood spurts from Thomas's neck. He has done nothing to defend himself.

I hear him fall, but now I cannot see him. All I can see is the blood-drenched knife and the blood-splashed hand that holds it.

Somewhere near my feet Thomas is dying.

The knife occupies my vision because it has turned to me. He is slowly moving in my direction. I tear my gaze from the blade and look into his face. The rush he's feeling emanates from him like white heat.

I glance at the poker but it's impossibly far away. The sofa blocks my route to the door.

I don't stand a chance.

Our gazes meet, each knowing what the other is thinking. He takes his final step. He's so close I can smell the scent of damp wool and night air on his coat.

CHAPTER ONE

Shauna Holt lay on her stomach on the cold ground, surrounded by tall clumps of dew-speckled grass. She'd been lying in the same spot since before dawn, and a chill had settled in her bones. Slowly and carefully, she rolled her shoulders and drew circles in the air with her toes, but the actions didn't do much to get her blood moving.

Propping herself up on her elbows, she took a peek between the clumps.

Nothing.

Rough grassland spread out before her in the first light of day, night shadows still clinging on among the tussocks. Wicken Fen was one of the few remaining wild fens in England. Over 800 acres of fenland, reed beds, marsh and farmland.

At this hour in the middle of winter, it was predictably deserted.

Plumes of warm breath puffed from her lips, obscuring her view. She lifted her binoculars and peered through them, gently adjusting the focus. Frustratingly, tantalising rustles sounded from several spots in the landscape, accompanied by swaying and quivering vegetation.

She couldn't cover all the potential sites at once. She would have to pick one to concentrate on. She focused on the area nearest her where the long grass had intermittently, subtly, moved.

When the moment came, she would have to be quick. She would only have time to get off a few shots.

Long minutes dragged out. Her elbows grew sore from constant pressure, and the awkwardness of her position made her back ache.

'Come on,' she muttered. 'I haven't got all day.'

The grass in her chosen spot shivered, and her stomach tightened. Was this it?

A loud, electronic buzz shattered the early morning quiet, and a startled owl broke from the place Shauna had been watching. The bird's broad wings silently beat the air, pulling it upwards. Within a couple of seconds, it was flapping away into the distance.

'*Shit*!'

She'd set her mobile's wake-up alarm to its loudest pitch, worried she wouldn't wake up in time to see the short-eared owls. Or she *thought* she'd adjusted the volume of the alarm. She'd clearly maximised the ring tone instead. Her phone was also vibrating in her back pocket like a trapped bee.

All hope of photographing an owl gone, she sat up. The remaining fen birds not already scared off flew up in a commotion, squawking warnings and threats.

Damn! It was—she pulled her phone out and checked the time—six forty-five. Wasn't she allowed any time off?

She thumbed the icon to accept the call. 'What is it?'

Before the caller could answer, she snapped, 'This had better be important.'

There was a pause before a female voice replied tersely, 'A man's been found dead in a house just off Queen Edith's Way. Uniform discovered the body about five minutes ago.'

'Right. So, an ambulance wasn't called?'

'There didn't seem to be much point. He's cold and lying in a pool of blood with his throat cut. DCI Bryant has put you on the case.'

Shauna could almost hear a question underlying the desk sergeant's words: *Is* that *important enough for you?*

'Okay. Text me the address.'

She began to trudge back to her car, parked in a lay-by a quarter of a mile away.

'Bryant has assigned DS Fiske to work with you. Would you like me to call him?'

'No, I'll do it. I have his number. Er...sorry for being sharp with you just now. You caught me in the middle of something.'

'Don't worry. I've had worse. Early mornings were a *special time* for me and my husband, too, when we got the chance. Before the divorce.'

'Oh, I wasn't...I mean...I'm at Wicken Fen.' The more exact response, *I was lying in mud trying to get a photo of a bird*, didn't seem wise, unless she wanted the desk sergeant to think she was completely insane.

'Wicken Fen?' The second portion of the sergeant's question —why on Earth would Shauna visit that desolate place at dawn on a freezing February morning—hung in the air, unasked.

One week into her new posting and she was already the oddball at Cambridge Major Crime Unit.

'Anyway, thanks. I'm on my way.' She slipped her phone into her coat pocket and took out her keys to unlock her old Corolla.

By the time she arrived at the city a foggy pall hung over it, the sun a spot marginally brighter than the rest of the misty grey sky. The early morning rush hour had already begun. The scene was nothing like the images promoted by the tourist companies —the grassy meadows of Midsummer Common, students lazing on the lawns of Jesus Green or punting on the Cam, the ancient, grand edifices of the University.

Those images were not what had drawn her to the place, so her illusions hadn't been shattered. Every city had its ugly side, in appearances and in people.

———

Crime scene tape stretched across the open gateway of number 23 Maiden Close. That, along with the incident tent erected in the street and the police presence had drawn out groups of neighbours to watch the proceedings, despite the cold. The local newspaper had sent out a reporter and photographer, too. Somehow, as Shauna reached the outer cordon, the two of them sensed she was someone important and rushed over. A uniform told them to keep back as she went into the tent to put on PPE before going into the house.

The central heating was on and the home was warm, though the front door must have been open for hours. An unfortunate effect of the warmth was to heighten the stench of blood and death permeating the place, though the smell didn't affect Shauna as much as it had at the start of her career. In her years in the police service, she'd encountered her fair share of victims of murder and suicide, and people who had died from what turned out to be natural causes. Death was no stranger to her, but she'd hoped her relocation to Cambridge would mean she wouldn't see quite so much of it.

It seemed her wish wasn't about to come true.

Number 23 seemed tastefully decorated and well-kept at first glance, as might be expected of a house in that expensive area of the expensive town.

She headed towards the sounds of activity coming from the first door on the right in the hallway. Will Fiske had already arrived and was easily identifiable as the only person who wasn't doing anything. While the SOCOs were taking evidence samples, he was looking down at the body, his arms folded over his chest.

Shauna had only met the young DS a week ago, during her general introduction to the team. He'd been working on a different case then. Perhaps it was wrapped up or DCI Bryant had pulled him off it to work with her. Perhaps Bryant saw potential in Will and was giving him the chance to show his worth. Or perhaps he wanted a local lad to keep an eye on the upstart who had just arrived from the Big Smoke.

From what she'd seen of him, Will fancied himself a bit. His choice of clothing epitomised the phrase smart casual. His hair was well cut and he kept his beard clipped to fashionable stubble. Not that trying to look good was necessarily a bad thing.

'First impressions?' she asked as she joined him.

The victim sprawled on his back next to the fireplace, his arms thrown up, legs akimbo, a look of profound astonishment on his face. A gash in his neck gleamed wetly, and the blood that had run from it spread out around the body, soaked into the carpet.

Will shot Shauna a glance before replying, 'Well, he's definitely dead.'

Her eyebrows rose. He certainly *was* sure of himself.

'Sorry,' he said, appearing to understand he'd overstepped.

Employing black humour was a way of coping with the gruesomeness of homicide investigations. She decided to let it go.

'Excuse me,' said the SOCO photographer. 'I hate to break into your comedy routine, but, if you wouldn't mind...?' She held up her camera.

Will moved out of her way. Shauna ran her gaze around the room. No furniture seemed out of its usual place and nothing else appeared to have been disturbed. An empty whisky tumbler lay on the floor a couple of feet away from the body. Blood had hit the fireplace before the victim collapsed. Other than the obvious, the scene wasn't telling her much.

She said to Will, 'Let's have a look around.'

As they left the bustle of the living room, he said, 'You should probably begin at the kitchen.'

'Upstairs first.'

The house was four-bedroomed. Two of the rooms had been turned into home offices, a third seemed to be a guest room, and in the fourth, the master, the king-size bed was made. Wardrobe doors and drawers were closed. Opening them, Shauna found women's and men's clothes.

She asked, 'Do we have a name yet?'

'Thomas Edwards. He's a solicitor.'

'Do we know where his wife is?'

'No. I checked for a handbag, couldn't find any except empty ones in the wardrobe.'

Downstairs, the kitchen looked exactly as she would have expected in that expensive area, with one exception. Gleaming saucepans hung from a rail, an Italian coffee machine stood on the worktop, tea towels were folded neatly on a shelf. The only thing out of place was the frosting of shattered glass from the outer door over the quarry tile floor.

'Attacker's entry point,' said Will.

'Yeah,' Shauna replied hesitantly.

'No?'

She looked around the room. 'The broken glass is the only evidence of disturbance. Like the rest of the place, nothing in here seems disordered. The murder doesn't look like a burglary gone wrong. If it wasn't a burglary, that means no burglar, and perhaps no forced entry.'

'You think the perp smashed the window after committing the murder to make it look like someone broke in?'

She replied, 'Just thinking aloud. Who raised the alarm?'

'Postwoman found the door wide open and no one around.'

A man in a crime scene suit walked in.

'Dr. James, forensic pathologist,' he said. 'I won't shake hands. Just had a look at the body.'

He was mid-fifties and tubby, the suit stretched tight across his belly. Like all the pathologists Shauna had ever met, he had a natural cheeriness about him.

She introduced herself and Fiske.

'It's okay,' said Will. 'We've already met.'

'Can you give me a rough estimate of time of death?' she asked.

'From the state of the body, I'd say about between ten last night and one in the morning.'

'The central's on a timer,' Will remarked. 'Assuming no one fiddled with it, the heating went off at eleven and turned on again at six.'

Perhaps Will Fiske wasn't all nice hair cut and trendy gear after all.

'A cold house for a few hours might push the death forwards a little,' said James, 'but, honestly, with a corpse as fresh as this, it won't make a lot of difference. Anyway, I'm heading off now.'

'All right,' said Shauna. 'Nice to meet you.'

When the doctor had left, she returned to the hall.

A tall, thin, corner cupboard stood to the left of the front door. China ornaments sat behind glass in the top half. On the shelf at waist height was a small pile of letters. She picked them up.

Most were unopened and appeared to be junk mail. One looked like a council tax bill.

'Mr T. Edwards and Dr P. Edwards,' she read aloud. 'Dr P. Edwards.'

'All the rooms and the garden have been searched,' said Will. 'There's no sign of her.'

Three detective constables were waiting when Shauna arrived at the incident room at Cambridge Central Police Station. She only remembered the name of one of them: Connor Payne. Pale, skinny, mid-twenties, acne-scarred and serious.

As she pulled off her woolly hat and unwound her scarf, she mentally scrambled for the names of the other two.

'Jas,' said Will, 'it's good to see you here. This is your first case, isn't it?'

Jasmine Singh. That was it.

The young constable blushed as she replied, 'Yes. Can't wait to get stuck in.' She was short, round-cheeked and probably the most harmless-looking police officer Shauna had ever met.

'Good,' said Shauna. 'There's plenty to get stuck into.'

She turned to the third DC. He was six feet tall plus some and had the chest and arms of someone who spent most of his free time in the weight machine section at the gym.

'Sorry,' she said, 'I'm terrible with names. You're...?'

'Alfie Hepplethwaite.'

How could she have forgotten?

'Alfie, great. So, Alfie, Connor, Jas, a man has been killed in cold blood in his own home in a respectable leafy suburb of

Cambridge. This isn't a pub brawl gone too far or drug deal gone wrong, and if the killer wanted to trick us into thinking it was an unfortunate outcome of a burglary, they did a piss poor job of it. Let's get started.'

The three DCs were giving her funny looks. It was then she realised she was still wearing her birdwatching clothes, complete with muddy knees and grass stains. Standing next to Will, who, despite the earliness of the hour, had somehow managed to dress like he worked in the City, she must look like she'd been dragged through a hedge backwards. There was no point in trying to explain.

She briefly outlined the details of the case before saying, 'We need to find the families of the victim and his spouse. DS Fiske and I will break the bad news to Thomas Edwards' parents, assuming they're still alive. But our immediate concern is locating the wife, Phillipa Edwards. Jas and Alfie, I want you to canvas the neighbours, not only about what they saw or heard last night but also what they know about the Edwards' relationship. Any loud arguments, door slamming, that kind of thing.

'There are two cars in the driveway. We can check if they owned any others, but it's probably safe to say if the wife left the house alone, she was either on foot or took a taxi or Uber. Connor, call the local firms and see if anyone picked up a lone woman in the area last night. Check the hospitals too. She might be injured. Then take a look on HOLMES for any priors for either of them. There might be a history of domestic violence. One spouse is dead, the other missing. I think as soon as we find Phillipa Edwards, we could have our murderer.'

The desk sergeant poked her head into the room. 'The DCI would like to see you, ma'am.'

'Isn't it more likely the wife was abducted?' asked Alfie.

'I haven't ruled it out,' Shauna replied, 'but there were no signs of a struggle or reports of a disturbance. If she *was* kidnapped, she went without a fight. And it's hard to imagine an abduction taking place around there. But you're right to keep an open mind. Connor, everything you can find on the deceased and the missing woman.'

As she walked to Bryant's office, she made a quick, rueful appraisal of her clothes.

Detective Chief Inspector Bryant was based in Huntingdon, but he'd been at Cambridge Central attending meetings for a couple of days. She didn't really have the measure of him yet and she didn't know what to expect. In her years in the Met, she'd worked under several bosses and they'd all been very different in working style and temperament.

'You asked to see me, sir?'

Bryant had taken a long time to reach his rank. Either that, or he'd joined the force later than most. Or he looked much older than his age. His hair seemed to have been beating a retreat for a long time and now only a few brave defenders clung on at the edges of his scalp. His red-rimmed eyes drooped into the heavy bags hanging beneath them, and liver spots thickly covered the backs of his bony hands.

'Take a seat, DI Holt.'

He laced his fingers and placed his elbows on his desk, opened his mouth to speak and then shut it again as he frowned at her clothes.

'I'm sorry. This isn't my usual work attire. I didn't have time to change before coming in this morning.'

'I see. Never mind. I wanted to find out how things are going.'

'It's hard to say. I only attended the crime scene half an hour ago.' She didn't mean to sound annoyed, though she did.

'I'm aware of that,' he replied, a note of annoyance also creeping into his voice. 'How are you getting on here in the Cambridge Office? This is the first time I've had the chance to catch up with you since you arrived, and I wanted to be sure you're settling in.'

'Oh, I'm getting on fine, thanks. Everyone's been very nice.'

'Good. I imagine things are a bit different from what you're used to.'

'In what way?'

'I mean we're probably a bit friendlier than they are in London. Bit more open and relaxed. We try to promote a cordial professional working environment.'

Was he really insulting the entire Metropolitan Police Service? Shauna considered herself the master of faux pas and awkward conversations, but Bryant was giving her a run for her money.

'As I said, everyone's been very welcoming. Thanks for asking.'

'Excellent. I decided to make you SIO as, frankly, you're the most experienced DI we have on the team at the moment and I'm up to my eyeballs. It looks like this is going to be a high-profile case.'

His meaning was unstated but clear: the public would be watching and judging how the police handled the investigation, and he was making her senior investigating officer because he thought she would put on a good show. The detective from the Met should know the ropes on that score.

'I understand. I thought murders are probably rare in Cambridge.'

'Yes, things are pretty quiet here compared to the inner cities, though we do have our share of the usual undesirables.'

'I'll do my best, sir. Talking of which...?' She half-rose from her seat.

'Yes, yes, I won't keep you any longer. Just wanted to touch base with you. I'll be back in Huntingdon tomorrow, but I expect regular updates.'

'Of course.'

On her way back to the incident room, Shauna had the sensation of being squeezed in a many-sided vice. There was the usual pressure of a murder case, plus the fact she was the new hire and all eyes were on her, and now the DCI had added public scrutiny and his own expectations.

When she arrived, Jas and Alfie had already left to talk to the Edwards' neighbours and Connor was on the phone. A white handkerchief in a transparent evidence bag sat on a central table.

Will looked up from his computer. 'A SOCO found it under the sofa. Thought it was a bit strange so they bagged it and brought it in.'

Wrinkling her nose, she picked the bag up. The handkerchief had once been white but someone had put them in with a darks wash and it was now an unpleasant grey. The edges were frayed and though the handkerchief wasn't obviously dirty, neither was it clean.

'Yeah,' said Will. 'Probably not significant. If I had a handkerchief like that I'd hide it too.'

Shauna put the bag down. 'Forensics going to collect it for testing?'

'Yeah. Hey, you'll never guess what Phillipa Edwards does for a living.'

'You're right. I won't. So you're going to have to tell me.'

'She's a psychologist.'

CHAPTER THREE

Sleet was beginning to fall as Dr Ruth Terrell pulled into the prison car park. She parked, picked up her briefcase from the passenger seat and climbed out of her car, the freezing winter air hitting her like a slap from a cold, wet towel. Ruing that morning's clothing choice of a cotton trouser suit, she shivered and trotted towards the prison entrance, calling out a greeting to Ronnie, the officer on duty in the security booth.

Ronnie, as always, was wearing his hat pulled low over his forehead, and as she approached him she noticed he was peering at her intensely from beneath the visor.

'I take it you've heard?' he asked.

'Um, heard what?' She slowed her pace only a little, hoping if she didn't stop, he might not launch into a long spiel.

The guard's face lit up, and a heaviness settled on her stomach. She wasn't a big fan of gossip, though it was hard to avoid in the prison system. The same couldn't be said for Ronnie. This item was apparently so juicy he was half leaning out through the window of his booth in his eagerness to tell all.

She stopped and waited.

Later, when it was all over, she would reflect how odd it was she remembered the inconsequential details of that day, like

Ronnie's hat and the glee on his face, as if her mind had put down markers to lead her back to the moment her life changed forever. But then she would consider it wasn't so strange. She blamed herself for everything. It was guilt that drove her to remember it all so well.

'I can't believe you don't know,' Ronnie said. 'It'll be all over the news by this afternoon, I bet. I might have to deal with reporters.'

He straightened up, watching for her reaction, delighted to be the first person to tell her whatever it was he'd heard.

She hesitated. The sleet had thickened to heavy, icy rain-drops, and now Ronnie had her attention he clearly intended to prolong the conversation as much as possible. She wasn't in the mood to be baited. She had a long day of assessments ahead, as well as the usual management tasks to tackle. 'Right. Well, I'd better be—'

'There's been a murder.' His eyes widened to convey the grave magnitude of the fact.

'Oh my goodness,' she blurted, dismayed. He hadn't been exaggerating, after all. A murder *was* significant news, and for him to be acting as he did, the victim had to be someone she knew.

He nodded, appearing satisfied.

'Not one of the officers I hope?' she asked.

'No, not a PO or an inmate.'

He let the pregnant pause play out.

She began to grow irritated. Someone had lost their life, and this grown man was making a game of discussing it.

She was about to say, *Well, I'm sure I'll hear all about it soon enough*, and make her getaway when he said, 'Detectives got here half an hour ago. They'll be wanting to talk to you. You'd better get in there.'

'Wanting to talk to *me*?'

Ronnie didn't seem willing to explain further. Leaving the

guard and his smug grin behind, Ruth hurriedly walked the final steps to the prison building.

The gate staff member opened the sliding door to the airlock. Once she was inside, she showed her pass at the window and the inner door opened, admitting her to the stuffy warmth of the interior. At the keys cabinet, she pressed her finger to the fingerprint scanner, triggering it to unlock, removed a key set and fastened it on a chain.

As she turned around, she found herself face to face with a woman and a man. She started in surprise.

'Dr Terrell?' the woman asked.

'Yes?'

'Sorry, didn't mean to make you jump. I'm Detective Inspector Holt and this is Detective Sergeant Fiske. We'd like to have a chat with you if possible.'

'Of course. Er...'

'It shouldn't take long,' said Holt. 'I understand you must be busy, but as head of the Mental Health Unit, you're important to our investigation. We'd like to ask you some questions about Phillipa Edwards.'

'*Phillipa?* Phillipa's been murdered?!'

She reeled. She'd seen her colleague and friend only yesterday, saying goodbye to her metres from where they were standing.

Holt glanced at Fiske before saying something Ruth didn't take in. Then she said, 'Do you have an office where you can sit down while we talk?'

'Yes, that's a good idea.' She crossed the admin section, acutely conscious of eyes upon her. After unlocking her office door she showed the detectives inside before taking her seat behind her desk.

'Would you like some coffee?' she asked weakly.

'Not for me, thanks,' said the detective sergeant, bringing over a chair from the side of the room while his partner took the one opposite her.

'I'm all coffee-d out,' Holt said. 'But make yourself some if you want. I can see this has been a shock.'

Ruth got up and started the machine, realising her face and hair were wet from the rain. She removed what moisture she could with her hands. Gurgles and spurting sounds from the percolator filled the vacuum of silence in the room, and hot coffee began to drip in the jug. Thinking of Phillipa again, she clasped her cheek, her attempt to maintain her usual professional demeanour falling to pieces. Whirling to face the detectives, she said, 'I can hardly believe she's dead. I only saw her yesterday. She was so young, in her forties! What on Earth happened?'

The detectives shared a look.

'Dr Terrell,' said Holt, 'please sit down.'

She returned to her desk with a mug of strong, black coffee, gripping it tightly though it began to burn her hands. A pile of documents sat in front of her—that day's work and more. The contents of the pile changed, but it never seemed to reduce. She put down her mug and slid the papers to one side.

'We're here to discuss the presumed murder of *Thomas* Edwards,' said the DI, 'Dr Edwards' husband.'

'Not Phillipa?' Warm relief washed over her. So her friend wasn't dead after all. 'Oh, poor Thomas! Poor Phillipa. She must be devastated.'

Ruth had talked to Thomas Edwards a few times at social functions and dinner parties. He'd always been quiet and reserved, but not unpleasant. And Phillipa had never said a bad word about him, which was unusual for someone in a long-term relationship.

'Mr Edwards' body was found early this morning,' Fiske said.

'How awful! Did Phillipa witness the murder?' Ruth mentally recoiled from the horrific images flooding into her mind.

Gravely, Holt replied, 'That's the main reason we're here. Dr Edwards' whereabouts are currently unknown.'

'She's missing?! Then she might still be—'

'Right now,' said Holt, 'we don't know where she is or what's happened to her.'

'You don't think...you don't think whoever murdered Thomas has kidnapped her?'

'As usual with this type of investigation,' said Holt, 'we're keeping our minds open.'

Fiske was rummaging in the inner pocket of his jacket. He pulled out a black flip notepad and a pen.

'Are you searching for her?' Ruth asked.

'Naturally,' said Holt. 'That's why we wanted to talk to you. Do you have any idea where Dr Edwards might have gone? Have you spoken to her or heard from her in the last twelve hours or so?'

'I spoke to her about six-thirty last night,' Ruth replied, 'when we left work at the same time. I haven't heard from her since.'

'Would you expect to hear from her outside working hours?'

'It wouldn't be unusual. We occasionally see each other at weekends, but we hadn't made any arrangements.'

'So you know Dr Edwards on a personal basis?'

For the first time, Ruth took a proper look at the detectives, the people who were responsible for finding her friend. For some reason, the woman was incongruously dressed in outdoor gear and hiking boots. She looked about thirty-five years old, her hair was shaggy and black and her eyes were almost black, too, strikingly so against her ivory skin. She had a determined, intelligent look about her, but also a degree of melancholy.

Her subordinate was a few years younger. He compensated for his slightly long face with a scrubby beard and was smartly dressed. He wasn't bad-looking and he appeared to know it.

'Yes, I would say so,' she replied, realising she was opening a floodgate of questioning that could take a while.

But the news had given her another cause for alarm.

'Before we start, I need to make an urgent phone call.'

CHAPTER FOUR

Molly Markson sat at her parents' breakfast table stirring sugar into her sweet, milky coffee. She usually took it sugar free, but today sugar was needed. Plenty of it.

The clatter of the spoon against the mug made her head hurt, so she stopped stirring and put it down. Resting her elbow on the table and her chin on the heel of her hand, she absent-mindedly watched Becky, her sister, demolish her Marmite on toast, crushing the slices in her hands and allowing the crumbs and broken pieces of bread to fall to the plate.

Molly's chest constricted. A sob forced its way up her throat, but she swallowed it.

Dad was making scrambled eggs. Molly could hear each scrape of the plastic spatula around the saucepan with painful clarity.

Returning home after a five-year absence was both comforting and utterly awful. Last night, to escape her conflicting feelings, she'd raided her parents' wine collection after they'd gone to bed and drunk an entire bottle of red while sitting alone in her old bedroom.

Now she was paying the price. Her stomach felt like it was

digesting itself in its own acid, and a headache was threatening to push out her eyeballs.

It had been the state of her bedroom that tipped her over the edge. Nothing in it had changed. Not a thing, as far as she could remember, was different from how it had been when she'd returned to uni after Easter, unaware she would not be coming home at the end of the semester.

Her A level and GCSE files from school still sat in a neat row on the shelf above her old desk; her anime posters remained stuck with Blu-Tack to the walls, dog-eared and faded with age; and her video game collection was thick with dust.

Dad had even made up her bed with her old Laura Ashley duvet set. She'd hated the set, but she'd never had the heart to tell her parents. The same was true now. Some things never changed.

Becky dropped the remaining pieces of destroyed toast on to her plate and sucked butter and Marmite from her fingers.

Only just noticing, Dad said, 'Becky, what are you doing?'

The saucepan hit the hob with an iron clang.

Molly winced.

He wet a flannel, wrung it out and then wiped his daughter's face. Becky sat passively, allowing him to tip back her head and then clean her hands one at a time.

'Why didn't you say something?' he asked Molly.

'I'm sorry, Dad. I must have faded out. Here, let me do it.'

'I've done it now.'

He rinsed the flannel in the sink, and then hung it up before returning to the table to pick up Becky's plate of toast and swipe the crumbs onto it.

Her father was looking more hunched than Molly remembered him. More tired and grey. He'd changed, moved forwards in time since she'd last seen him, unlike everything else in the house.

Her room reminded her of a shrine. Or a punishment.

Here, look what we did when you stopped answering our phone calls and replying to our emails. We acted like you'd died.

Becky slapped the table with both hands and gave a guttural moan.

'Oh, please don't,' Molly said, cradling her head in her hands.

'She's happy you're back,' said Dad.

He'd said the same thing last night. So had Mum.

'Is she?' Molly asked.

'Of course. Can't you tell?'

Honestly? No, I can't tell. I've never been able to tell what my autistic sister is feeling or thinking. I've never had the magical ability you and Mum have. You know that. It's the great unspoken truth in our family.

'I missed her,' Molly said. 'I've missed you all.'

Dad's eyes glanced up from under his greying, unruly brows, questioning her sincerity. He returned to the stove and picked up the saucepan.

She had to admit her behaviour couldn't have given him any cause to believe her.

'I've made you some, too,' he said, scooping out eggs and putting them in front of Molly.

'Oh, I didn't ask...I really can't eat anything. Coffee's enough.' She took a sip of the warm, stomach-settling liquid.

'Don't touch it yet, Becky,' said Dad as he gave her some eggs. 'It's hot.'

He replaced the pan on the stove more heavily than Molly thought was warranted. Then the way he scraped the chair on the kitchen tiles as he drew it closer to the table caused her to wonder if he was doing it on purpose.

Had he noticed the missing bottle of wine? Was he passive-aggressively getting his revenge?

Perhaps not for the wine, but for the five years' absence.

Probably.

She certainly deserved it.

'I'll drive Becky in for you this morning, if you like,' she offered.

'She isn't at the same place any more,' he replied without looking at her. 'She moved to a new school when she turned eleven. Didn't Mum tell you?'

He blew on the scrambled eggs in Becky's bowl and chopped them up to release the steam before pushing the bowl closer to her and handing her a spoon.

'If you give me the address I'm sure I'll find it. I can use the GPS on my phone.'

'There's really no need, love. I can manage. This is what I do, remember? You just stay home and rest today. You should relax, take it easy for a few weeks. You need time to get over things. You've been through a lot. You know you're welcome to stay as long as you like.'

'I know, Dad. Thanks. I appreciate it.'

Becky jabbed at her eggs with her spoon.

Molly watched her sister, who had grown from a child to an adolescent while she'd been gone. As always, Becky betrayed little sign of what was going on inside. Though she sat within Molly's reach across the table, a nameless gulf stretched out all around her—a gulf she maintained with an intractable vigilance.

'I'll see if I need to scrape ice off the car,' said Dad.

As he left the kitchen, Molly got up to wash the breakfast dishes. While Dad was gone she would vacuum and do whatever housework needed to be done. She would make herself useful. It was the least she could do.

When her father returned a moment later and saw her running hot water into the sink, he said, 'For goodness' sake, sit down. There's no need to do that. Everything goes in the dishwasher.'

She turned off the tap and gripped the sink, tensing as she fought back tears. 'I'm just trying to help.'

She felt her father come up next to her. He put an arm around her shoulders.

'I know you are, love. And the best way you can help is to sit down and rest. Watch some television. What is it they say these days? *Zone out.* Maybe you could play one of your games like you used to.'

'I'm not twelve, Dad.'

He gave her shoulders a squeeze, and then walked away. 'Come on, Becky. Time for school. Let's put your coat on.'

Becky voiced her disagreement.

'Come on,' he said. 'Coat on, then in the car, and then you'll see Matthew and Diane, remember?'

This statement had the desired effect. Becky pushed back her chair and got up before walking with her awkward gait into the hall.

'That was easier than it used to be,' Molly said. 'Are Matthew and Diane her friends?'

'No, they're two new staff members. She's taken quite a shine to them. I'm not sure why, but I'm not questioning it. Help yourself to whatever you want while I'm gone. I'm going to pop into town and do a bit of shopping so I'll be a while. Those eggs are still warm. You should eat more. You're looking thin.'

'See you later, Dad.'

'See you later.'

At the sound of the front door closing, Molly relaxed.

Alone at last. Unobserved.

She climbed the stairs to the bathroom, where she found the paracetamol in its usual place inside the bathroom cabinet.

She ran the water until it was cold, then washed down two tablets with a mouthful of water from the tap. Dipping her head down made the pain behind her eyes pulse strongly. She clung to the washbasin, refusing to look in the mirror. Then she sneaked a peek, catching a glimpse of a wild-haired, shadow-eyed woman, and ducked down again.

Waiting for the painkillers to take effect, she took the opportunity to wander through her old home, recalling the memories.

In her bedroom, she recalled lying face-to-face with her first crush, Armand. Both fourteen, they'd talked excitedly about what they would do when they were famous artists. How naive they'd been. What had happened to him? She had no idea.

Becky's room had transformed. It had once been a pretty little nursery. Now it was a place designed to calm her: soft pastel shades, a dimmer switch on the light and a white noise machine. In the kitchen she remembered Dad dropping a casserole he'd made to serve at a dinner party and swearing loud enough for the neighbours to hear.

She stepped into the living room. Here, the scene that flashed into her mind was of Mum wandering in as if lost and announcing Becky's diagnosis in shocked tones. Her sister had been three at the time. Molly recalled her own surprise that her mother, of all people, had apparently missed or explained away classic symptoms of autism in her own daughter.

Now she thought about it, she realised that, with the exception of Becky's room, very little in the house had changed. Her own bedroom hadn't been preserved so much as forgotten, neglected, along with the rest of her parents' home.

She returned to her room. It was time to unpack her things and finally admit she was there for a long stay. When she'd arrived the previous evening, she'd dumped her bag on her bedroom floor, pretending to herself she would only be there a few days. But, in reality, she had nowhere else to go, no money to pay a deposit or rent, and not really much more to her name than the contents of her duffel bag.

You know you're welcome to stay as long as you like, Dad had said.

It was just as well.

The phone rang in the hall, the sudden, loud jangle making her jump and her headache surge. Pressing a hand to her forehead, she trotted down the stairs and, grimacing, picked up the receiver.

'Hello?'

'Molly, how are you feeling? Did you sleep well? I didn't want to wake you before I left.'

'I'm okay, Mum. I'm fine. Is something wrong?' Unless things had changed, her mother rarely phoned home while she was at work.

'Something terrible's happened. A murder. A colleague's husband has been killed and she's missing. The murderer is still on the loose. Please stay inside today, Molly. I'd feel better if I knew you weren't going out anywhere. Stay inside with all the doors locked. Will you do that?'

'Yes, I will. I didn't plan on going out today anyway.'

'Good. Tell your Dad what's happened too. He must have left with Becky by now. Tell him when he gets back.'

'Yes, he's left. I'll tell him as soon as he's home. I promise.'

There was a strained silence at the end of the line.

'Are you all right, Mum?'

'I know the missing woman very well, and I met her husband several times. But I can't talk now. I have to speak to the police.'

'Okay. I'll see you tonight. Take care.'

Ruth hung up, noticing her hand was shaking. Two shocks in as many days, the first being Molly's surprise return last night, seemed to be getting to her. She folded her hands together on her desk.

'Thank you. It's just…If the murderer is a former inmate…'

'We understand,' said Holt.

'Is that likely, do you think?' Ruth asked. 'Could it have been one of Phillipa's patients?'

'We're still in the process of gathering information so it's impossible to say, but, given the line of your profession, we can't rule it out as a possibility. Are you Phillipa Edwards' supervisor?'

'I'm the senior member of the mental health team, though my discipline is somewhat different from the others'. I'm a psychiatrist and my colleagues are psychologists.'

'What's the difference?' asked Fiske.

'I'm a medical doctor. Psychologists aren't usually doctors.'

He frowned. 'But Phillipa uses the title 'doctor'?'

'She's a clinical psychologist who has completed a doctorate degree.'

Ruth gripped her coffee mug, trying to steady her nerves. It wasn't the first time the idea that a former inmate might target someone in the team had crossed her mind. Many of the people she worked with were extremely troubled, affected mentally by experiences unimaginable to most, and the prognosis for their recovery was usually poor. The best to be hoped for was that medication would keep the worst of their symptoms and behaviours at bay—providing they took it. The threat of violence was ever present. Precautions could be taken within the prison, but once inmates were released there was essentially little to be done to protect the staff.

'Perhaps you could start by telling us what you know about Phillipa Edwards,' said Holt.

'She joined us about five years ago. I would have to check her file for the exact date. She's reliable and good at her job. A pleasure to work with, in fact.'

'You said you know her on a personal basis. Are you close?'

'We're fairly good friends, I suppose. We share a love of botanical art and sometimes visit Cambridge Botanic Garden together or go to an exhibition if one is on locally. She noticed my paintings when she came into my office not long after she joined the team, and she told me she'd always been interested in the subject.'

Holt looked up at the paintings.' All your own work?'

'Yes. They aren't very good and they're quite old now. I haven't painted anything new in years. Too busy.'

The detective rose to her feet to study a painting of an iris flower.

'I'm not sure how this is going to help Phillipa.'

'We have a team of officers doing all they can to find Dr Edwards,' said Holt. 'DS Fiske and I are trying to build a picture of her as a person, which may help us locate her.'

'Perhaps you should dispatch officers to the Garden then,' Ruth said, sudden bitterness staining her tone. Now her initial shock was wearing off, her concern about her friend was growing stronger. What could have happened to her?

'I know you're worried,' said Holt, 'but it's best if you let us do our job our way.'

Fiske kept his head down, scribbling.

'How would you describe Phillipa's personality?' Holt asked, her gaze remaining on the watercolour.

'I fail to understand what any of this has to do with locating her kidnapper...' Ruth paused. 'Oh my goodness. You aren't looking for the person who murdered Thomas and abducted his wife. You think Phillipa did it.'

She'd worked within the criminal justice system long enough to know that in murder cases the police's first suspicions often fell on spouses, and with good cause. But she also knew that in this case, the detectives were mistaken.

'We're simply exploring all avenues,' said Holt. 'As I said, it's too early to draw any conclusions. But now you've brought it up... You deal with murderers all the time. Do you think Dr Edwards is capable of murder?'

The detective sat down again and folded her arms as she gazed at Ruth intently.

'Phillipa Edwards, a murderer? I'm sorry, but that's preposterous. A happily married woman with the freedom to retire tomorrow if she wanted to, suddenly turns around and murders her husband for no reason whatsoever?'

Holt's expression hardened. 'As I said, we must explore all avenues. You said she could retire tomorrow if she wanted to. She's only forty-four. The prison service can't pay any better than our line of work. Was her husband wealthy?'

'Thomas's father died last year and the inheritance came through a few months ago. Phillipa didn't tell me the exact amount, but she did say Thomas had suggested she gave up her job.'

'It must have been a lot of money if it was enough for her to retire on. Any idea why she didn't give up work?'

'She loves what she does,' Ruth replied. 'Not many of us can come into the office day after day with her kind of positive attitude. She said she had no intention of retiring. She only told me what Thomas had said in relation to mentioning the money had finally arrived.'

'Was he pressuring her to stop?'

'She only said he'd *suggested* it. He'd bought an expensive car. Perhaps he was feeling a little guilty.'

Fiske looked up from his notebook and asked, 'Was she angry with him for spending his inheritance frivolously?'

'No!' Ruth shook her head. 'You have entirely the wrong impression. I understand why you're focusing on Phillipa's role in this, but you're wrong. She's a victim here.'

'From what you say,' Holt said, 'now her husband is dead she stands to inherit all his money. How would you describe their relationship? Did she ever mention any arguments or disagreements?'

'Detective Inspector, your line of questioning is nonsensical. You seem to be here to uncover information implicating Phillipa in Thomas's murder. I'm sorry to disappoint you.'

'I'd like to see her file.' said Holt.

'You'll have to take it up with HR. I don't have the authority to hand it over to you.' In truth, Ruth was hazy on the exact regulations, but she wasn't about to make the detectives' job any easier now she knew they were searching a blind alley.

She stood up. 'I have a busy day ahead, so unless you have any more questions...?'

The police officers didn't move. Holt gazed up at her with an inscrutable look. After a pause, she said, 'We'll get a warrant to see Dr Edwards' file and the files of the prisoners she treated recently. Do you know of any who were released in, say, the last two or three months who might wish her harm?'

Ruth mentally sighed and sat down again. 'Give me a minute.' She started up her computer. She was familiar with some of Phillipa's patients but not all of them, and she wasn't sure if any had been released recently.

'If an inmate had threatened you, would you be able to do anything about it?' Fiske asked.

'Not as such, no. If we think a patient is a danger to the public we include our opinion in the report.' Phillipa's schedule for the previous month appeared on her screen.

'Are you often threatened?' asked Fiske.

'Probably less often than you might think,' Ruth replied. 'You...I mean, the police...probably receive more threats than us. *We're* here to help, essentially. I think most inmates understand that. I would say our largest area of conflict is around prescriptions. Inmates often attempt to obtain medications they can use as a form of currency within the prison. I have to be very careful about what I prescribe.' Realising an administrator would be better equipped to deal with the enquiry, she added, 'Excuse me a moment.'

She buzzed through to Stella's phone and asked her for a list of inmates fitting the detectives' description.

'It's difficult to truly know a patient's feelings about you,' she said to the officers after hanging up. 'An inmate with no record of violent behaviour might make a veiled verbal threat, while another may be perfectly pleasant to your face but have a list of assaults as long as your arm and be secretly fantasizing how he'll kill you.'

'We'll check out the recent releases,' said Holt. 'If they turn out to be dead ends, we'll cast the net wider. Do you know where Phillipa was working before she joined you here?'

'This was her first appointment after she qualified, which may go some way to explaining her enthusiasm. This line of work takes it toll after a while.'

There were two quick knocks at the door and then it immediately opened. Stella walked in triumphantly, holding a piece of paper. 'I thought you might like a hard copy,' she said to the detectives.

She moved to give the paper to Fiske, but Ruth held out her hand and took it. She scanned the names: Derek Abelton, Joshua Drake and Baram Scott. None rang a bell. She gave the paper to Holt.

'Thanks for your time,' the detective said. 'We'll be going now. Would you mind giving us your personal number in case I need to contact you again?'

Ruth recited it and Fiske wrote it down. Then Holt took out a card and placed it on Ruth's desk. 'You can contact me directly on my number if you think of anything else that might be relevant, no matter how small.'

Ruth picked up the card. 'Do you think it's likely whoever murdered Thomas might go after other psychiatrists' families, too?'

'Likely?' said Holt. 'I wouldn't say so. If this does have something to do with an inmate who knew Dr Edwards, it's probably a personal thing, not something directed at the whole profession. Is it impossible, though? I don't know. You tell me.'

Ruth thought of Molly and Dom at home and decided to call them again after the detectives left.

Someone's mobile rang.

'That's me,' Holt said, pulling a phone from her pocket. She made her way to the door as she listened. Then she stopped. 'Really? Where?' A pause. 'How is she?' Another pause. 'Okay. Thanks.'

She put away her phone and turned to Ruth. 'She's been found.'

'Thank goodness! Is she all right?'

'She's in hospital, but I don't know any more at the moment.'

Tears sprang to Ruth's eyes. 'She's still alive! What a relief. I'd like to see her. Will I be allowed, do you think?'

Holt replied, 'Not yet, sorry. We have to go. Thanks, you've been very helpful.'

The two detectives departed.

Ruth noticed Stella was still in the room.

'Good news, eh?' said the admin assistant.

'Yes, very good news,' Ruth replied, though she remained worried about her friend.

CHAPTER SIX

'That was Connor,' Shauna told Will as soon as they were out of earshot of anyone else after leaving the prison. 'Phillipa Edwards is at Addenbrookes. She was found wandering around a supermarket car park. The staff called an ambulance because she seemed confused.'

'Which one?' asked Will, pressing the key to open the doors of their unmarked police car.

'What?'

'Which supermarket?'

She gave the name of the large, mid-range chain.

'That's a couple of miles from her house,' said Will.

After climbing into their frigid vehicle, she rang Connor back to give him the names of the ex-prison inmates Edwards had treated. 'We need to know where they are now.'

'I'll see what I can find,' Connor replied. 'I asked around the taxi companies and Uber, but there were no pick-ups near Maiden Close in the last 24 hours. Oh, and Thomas and Phillipa Edwards have no priors. The deceased doesn't have any living family. Sending you his workplace. I couldn't find any relatives for Phillipa either. Do you want me to carry on looking?'

'Yes, please. Thanks. Good job.' She hung up and waited for

the address to arrive via text. Knowing she wouldn't have to inform the victim's family of his death was a relief. It was one of the worst aspects of her job.

While she'd been talking to Connor, Will had started the engine and turned up the heating to full.

She pushed her hands into her pockets. 'Right. It's been...' she peered at the clock on the dashboard. '...three hours since the body was found. Assuming Edwards left directly after her husband was murdered, that leaves a long period of time unaccounted for.'

'If she's confused she could have been wandering around.'

'All night, in this weather? I suppose it's possible. We'll see what condition she's in when we get to the hospital.' Shauna peered at the sky. The icy drizzle had finally stopped, but the dark clouds threatened an encore.

'Maybe she was at home all night,' said Will. 'The beds were made, but that doesn't mean she didn't stay there.'

'Doing what?'

'Sitting in shock? Sleeping? Though it would be a cold-hearted person who could sleep with their husband's corpse lying downstairs.'

'Murderers *are* cold-hearted,' Shauna said. 'The ones who plan it, anyway.'

'You think she did it?'

'I don't want to point any fingers yet. Let's wait and see what she says and what the forensics tell us. But most murder victims know their attackers, and she wouldn't be the first woman to murder her husband.'

'She had a spouse sitting on a fat inheritance,' said Will as he drove, 'and a job working with violent criminals, potential suspects to divert attention away from her. If she *did* want to commit murder, staging an intruder break-in makes sense.'

'Doesn't quite work, though, does it? If an offender had a problem with his psychiatrist he would murder *her*, not her husband.'

'She could argue the murderer didn't want to kill her, only hurt her by killing the person she loved. There are some twisted people out there.'

'Yeah, you're not wrong.'

While they'd been talking, they'd reached the A road leading from the hospital into town. Most of the other cars' headlights were shining out, but their bright beams did little to dispel the dreary dullness hanging over the city.

Shauna was slowly becoming familiar with Cambridge roads. Their layout had been designed to carry cars around the outskirts. Heading into the centre was only for people with plenty of time on their hands, as low traffic speeds and traffic controls favouring pedestrians, bikes and buses inevitably reduced progress to a crawl.

'The supermarket will have CCTV in their car park,' Shauna said. 'I wonder if there's any between her house and the shop, too.'

'Doubt it,' said Will. 'It's mostly residential. Some home-owners might have security camera recordings for us to take a look at. Jas and Alfie might turn up something from the door-to-door.'

Keeping one hand on the wheel, he pulled a bag of sweets out of his pocket and offered it to Shauna.

'What are they?'

'Chocolate limes.'

'Chocolate limes? That takes me back. I didn't know you could still get them.'

'I know a place,' said Will in the tone of a conspirator. 'Do you want one?'

'Thanks,' said Shauna taking a sweet.

She knew what was coming next. It was a classic manoeuvre. Put the suspect at their ease. Pretend you're their friend.

Here we go.

Will waited until she'd unwrapped the cellophane popped the sweet into her mouth.

'So, what made you transfer to Cambridge?' he asked.

DS Fiske's interrogation technique was best described as unsubtle.

'Nothing much. I fancied a change of scenery.'

Her obvious, lazy lie hung in the air between them. She was unembarrassed. She wasn't about to dignify his nosiness with honesty, even if she'd been inclined to reveal the truth, which she wasn't.

'Really?'

When Shauna didn't answer, he followed up with, 'Seems odd for someone in your position to relocate to the sticks. It's a step down, career-wise.'

She watched the road in silence, her mind's eye on a different scene. The pall of winter had drained the colour from the day, but the dingy, damp view was far more pleasant than the images Will's question conjured in her inner perspective.

She allowed the awkward silence to play out. As a young woman she would have felt obliged to smooth the conversation so no one felt uncomfortable. She would have made up a joke reply, politely signalling that his enquiries were too personal. But she no longer took responsibility for others' feelings. Something had changed. She'd grown too old or too hard, perhaps.

When enough time had passed for the awkwardness to ease into boredom, she asked, 'What did you think of the psychiatrist, Terrell?'

'*Phillipa Edwards, a murderer? I'm sorry, but that's preposterous.*' he said, mimicking Dr Terrell's posh accent.

Shauna smiled. 'She wasn't very forthcoming, was she? As soon as she got wind her friend could be a suspect, she clammed up. I suppose it's only to be expected, but she works in the criminal justice system. You'd think she would understand we have a process to follow.'

'Yeah,' said Will, 'but she seemed pretty shaken up. Maybe when she calms down a bit she'll be more cooperative, if we have to speak to her again. She knows Phillipa Edwards fairly well from the sound of it.'

'She knew about the inheritance,' Shauna said. 'And the other stuff, the flower paintings—they have a hobby in common, and they've worked together for years. She might be able to shed some light on what's been happening in the Edwards' home lately.'

Will flipped up the car's indicator switch before pulling into the hospital car park.

After crunching up the remains of the chocolate lime, Shauna remarked, 'Let's see what the victim's wife has to say.'

CHAPTER SEVEN

Molly's parents' house was just as much as mess as it had been while she was growing up, or, rather, since Becky had been diagnosed and Dad had given up work to look after her.

Until then, as far as Molly remembered, her mother and father had split the housework fairly evenly, but when everything devolved to Dad somehow much less was done than before. He cooked and did the laundry but rarely cleaned or vacuumed. Molly's room was a bastion of order and cleanliness in the chaotic, dirty clutter. If the situation bothered Mum, she didn't say anything about it.

Molly began tidying up the living room, picking up weeks' old newspapers—who read newspapers anymore?—mouldy coffee mugs, dried-up orange peel, junk mail, toys and take-away containers. The room was disgusting. How could her parents live like this? A faint musty, rotting smell she hadn't noticed the previous night thickened the stale air.

She continued to work, gradually filling Becky's toy box, the dishwasher, kitchen bin and recycling containers. When the living room was empty of everything that shouldn't be there and she'd straightened the cushions on the sofa, she began to dust the surfaces, moving the ornaments to wipe underneath them.

The decision over who would stay at home had made financial sense to her parents, even though Dad wasn't a great househusband. Teachers were paid less than psychiatrists and someone had to be around to care for Becky, whose needs would only increase as she grew older. And Mum had found with the stresses of her job she couldn't cope with housework too. She needed all the time she could get to unwind.

Had the pang of jealousy towards her sister Molly had felt when she heard this explanation been the first she'd felt? Probably not. Until Becky came along she'd been an only child, the focus of Mum and Dad's attention. She must have been at least a little upset at the change of her status in the family, though she couldn't recall clearly.

When the household roles shifted was the first time she remembered a strong response. She'd always gone to a childminder after school, and when she started secondary school she'd come home to an empty house. From the age of eleven she'd been a latchkey kid. Her instinctive reaction to finding out things wouldn't be the same for her sister had been: *Don't I have parenting needs too?* That was what she'd thought, but she hadn't said anything.

She was glad she hadn't. Her parents' world had been turned upside-down by the bombshell that their non-verbal, late-walking toddler had a lifelong, incurable neurological condition. Her role from then on should have been doing what she could to make their lives easier.

She had screwed up badly. Now was her chance to put things right.

She began to imagine the house tidy and spotless. The kitchen was to be tackled next, then the dining room, which, though rarely used, had also built up its own share of rubbish and grime.

When Dad got back from shopping and Mum returned home from work, they would be amazed and delighted at the difference.

She went into the kitchen to get a washcloth. The one hanging over the tap was little more than a rag: grey, full of holes and probably smelly. She wasn't going to sniff it to find out. There would be more under the sink. When she opened the door, a laundry liquid container fell out. Cleaning products of many kinds crowded into the small space, some appearing new and unopened, others years old and probably empty.

A packet of thin yellow sponges sat on top of the jumbled containers. Why Dad continued to use a bacteria-laden rag when he had new cleaning cloths less than a couple of feet away was a question Molly decided to leave for another day, or perhaps forever. She was getting into her stride. She couldn't do much to help her parents, but if the previous five years had taught her anything, she could clean.

She took one of the sponges out of the packet.

As she straightened up, something moved in the corner of her vision.

She froze.

A figure had stepped quickly away from the kitchen window. A man in dark clothing, a scarf wrapped around his face had been looking in...looking at her. She couldn't be sure.

She stood absolutely still, the sponge in her raised hand.

The view through the window was clear. Frost silvered the long grass of her parents' lawn. The bare limbs of the ornamental cherry were silhouetted against the off-white sky. Overgrown shrubs reached across the grass, creating deep black shadows.

Breathing shallowly and fast, she leaned over the sink, half-expecting someone to leap into view. But the wider vision revealed nothing but more garden and the icy path running under the window. Where had the man gone?

Or perhaps he'd never been there at all. Perhaps her mother's phone call had made her expect a threatening stranger. And she was still a little hungover.

She didn't believe her doubts. She *had* seen someone. She was sure of it.

A deeply uncomfortable tingle traced a journey up her back and into her scalp. She turned. The kitchen was empty. She'd almost felt as though the man was standing behind her, watching her.

What should she do? Mum had only said to lock all the doors and windows. She hadn't said what to do if someone turned up.

What was she thinking? The man was a murderer and he was targeting the prison's psychiatrists. He'd come there to kill someone like he'd killed the husband of Mum's friend. She had to phone the police. Where had she left her phone?

She ran into the hall. Her phone was in her bag upstairs in her bedroom. The living room door was open and through it she could see the patio windows.

The man darted across them.

Her throat and chest tightened to scream, but she only gasped soundlessly.

Feeling her legs about to buckle beneath her, she made it to the stairs. She ran up three steps before a bubble of common sense welled up and burst in her mind. The landline. She'd sped right past her parents' house phone. She flew downstairs, the bannister rail sliding through her hand.

Just as she grabbed the receiver, three thuds resounded from the front door. The strange man was standing there, dark and indistinct through the frosted glass. Her parents had a doorbell. There was no need for him to knock, but he'd struck the door with his fist, intent on intimidating whoever was inside. It had to be the murderer.

Her hands were shaking so hard she could barely hold the phone. She jabbed the 9 on the keypad, almost missing it. She jabbed the 9 again.

The letterbox on the front door opened and a pair of bearded lips appeared on the other side.

'Molly! Open the door. I know you're in there.'

CHAPTER EIGHT

Derek Abelton. Joshua Drake. Baram Scott.

As Ruth lifted her hands to type the first name into the prison data base search bar, she noticed her fingers were trembling again. She clasped her hands together.

The news about Thomas and Phillipa had been devastating. Coupled with Molly's sudden return yesterday evening after five years' absence, it was no wonder she was deeply disturbed. She took a few deep breaths.

Over the five years they'd known each other, she and Phillipa had become such good friends. They'd spent so many lovely days together. She loved Dom dearly, but only someone working in the same profession can really empathise with work struggles. And when Molly had cut off contact, Phillipa had been so supportive. She couldn't imagine how the poor woman must be feeling. She had to do something to help.

She took a sip of her cooling coffee and a couple more deep breaths before trying again.

Derek Abelton.

He was a career criminal. Aged thirty-four, he'd spent...she totted up his many sentences... fifteen years of his life incarcerated, firstly in juvenile offender institutions and then in Category

C and B prisons. At Shelby, he'd served two years of a three-year sentence for grievous bodily harm and had been released three weeks previously on licence. If his past history was anything to go by, he wouldn't remain at liberty for long. Recidivism was almost a certainty for people like Derek Abelton, who were often institutionalised and lacked a social network on the outside. He certainly had a history of violence predisposing him to murder, though there was nothing obvious in his file to give him a motive for killing Thomas.

Joshua Drake.

Ruth frowned. How had *he* ended up at Shelby? His offence had been fraud—specifically, embezzlement. It was unusual for white-collar criminals to be sent to Cat C prisons. If the crime was sufficiently serious to warrant a custodial sentence, people convicted of fraud were usually deemed low-risk and placed in open prisons. She scanned the details. He also had charges related to domestic violence: false imprisonment, coercive control, harassment and actual bodily harm. The final charge might explain his presence in Shelby if the attack had been particularly brutal.

Phillipa's husband had been a solicitor. Had he been involved in Drake's conviction for fraud? But Thomas had practised family law, so it seemed unlikely. Perhaps he'd represented Drake's wife in a divorce.

She closed the file on Drake and typed in *Baram Scott*. As the result appeared, the words 'First Degree Murder' leapt out from the screen. She clicked. Scott had served twenty-one years and had spent the last three years of his sentence at Shelby. He'd been released two weeks previously, aged forty-six. A one-time murderer could murder again, and it must have been a shock to return to normal life after such a long period of incarceration, but, again, there was nothing to indicate why he might have a particular grudge against Phillipa. His case was so old, the file contained no details on his crime, only the outcome.

None of it made sense. If the perpetrator was one of Phillipa's former patients, why hadn't *she* been the target, not her innocent, anonymous spouse?

She took another sip of coffee.

Had the murderer grown romantically attached? Transference was a common problem in psychiatrist/patient relationships. Perhaps the attacker had been jealous of Thomas. Murdering the partner of the person you love wasn't the most sensible approach to winning their affection, but if people behaved sensibly, Ruth reflected, she would be out of a job.

What if it wasn't transference? What if the killer had wanted to kill Phillipa but Thomas had protected her? He might have bought her enough time to escape, and then...? Had she been lying somewhere for hours, injured, before someone had happened to find her?

Ruth swallowed as a hard lump formed in her throat. It was all so dreadfully awful. Thomas's killer had to be found.

She closed Scott's file, and then brought up the medical histories of each man. In the duration of her career, she'd read thousands of psychiatric assessments of prison inmates and she saw nothing out of the ordinary in these in terms of their mental health. All their discharge summaries had been completed correctly. There was no mention of a verbal or physical threat made to Phillipa or anyone else. However, that didn't mean none had been made.

Ruth walked out into the main office area. Until then, she'd been unaware of the buzz of conversation going on among the staff, but she noticed it fade to a hush as she appeared.

'Terrible news about Dr Edwards' husband,' Stella offered.

'Yes, it is,' Ruth replied tightly, not slowing her pace as she headed towards Phillipa's little room.

'What did the detectives say?' asked Stella. 'Anything interesting?'

The quiet intensified as the ears of the support staff strained to hear her reply.

'I'm afraid I don't know any more than you do. I'm just glad

Dr Edwards has been found. I plan on going to see her later if I'm allowed.'

'I hope she's all right. We've been talking about sending her a Get Well card and some flowers. What do you think?'

'I think that's a lovely idea. I'm sure she would appreciate it.'

Ruth had reached the sanctity of Phillipa's office. She slipped inside and closed the door with some relief. She was sure the concern Stella had voiced on behalf of the other staff members was genuine, but there was also something vulture-like about the way they fed upon the scandalous events.

Before she had a chance to turn on Phillipa's computer, the door opened again.

She stiffened but then relaxed when she saw the person looking in. A bespectacled man in his mid-forties, Dr Anders Nilsson had joined the psychologists in the Mental Health Unit seven months ago after migrating to the UK to marry his British girlfriend. He generally kept to himself, but he'd been reliable and professional.

'I only just heard,' he said. 'What a nightmare.'

'Yes.' She pressed the computer's power button. 'That's a good word for it.'

'Is there anything I can do to help?'

'I appreciate the offer, but I don't think so.'

Her legs suddenly felt weak, and she sank into Phillipa's chair.

'Are you all right?' Anders asked.

'Yes, I'm just a little shocked, I think.'

'It's been a shock for everyone, but you must be feeling it especially badly. You get on well with Phillipa, don't you?'

Ruth nodded, barely hearing him, hunching over the screen. The computer was progressing slowly through its start up sequence. The department was in need of an IT upgrade. She'd been asking for one for a couple of years, but the answer was always the same: the budget wouldn't allow it.

'So they suspect it was a former prisoner?' asked Anders.

'They're looking at all the possibilities at the moment.' She didn't mention the detectives' insinuations. She didn't want to cast aspersions on her friend's character to one of her colleagues.

'Something similar happened when I was working in Stockholm.'

Ruth looked up at him. 'Really?'

'It was a while ago, a year or two after I started practising.'

'What happened?'

'An inmate escaped—the security at the prison was a little lax. Things were tightened up after the incident, though to be honest I don't think it would have helped. The prisoner was due to be released in a few months, and he would probably have done the same thing as soon as he was free. He murdered his psychiatrist and her family. How he'd discovered the address, no one ever found out.'

Her hand had risen to her mouth. 'The whole family?' She didn't remember the case, which was odd. She was sure she would have heard about something so horrible, even if it had occurred abroad.

'Her, her husband and their two little girls.'

'How awful.'

'It shook up the entire psychiatric community. I didn't know the woman, but naturally I was shocked too. I reconsidered my career choice, wondered if I would be better off working at a hospital or perhaps setting up in private practice.'

'I imagine you would. But you decided against it in the end.'

He paused before replying in his usual mild, even tone, 'There are many dangers in life. One of them is to not be fulfilled by what you do. Do you understand what I mean?'

'I think so.' She had also passed through points of crisis when she'd considered giving up her job, but even after all these years she still clung to the belief she was making a positive contribution to society. 'So you think it could have been one of Phillipa's patients?'

'Who knows?' said Anders. 'I hope you find what you're looking for, Ruth.'

'What?' She'd forgotten why she'd come into Phillipa's office. 'Oh, yes. Thanks.'

Anders left.

His story from his early days of practice hadn't left her feeling any better. She thought of Becky, Dom and Molly. Anyone who was determined to break into her home could do so without much difficulty.

Her resolve renewed, she returned her attention to Phillipa's computer.

Then she remembered she was here to find her friend's hand-written notes, not look at her digital files. The surface of the desk was nearly bare except for the monitor, keyboard and a container of biros. Phillipa kept her office extremely neat and tidy. Psychology textbooks lined the shelves, and her qualifications hung framed on the walls.

Ruth tried the larger of the two desk drawers. It was locked. The smaller, upper drawer opened. Inside was a tray organiser containing stationery but nothing else of interest. If the hand-written session notes were in the desk, they were in the large drawer.

She slammed the upper drawer shut, the sound of the impact loud in the little room.

She sat motionless.

Phillipa's husband had been murdered before her eyes. She must have been terrified. She was such a sweet, kind person. It seemed doubly unfair it was she who had experienced such a devastating event.

Would the detectives investigate the case properly? They appeared to have already seized upon Phillipa as the murderer, which was clearly nonsense.

Abelton, Drake, Scott. The names of the three potential suspects repeated in Ruth's mind as she returned to her office.

CHAPTER NINE

The dark figure of the man was fuzzy behind the frosted glass of her parents' front door, but Molly was in no doubt now as to who he was. How on Earth hadn't she recognised him? Though, she'd only caught a glimpse of him and his scarf had been wrapped around his face. And the news a killer was on the loose —a murderer who might be targeting psychiatrists—might have muddled her mind.

The figure ducked down and the letterbox opened again.

'Molly! Don't you bloody dare leave me standing out here. Open this door, now!'

She backed up to the wall, the small shelf that held the telephone jabbing into her ribs. She reached behind and grabbed it as if it were a secure hold aboard a ship on a stormy sea.

Could he see her through the glass?

Pressure seemed to crush her chest, making her pant.

She took a deep breath in and slowly let it out.

You're being ridiculous. He's never physically hurt you. Stand up to him for once, Molly. Show him he has no hold over you.

She shouldn't be afraid. And yet...

'Molly, I'm sorry,' the bearded lips said. 'I'm sorry for shouting. I didn't mean to frighten you. I'm just angry about what you did. Let me in so we can talk. Sort things out. If you really want to leave, that's fine. But we need to talk about it. You can't just walk out on me. It isn't fair, not after everything I've done for you. Come on, be an adult about this. Open the door. Don't hide from me like a fucking kid.'

She remained still. She didn't think he could see her, but if she moved he might.

Opposing forces pulled at her.

You don't owe him anything. He doesn't deserve your attention or respect.

Face him. Tell him it's over and you're never coming back.

Maybe he's right. Maybe you can figure things out. Things were good once, perhaps they can be good again.

The letterbox rattled as it closed.

The doorbell rang, long and loud.

She stayed frozen in her position in the hall, staring at the indistinct silhouette.

Abruptly, it moved away, and bright sunlight gleamed through the glass.

The tension in her muscles eased. She let go of the shelf.

Had he gone?

Her only view of the front of the house was through the glass pane in the door. She could go into the living room or dining room to peek out, but the glass in the other windows was plain and the curtains were open. She would be able to see the road but she would be visible too.

On the other hand, cowering in the hall was stupid and cowardly. So what if he saw her? She wasn't obliged to let him in. She could just ignore him.

Despite all her rationalisations, she didn't move.

She imagined him roving around the outside of the house, peering in at the windows. That's what he'd been doing when she was in the kitchen. Had he seen her? She'd been bent down at the under-sink cupboard when he looked in. Did he even know for sure she was home? He must have seen the empty driveway and guessed her parents weren't here. He'd decided to take the opportunity to try to speak to her and persuade her to give things another try, as he'd done every time she'd threatened to leave.

When was Dad due back? It had to be soon. Though she recoiled at the idea of her father coming face to face with Daniel, the thought also calmed her. She would not have to deal with him alone.

She waited.

He would have to give up and leave eventually. He must have parked on the road. She would hear the engine start and his—their—car pull away. He had to finally accept she was out or determined to not let him in and speak to him.

Her skin felt hot and uncomfortable as she thought of him phoning around the friends she'd once had and them telling him they didn't know where she was. They would have guessed what had happened, that she'd slipped out and abandoned her husband and marriage without telling a soul.

An age seemed to pass.

How long had she been waiting?

Had he already gone?

She listened, but all she could hear was the distant hum of traffic on the main road.

CHAPTER TEN

Before going in to see Phillipa Edwards, Shauna peeked through the small window in the door to the single-occupancy room. The woman was perched on the edge of the hospital bed, her legs dangling and her hands nervously clasped in her lap. A small, slim woman in her forties, Edwards looked the antithesis of a vicious murderer. Yet neither did she look like someone who had spent the night on the streets. Her short, mouse-brown hair was only a little messy, and her clothes were clean and unrumpled. Her attire was simple but expensive-looking: court shoes, a knee-length woollen skirt, matching jacket and thin turtleneck jumper—definitely not clothing suitable for a night at subzero temperatures.

'She refused to change into a hospital gown,' said the doctor who had admitted her, a diminutive middle-aged man named Patel. 'She's been quite difficult, in fact. Not combative, like some we get in A&E, but...obstructive. Probably not surprising, considering she's confused and upset. I did manage to get some blood samples out of her.'

'Great,' said Shauna.

'She's tried to leave, several times, but the nurses managed to dissuade her.'

'Right. Will, could you request a uniform to watch her?'

The last thing they needed was their prime suspect walking out, taking all the precious evidence on her clothes and body with her. Shauna was surprised Bryant hadn't sent someone to watch Edwards already.

'She has no obvious injuries and she's aware of who and where she is,' said Patel, 'but she...well, I've requested a psychological assessment. I'll leave the rest up to you.'

'Thanks. I might need to talk to you again after we've finished.'

'No problem. Just ask a nurse. They'll know where to find me.'

While Will was on the phone to the station, Shauna pushed the door open and introduced herself.

'A detective?' Edwards asked, hopping down from the bed. She approached Shauna, her eyes wide with alarm. 'Can you please tell me what's going on? I feel like I'm being held prisoner, and no one will explain why. I'm perfectly fine. Why won't they let me go home? I need to call my husband, but I've lost my handbag with my mobile in it. Could you contact him for me? I asked the nurse if someone could phone my home but I don't think anyone has or he'd be here by now. He'll be worried about me.'

Shauna hesitated. Delivering the news of a fatality was always horrible, no matter the circumstances. She stalled. 'How are you feeling, Dr Edwards?'

A creak of the door signalled Will coming in.

She asked Edwards, 'Could you tell me what you remember of last night and where you've been since then?

Frustration crossed the woman's features. 'I need to speak to my husband.' When Shauna didn't reply, she went on, 'Oh, very well. I don't remember last night, for some reason. I went shopping this morning, but when I came out of the supermarket I-I couldn't find my car. I wandered around for a bit, and...I'm not sure what this has to do with anything. I want to go home. I admit I'm not feeling my best, but I'm not so ill I need to be in hospital. Why am I being kept here against my will?'

'I'll explain everything,' said Shauna. 'It's probably best if you sit down.'

'I don't want to sit down. I've been sitting here for an hour or…Oh my god. Has something bad happened?' Her mouth hung open.

'Please take a seat, Dr Edwards.'

She backed up to the bed. 'What's happened?'

'I'm afraid it's bad news,' said Shauna. 'We don't have a positive identification of the body yet, but we believe your husband is dead.'

She watched the woman's reaction carefully.

At first, Edwards frowned. 'Thomas is *dead?* But…' She looked from Shauna to Will, incredulous. Then she buried her face in her hands and shook her head. 'I can't believe it. How? What happened to him?'

'We believe he was murdered.'

As Shauna replied, the image she'd seen a few hours previously flashed into her mind—the darkened, congealed pool of blood, the splashes on the fireplace, the staring eyes and look of horror and disbelief frozen on the victim's features.

'No, no, no, it can't be true!' Edwards' voice was muffled by her hands. 'How? Why?' She stared at the two detectives. 'Why would anyone want to kill Thomas? He never did anyone any harm. He was…There has to be a mistake. Maybe it isn't him.'

'I'm sorry,' said Shauna, 'but we're confident, pending the formal identification.'

'No, I…' The psychologist's head dropped and she touched the bedclothes she was sitting on, as if to reassure herself of their reality. Her shoulders slumped.

'Dr Edwards,' Shauna said, 'can you think of anyone who bore a grudge against your husband, for whatever reason, or might have wanted to hurt him?'

'No one at all. Thomas wasn't the most sociable person, but

as far as I know no one even disliked him. Are you sure it wasn't an accident?'

'We understand this is a difficult time...' said Will.

'I have to ask you again, Phillipa' said Shauna, 'where were you yesterday evening?'

She took a moment to answer, and when she did her voice was soft and trembling. 'I must have been at home, where I am every weekday evening.' Her gaze remained on the bedclothes. 'Is that where he was found?'

'Are you saying you were definitely at home?' Shauna pressed. 'Is that what you remember?'

'I don't remember anything of last night. I'm sorry.'

'What about this morning?' asked Will. 'You said you couldn't find your car at the supermarket car park. What model do you drive?'

When Edwards told him, he shot Shauna a glance. 'Your car is parked in your driveway. You must have walked to the super-market or used some other transportation.'

'I suppose I must have. To be honest, I don't recall. I just knew I was at the shop, so I guessed I must be there to do some shopping, and that I must have driven there as I usually do.' She touched her forehead. 'I really don't feel very well. I'd like to go home now. I'd like to...' her voice caught in her throat, 'I'd like to see my husband.'

'I'm afraid you can't go home just yet,' said Shauna. 'Your house is currently a crime scene. And we'll need your—'

The door swung open and a SOCO she recognised from the murder scene walked in. He was a tall, thin, middle-aged man. *Paul? Peter?* At least Bryant had sent one without being prompted, unlike the uniform required to watch the suspect. The SOCO put his kit on the table.

After nodding hello, Shauna continued to Edwards, 'You might have been present at the murder, so we have to collect evidence from you. Your clothes, nail scrapings, that kind of thing.'

Edwards recoiled, gawking at the newcomer. 'I don't want... What if I refuse?'

Considering the woman's line of work, Shauna found her question a little odd. But then maybe Edwards wasn't familiar with the fundamentals of crime investigation. 'We need to gather all the relevant details to find your husband's murderer, especially from yourself.'

'Why? I wasn't even there.'

'We don't know that. You said yourself you're usually at home on weekday evenings.'

'I think I would remember someone killing Thomas.'

Shauna paused. 'It would be helpful to the investigation if you were cooperative.'

Edwards hung her head again. 'I suppose it would.'

'Thank you. We'll be back to ask you more questions later.'

Outside the hospital room, Will asked, 'What do you think? The news did seem to come as a shock.'

Before Shauna could reply, her phone rang. It was Connor.

'I got the information on the ex-inmates,' he said, his voice thin and high, perhaps due to nerves. 'I've forwarded all the details to your email, but I thought you might want their last known addresses as soon as possible.'

'You're right, I do. Text them to me, would you?'

She hung up and then said to Will, 'Yeah, she did seem genuinely surprised and shocked. Doesn't mean she didn't do it.'

'You think she was so traumatised by murdering her husband she blanked it from her memory?'

Shauna shrugged. 'It's possible.' She was wary of dismissing the grieving widow from the list of suspects. She couldn't allow sympathy to cloud her judgement. Murderers sometimes *were* remorseful when looking back at what they'd done in the cold light of day, but remorse didn't make them innocent.

'One thing we know for sure,' she said, 'Edwards didn't spend the night in a ditch. So where has she been all this time?'

Before paying the ex-prisoners a visit, she had another line of enquiry to pursue. Would she be the bearer of bad news once more? Bad news travelled fast.

CHAPTER ELEVEN

The solicitors' office where Thomas Edwards had worked stood five minutes' walk from Cambridge station. The blocky, sixties-style building was in prime view for commuters trudging home after a long day's work in London, perhaps questioning their life choices. Shauna wondered how many divorces had been triggered by the sign Barker and Partners Family Law?

From the receptionist's lack of surprise when Shauna and Will showed their badges, she knew why they were here. However, she had the decorum—probably from years of dealing with people in the throes of painful marriage breakdowns—not to comment. She politely asked them to wait and said Mr Barker would see them shortly.

As Shauna and Will entered his office a few minutes later, Mr Barker rose and extended his hand. He seemed old enough to have retired from practising as a solicitor. His face was heavily lined though he was pudgy, his belly barely fitting behind his desk as he sat down. The smell of the green leather desktop filled his office along with the odour of dusty books.

'This is about Thomas?' he asked.

'I'm afraid so,' Shauna replied, sitting down.

'I heard it on the radio as I was driving in. We're all in absolute shock, as you can imagine. I'm not sure I quite believed he was gone until just now when Belinda told me detectives had arrived. And...' he lowered the volume of his voice a notch '...he was definitely murdered?'

'We are treating the case as a murder, yes,' replied Shauna.

As Barker sadly shook his head, his jowls wobbled slightly. 'Never heard of such a thing. Not in all my years. Family law is generally the quieter side of the business. No vicious criminals, no ruthless corporations, just people having relationship problems, trying to work their way through life the best they can. Like all of us.'

He suddenly looked so sad Shauna feared he might begin to weep.

But he held himself together. 'I assume you aren't only here to inform me of the loss of a member of our team?'

'We *would* like to ask you some questions,' she said.

'I can spare you ten minutes,' he answered, a professional veneer descending over his features. 'After that, I'd prefer it if you would email your questions to Belinda, who will forward them to me.' The mask lifted, and he continued in a friendlier tone, 'I do want to help, naturally, but having detectives around the place will give our clients the wrong impression. I do hope you understand.'

'We'll be as brief as we can,' said Shauna, 'but we would also like to talk to everyone who worked with Thomas Edwards.'

'I'll see what I can arrange. What would you like to know? Thomas has only...he only started at the practice six weeks ago. I had no complaints about his professionalism, but I can't say I knew him very well.'

Barker proved to be a poor source of knowledge. As well as having little to say about Thomas Edwards as a person, he also didn't know anything about Thomas's cases or if he'd experienced any difficulties with his clients.

After they left his office, Will said, 'I suppose it's only to be expected he wouldn't be able to tell us much. The people at the top usually don't have a clue what's going on. Take Bryant, for instance.'

'DCI Bryant?' Shauna asked.

Will's head jerked slightly as he appeared to realise he might have been too free with his opinion.

'I just mean, the higher ups—'

'I know what you mean,' she said. 'It's okay. You're right, Barker might not have the dirty on the other solicitors due to his place at the top of the hierarchy here, and even if he had, he might not tell us. He wants to protect the rep of his practice. On the other hand, he didn't seem worried. I think he genuinely doesn't believe the killing has anything to do with Edwards' work here.'

'I wonder what Belinda can tell us.'

Belinda was probably the hardest worker in the practice, Shauna guessed. She was the receptionist and, it turned out, also performed secretarial duties for several of the solicitors, including the late Thomas Edwards. They spoke to her in a tiny kitchen and rest area tucked away at the back of the building.

'Sorry to take up your lunch break,' Shauna said.

'It's fine,' Belinda replied, sitting on the edge of a cheap, threadbare two-seater sofa, her knees clamped together. 'As long as you don't mind if I eat.' She took a bite of a sandwich.

Shauna remained standing. There wasn't room to do anything else unless she wanted to squash up close to the secretary. Will hovered at the open door, his notebook and pen at the ready.

'Go ahead,' said Shauna. 'Do you know if Thomas Edwards had been having any problems lately in his work—with clients or his colleagues?'

'I thought you'd want to ask me that. The answer's no. I even checked his meeting notes to see if there was anything out of the ordinary in them. It was all the usual stuff.'

'What about the other solicitors?' asked Shauna.

'They're pretty friendly with each other. We had a little party to welcome Mr Edwards when he joined the practice. Everyone brought their other halves. It was lovely. Nice food.' She took another bite of her sandwich.

'Did Mr Edwards bring his wife?'

Belinda chewed before replying, 'Oh yes, she came. Poor woman. Was she hurt in the attack?'

'Did Mr and Mrs Edwards seem to get along all right?'

'If they didn't, I didn't notice.' Her eyes widened. 'Do you think she might have done it? No, that's silly.'

'We're just exploring all avenues. How was the atmosphere at the party? Were there any arguments or fallings out?'

'No, everyone had fun as far as I could tell.'

Shauna had the sensation of running up against a dead end. 'Okay, thank you. We'll be applying for a warrant for Mr Edwards' files.'

'I thought you would. I'll make sure they're ready for you, but I don't think you're going to find anything suspicious.'

Will put away his notebook, and they were on the way out when Belinda added, 'I know people say you can never tell what goes on behind closed doors, but I'm sure it was a complete stranger who killed Mr Edwards. We're all very normal here.'

———

'It's Donne Crescent,' said Shauna, checking the address Connor had texted of one the former inmates of Shelby Prison, Baram Scott. She'd just hung up after talking to the SOCO at the hospital. He'd rung to let her know he was finished and Phillipa Edwards had refused a rape kit. She passed the information on to Will, then asked, 'Do you want me to set the GPS?'

He moved the car into a gap in the traffic and replied, 'No, I know where it is.'

Road works had slowed the traffic speed to walking pace on the most direct route to Arbury, and they were caught in the queue. Will relaxed in his seat, resting one hand on the top of the steering wheel and the other in his lap as he edged the car forwards.

'Did you grow up in Cambridge?' Shauna asked.

'Yep. It isn't a big place. After a few months on the beat you get to know it pretty well.'

A bicycle whizzed past them on the pavement.

'You must like it here, to stick around so long.'

Keeping his eyes on the road ahead, Will replied, 'Is it strange to live all your life in one place? It isn't as exciting as London, but Cambridge has its charms.'

'Excitement can be overrated,' Shauna said.

He shot her a look and didn't respond, as if hoping to tease something out of her with his silence, but she already regretted saying too much.

The temporary traffic lights for the road works had come into view. In another few minutes they should be past them.

'Why do you think Edwards refused to find out if she'd been sexually assaulted?' Will asked. 'I mean, wouldn't you want to know?'

'I can understand her reluctance. It's an invasive procedure.'

'But she's a psychologist. Maybe not exactly a medical professional, but close. You'd think that sort of thing wouldn't bother her.'

'Well, it does, and that isn't necessarily suspicious.'

The traffic lights turned green.

'At last,' Will said, putting the car into gear and pulling forwards quickly as he attempted to make it through before the lights changed back to red.

———

Shauna spotted Baram Scott's house before she identified the number. It stood out in Donne Crescent, but not in a good way.

The area was undergoing gentrification. She'd read about how the house prices in the fashionable south and east of the city had risen too high even for the Silicon Fen tech workers and London commuters, and they were pushing west and north in the search for properties. The traditionally less trendy parts of Cambridge were undergoing a transformation. Doors and windows were shining with new paint, scrubby, overgrown lawns were being mown and tended, and expensive cars were appearing in driveways.

The same could not be said for the place Scott was calling home after his two decades of incarceration. The windows looked as though they hadn't been painted since before he'd gone away, and they were visibly rotting. The small front garden was a wildlife haven in the heart of the city, and the front door was so faded it was hard to tell its original colour.

Will parked on the road directly in front of the house.

'No car,' he said, looking at the empty driveway, 'but he might not have one.'

'He's only been out for three weeks,' said Shauna. 'Let's see if he's home.'

When she pressed the doorbell, no resulting sound came from inside. She rapped the bleached wood with her knuckles.

A few beats later the door handle turned and the door jerked, but it didn't open. Someone in the house swore, then said, 'Come around the side.'

Shauna and Will walked around the semi-detached property, stepping over broken stems of weeds lying forlornly across the path. They approached a side door, which was already open.

An old woman in a grey jersey top, open at the neck, and baggy jeans stood waiting. She blinked in the sunlight and as she took in their appearance, her expression grew closed and sullen.

'Is Mr Scott home?' asked Shauna, pulling out her badge.

'Put it away,' the woman replied. 'I know who you are. What do you want?'

'So you were expecting us?'

'I wasn't. Pigs are just easy to spot.'

Shauna studiously avoided sharing a glance with Will.

'We wanted to ask Mr Scott a few questions to rule him out from our enquiries,' she said. 'Are you his mother? Do you mind if we come in?'

'Yes, and yes, I do mind.'

'Come on, Mrs Scott,' urged Shauna. 'If it's so obvious we're police officers, do you really want your neighbours to see us standing on your doorstep?'

'I don't give a fuck what my neighbours think. They're all a bunch of toffs anyway. It'll give them something new to gossip about.'

'We would like to talk to your son about a murder that took place last night,' Shauna said, 'and we'd rather not force him to come into the station for questioning.'

'He isn't here and he doesn't know anything about a murder.' The woman leaned out from the doorway, bringing her face closer to Shauna's. 'He was home with me last night. Your lot pinned one murder on him he didn't do, and he paid for it with half his life. You're not pinning another one on him.'

She drew back and slammed the door shut. A different voice could be heard, a man's voice. The woman shouted something indistinct and the man yelled back. An argument ensued.

Shauna called out, 'When Mr Scott comes home, ask him to call me.'

At the front door, she took out her card and pushed it through the letterbox.

Will remarked, 'Looks like we aren't very popular today.'

'Face it,' she replied. 'We're never going to be popular.'

The evening was turning frosty as Ruth walked across the hospital car park. She stepped carefully to avoid slipping on ice. Though, she reflected, if she was going to break a leg, she was in the best possible place.

What had happened to Phillipa after Thomas was murdered? Had she wandered around outside all night?

Ruth gave an involuntary shiver and stepped into the hospital reception.

She was so glad she'd called to check if she could visit her friend. The detective, Holt, had said she wouldn't be allowed, but the person she'd spoken to had said it was fine, only visiting hours would soon be over. Leaving work early meant asking Anders to take her final session of the day, but he hadn't minded and had asked her to pass on his well wishes.

The reception area was quiet and the hospital shop was closed. She would have liked to buy chocolates or another small gift as was customary, but her time was short anyway. She quickly crossed to the lifts.

A nurse at the central station in the ward pointed out Phillipa's room, but it turned out there was no need. When Ruth looked down the hallway, only one room had a policeman standing outside the door.

She paused and looked back at the nurse, who only shrugged.

'Is Dr Edwards under arrest?!'

'I'm sorry, I can't give out information on patients.'

'But she *is* allowed visitors?'

'Yes, but you'll have to be quick.'

Surely the police couldn't have arrested her, so why were they watching her? Or were they protecting her, thinking the murderer might not have finished his work? Ruth patted her pocket, where she kept her phone. She'd called Dom from the car park and he'd said they'd had an unexpected visitor but it was nothing to worry about, yet she couldn't shake the fear that her family was threatened, too.

Conversations going on in other rooms leached out into the corridor, and some of the visitors were beginning to make their way out. As she approached the door to Phillipa's room, the officer nodded at her.

She returned the greeting with a faint smile. 'I was told I could see Dr Edwards. I'm a friend of hers.'

'Don't let me stop you.'

Ruth peeked through the narrow, vertical window in the door. She didn't want to disturb Phillipa if she was sleeping, but she was awake, reclining in bed and watching television. She was wearing a hospital gown and she appeared uninjured, as the detective had said. She also appeared to be in shock, judging from the way she stared at the screen blankly, expressionless. Ruth supposed it was only to be expected. Her friend was obviously still suffering the effects of her ordeal.

She went in.

'Ruth!' Phillipa pulled herself upright. 'How lovely of you to come and see me.'

'How couldn't I? I only wish I'd known you were allowed visitors earlier.' She walked quickly to the bedside and hugged her. 'You poor, poor thing.'

The gesture seemed to trigger something, as Phillipa hunched over and her shoulders began to shake with sobs. Ruth held her. The spate lasted a minute or so, then Phillipa grew calmer and wiped her eyes. Ruth took one of Phillipa's hands in her own.

'I can't imagine what you must be going through. Is there anything I can do…?' Her words dried up as she realised their fatuousness. What could she possibly do to help someone who had, presumably, witnessed her husband's murder?

Phillipa's other hand covered her face, and her head slowly shook from side to side. 'No one can do anything. No one can bring Thomas back.'

'Oh, you poor dear.'

Ruth bit her lip. In her professional life she'd spoken with countless individuals about terrible events they'd witnessed or taken part in, but she didn't want to slip into the psychiatrist's role with her friend. It was too distant and impersonal. She wanted to support her, but she felt ill-equipped. Her life was humdrum. Aside from Molly's disappearance a few years ago, she'd never had to deal with much drama or disaster, and certainly not anything as monumental as a murder.

'How have you been, since…?' she asked.

'Terrible. Just terrible.'

Ruth gripped her friend's hand tighter.

Phillipa lifted her head. 'The doctor wants me to stay at least twenty-four hours. *For observation* he said, though there's nothing physically wrong with me. The funny thing is, if I don't think about what's happened, I feel fine mentally too. It's all a blank, you see. The last thing I can remember from yesterday evening is having dinner, then suddenly I was wandering around a car park this morning. So although I know what the police told me about Thomas must be true, I can't quite take it in. I think the doctor is worried about my mental state. Isn't that ironic?'

'You mean because you're a psychologist? Not ironic at all.

How could you think it was? You're reacting to an extremely traumatic event. We're human the same as everyone else, and just as vulnerable to mental ill health.' Ruth smiled wryly. 'Maybe even more so.'

She gently squeezed her hand once more. Phillipa appeared to be experiencing dissociative amnesia. However, it wasn't the time or place for a discussion about it.

'Have the police said anything?' she asked. 'They enquired if any recently released offenders might be harbouring a grudge against you.'

'What did you tell them?'

'Stella gave them a list of three possible leads.'

Phillipa slumped against her pillows, her expression pensive. 'I suppose it could have been someone I treated. I just don't know.'

'I have the list, too. I-I...I'm going to do some digging of my own.'

'You?' Phillipa said, pushing herself upright again. 'Why would you do that? Wouldn't it be better to leave it to the police?'

What to tell her?

The police suspect you.

She couldn't add to her friend's already heavy mental burdens. It was one thing to know murder investigations often focus attention on the victim's family and friends; it was quite another to know you're suspected of murdering someone you loved.

She replied, 'I just want to help. We know the inmates better than most people, don't you think?'

'Yes, maybe, but...I really wish you wouldn't do it. Whoever killed Thomas is extremely dangerous. I don't want you to put your life at risk on my account.'

'Don't worry. I doubt I'll approach anyone. All I've done so far is read the former prisoners' files, but I was thinking, if I could read your session notes, I might find something that would—'

'No, Ruth. It isn't safe for you to become involved. If Thomas's murderer is targeting the mental health team—'

White noise briefly burst from an overhead speaker, followed by the announcement that visiting hours were over in five minutes.

'Oh dear,' Ruth said.

'It's fine. I'm glad you came.'

Still holding her friend's hand, Ruth said, 'You will get through this, Phillipa. I promise you will. I'll help you.'

'You're such a good friend, Ruth.'

'You've been a good friend to me. Things have been hard over the last few years, and you've always been there with a smile and a listening ear. Returning the favour is the least I can do. What will you do tomorrow, assuming the doctor discharges you? Where will you go?'

'I don't know exactly, but I'll be okay. I'll find somewhere.'

'I imagine your house is off limits for now. You're very welcome to...' Ruth paused, remembering about Molly.

'What?'

'I was about to invite you to stay with us, but Molly turned up out of the blue yesterday.'

'She did? How wonderful! Did she say why she hadn't been in contact?'

'Not yet. We haven't had time to talk, but it means her bedroom isn't spare anymore. Otherwise you could have had it.'

'I couldn't possibly impose,' said Phillipa. 'It's out of the question.'

'No,' Ruth said firmly. 'We can't have you staying in a hotel. You must come and live with us. I insist. We'll find a way. We have plenty of space, it's just a matter of jiggling things around a bit.'

Phillipa looked doubtful, but then she suddenly relented. 'If you insist...'

'I do. If you don't stay with us I'll worry about you.'

'I need some clothes. The police took mine.'

'That's easily fixed. We're about the same size.' Ruth stood up. 'I'd better go. Call me tomorrow when you're ready and I'll ask Dom to pick you up. He won't mind. He'll be happy to have you. We all will.'

CHAPTER THIRTEEN

Thomas Edwards' body lay cold and blue on the slab in the hospital's pathology department. Except for the parts of it exposed to the world. They were red and meaty.

Witnessing a post-mortem was not the kind of thing Shauna enjoyed at the best of times. Now, before she'd even had her morning coffee, the sight and smell were making her woozy. It was strange. Murder scenes, she could do. But there was a clinical awfulness about seeing a body deliberately opened up for inspection.

'You can take a seat if you like,' said James, his eyes cheerily smiling over his mask. 'I keep a few around for the medical students. There's one over there.' He nodded at the corner of the room, his hands otherwise occupied by Thomas Edwards' internal organs.

'I'll be okay,' she replied. She didn't know James well yet and didn't want to risk a rumour she was weak-stomached getting back to the team. Respect was hard won and easily lost in her job.

She wouldn't normally be so ill-prepared. If she'd known she would be the police representative present for the medical examination of the murder victim, she would have steeled herself to the task and taken a travel sickness tablet. But she'd only found out when Bryant had called her at seven that morning to tell her 'something had come up' and he needed her to take his place.

She hoped the 'something' wasn't that he didn't fancy doing it and was taking the opportunity to delegate to the new DI, setting a precedent.

After taking slow, deep breaths until her dizziness passed, she commented, 'I can't see any defensive wounds.'

'No, no sign of any,' said James, lifting out a large, soft, deep red object and placing it on a scale. The organ quietly squelched. 'His hands and arms are completely unmarked.'

'Maybe he didn't have time to put up a fight. Or he froze. There were no signs of an altercation at the crime scene.' She was aware she was thinking aloud, but speaking was a welcome distraction. 'The blood spatter is on the wall and fireplace. I'm guessing he was standing when he was stabbed.'

'That would be my guess too,' James commented, 'from the angle of the entry point. Has the murder weapon been found?'

'A SOCO spotted it in the garden, under a hedge. It was covered in blood and it matches one missing from the knife block in the kitchen.'

'Any fingerprints?'

'No.'

'Someone knew what they were doing.'

He extracted something else from the body. Shauna recognised this organ: The victim's heart, gilded with yellow fat. James made a comment into his recording device and placed the heart on a scale.

'If I had to take another guess,' he said, 'I'd say the murderer knew how to kill too.'

'You mean the single stab wound?'

'Yes. It's severed the carotid artery neatly.'

The pathologist was echoing Shauna's own thoughts. The skilful killing would also explain why the victim showed no signs of fighting back. He wouldn't have had much time before blood loss overcame him.

Her mobile rang.

It was Will. 'We're bringing Phillipa Edwards in for an interview today, right?'

'That's right. I'm already at the hospital for the post-mortem.'

'Great. I wondered why you weren't at the station.'

'Sorry, forgot to leave a message.'

'I'll meet you there. How's it going?' Will asked.

'It's as fun as you might expect. I'll fill you in when you get here.'

'Do we have Dr Edwards' medical report yet?'

'The email arrived last night. I'll forward it. Nothing useful in it, unfortunately. No signs of physical trauma. Blood tests show no alcohol, drugs or medications. The psych assessment says she's suffering from amnesia and disorientation but she's mentally sound.'

'I had an idea about her refusing a rape kit,' said Will. 'Maybe she's been having an affair, and after the murder she spent the night with her boyfriend. The SAK would pick up that she'd had sex and if we checked the DNA, it wouldn't be her husband's.'

Shauna thought he was grasping at straws. On the other hand, jealousy was a common motivation for murder. 'You think the boyfriend could be the perp?'

'Exactly. He could be someone Thomas knew, too, who was at the house on the night of the murder. He broke the glass in the kitchen door and tossed the knife under the hedge before leaving with the wife in his car.'

'Alfie and Jas can tell us if the neighbours saw another car parked on the street that night.' She briefly relayed James's comments about the expertise of the murderer, adding in explanation, 'The carotid artery's quite hard to reach. The jugular vein is nearer the surface, but if that's cut, it takes longer for the person to die.'

'Thanks, boss,' said Will. 'That's useful to know.'

She sighed. 'I've been in this business too long.'

'Me too,' echoed James. 'But I have to admit, I still enjoy it.'

Shauna had forgotten where she was. The pathologist had continued quietly slicing and measuring Thomas Edwards' remains while she'd been speaking to Will.

'I've nearly finished,' he went on, 'if you need to go soon.'

She shifted position, easing her stiffness from standing in one place too long. 'I've got a few minutes.'

———

There was no uniform outside Phillipa Edwards' hospital room. Shauna marched to the door and pushed it open, only to find the bed empty and made up, ready for the next patient.

'Where's she gone?' she asked, swinging her head from side to side in a daze, as if hoping to see Edwards in a corner of the small space.

'Didn't you hear?' asked Will. 'Bryant rescinded the order last night.' He was looking out the window as he replied, probably trying to be diplomatic.

'What?! Why?'

'I don't know, but she wasn't under arrest. He must have thought she wasn't in any danger either, so...'

Why hadn't the DCI mentioned that little tidbit of information when he called her this morning? Shauna clamped her lips together before she said something unwise. She couldn't trust Will yet.

When they tracked down a nurse, she explained, 'Dr Edwards discharged herself early this morning. I'm sorry you missed her. You should have been notified,' she added, her cheeks reddening. 'I was just about to do it, but I've been rushed off my feet.'

'Do you know where she went?' asked Will.

'No, sorry. A man came to pick her up. She didn't mention

who he was. She signed the AMA form, then she was gone. About six thirty.'

'Right,' said Shauna tightly. 'Thanks.'

There was nothing to do except try to track her down.

As they walked to the lifts, Will said, 'My boyfriend theory is beginning to sound more credible, right? But would she really have the brass balls to walk out of here arm in arm with the murderer?

'Clever or stupid, killers are often arrogant,' said Shauna. 'That's where they slip up.' She pressed the button to call the lift.

'I suppose you must have worked on a lot of murders in the Met,' Will commented.

'I've dealt with my fair share.'

'You must have been expecting things would be quieter in Cambridge. But now you're back to the same old.'

She didn't answer. After the snub from Bryant, she was in no mood to tolerate Will's continued blatant snooping.

There was an awkward pause, then he asked, 'Do we have Edwards' contact details?'

'Only her office number. Her handbag with her phone is still missing.'

'She must have gone home with whoever picked her up. Her house is still taped off.'

The lift arrived and the doors opened.

Shauna said, 'I think I know where she's gone.'

She took out her mobile, looked up a name, and called the number. To avoid losing the signal, she didn't step into the lift. The occupants watched her expectantly as the doors closed and the lift continued down.

'Hello?' Shauna said when her call was answered. 'I'd like to speak to Dr Terrell.'

———

It was no great surprise Edwards had gone to stay with her colleague and friend. Nor was it a surprise that Terrell lived in an expensive area of the city. What did surprise Shauna was the state of the house. Though it was in nowhere near as bad a condition as Baram Scott's, it had a similar air of letting down the side for the others in the street. The lawn hadn't seen a mower for months and years-old grime lay thick on the windowsills.

The car sitting in the driveway complemented the image of neglect perfectly: old and unwashed, bubbled paint on the wheel arches betrayed underlying rust.

Will rapped the door knocker.

Within seconds, the door was wrenched open and an angry-faced, middle-aged man said, 'I've *told* you...oh.' When he registered them, his anger was overtaken by surprise and then embarrassment. 'I'm so sorry. We don't normally get callers and I thought you were someone else. How can I help you?'

Shauna introduced herself and Will.

'Ah, that makes sense. You must be here to see Phillipa. Terrible business. I'll go and get her for you. Would you like to come in?'

He left the door open and disappeared into the house.

Shauna stepped inside with Will and waited in the hall. Through an open doorway she saw a messy living room, the back of a shabby sofa and piles of dog-eared magazines stacked on worn carpet. Dusty, full bookshelves occupied one wall from the floor to the ceiling, and a bulky, old-fashioned television broadcast a morning chat show.

Then the door closed, pushed by an unseen hand.

Footsteps sounded on the stairs and Phillipa Edwards appeared, closely followed by the man who had answered the door, probably Dr Terrell's husband.

'You can talk in the living room,' he said. Then he noticed the closed door. 'I'll just ask my daughter to—'

'Actually,' said Shauna, 'we'd prefer it if Dr Edwards came to the station with us.'

The woman had reached the bottom of the stairs. 'Yes, of course. Anything I can do to help.'

As they walked down the garden path, Shauna wondered who Terrell's husband had mistaken them for. Whoever it was, he'd taken a strong dislike to the person, that was for sure.

CHAPTER FOURTEEN

Molly turned down the television and tried to hear what was going on in the hall, but she couldn't make anything out. Now her curiosity had the better of her, she regretted closing the door in a fit of shame over the state of her parents' house. Though she'd done a reasonable job of tidying up and cleaning, Dad had insisted she take the magazines out of the recycling and return them to the living room, so they remained there in their sad stacks.

All she knew was the police had arrived to see Mum's friend. When she'd heard the knock at the door she'd made the same mistake as Dad. She'd thought Daniel had come back. Yesterday, it had taken half an hour to persuade him to leave, and since then he'd phoned fifteen times or more, trying to speak to her, after somehow finding out her parents' number.

She wasn't rid of him yet, not by a long chalk.

'Give me a ring when you're finished, Phillipa,' Molly heard her father say. 'I'll come and pick you up.'

If the woman thanked Dad, Molly didn't hear it. Footsteps crossed the wooden floor, and then came the sound of the front door shutting.

A moment later, her father walked in, rubbing his thinning, grey hair. 'First *you* turn up, then someone's murdered, and now we have the victim's wife living with us. Life has never been so dramatic.' He smiled. 'Did you have your breakfast? Becky missed you this morning.'

Molly strongly doubted her sister had shown any reaction to her absence from the breakfast table, but she didn't mention it. 'Sorry, I overslept.'

'I wasn't complaining, dear. It might be the last night you spend in your bed for a while. It's generous of you to give up your room for Phillipa.'

'I don't mind. I've been away so long I hardly feel like it *is* my room anymore. And Mum's friend's problems trump mine. If anyone needs a good night's sleep, it's her. It's kind of you both to take her in.'

'It was your mother's decision. You know how it works around here. She's the boss. Now...' he rubbed his hands together '...I bet you haven't eaten yet. Let me make you something. What would you like?'

'There's no need. I can make something myself.'

'No, no, I insist. Scrambled eggs on toast sound okay?'

Molly wasn't remotely hungry, but she didn't have the mental or emotional strength to put up a fight. And feeding her seemed to make her father happy. 'That sounds great. Thanks, Dad.'

As he left, she relaxed into the cushions and turned up the volume on the television.

But after several minutes of trying, she found she couldn't concentrate on the programme. The horrible encounter with Daniel the previous day kept playing through her mind. That was the reason she'd slept badly and woken up late. She'd gone over the incident again and again, yet thinking of it still made her heart race and her mouth turn dry.

After Daniel had stopped shouting through the letterbox, she'd waited in the hall, not moving for about half an hour, until she was finally convinced he'd left. Then just as she'd dredged up the courage to continue cleaning the house, the sound of a key in the front door made her jump. She'd calmed herself, realising it had to be Dad.

Her father had stepped through the door and was on the verge of saying something, when Daniel suddenly loomed up behind him. Though it had only been a couple of days since she'd seen him, he looked different. His thick, dark hair and beard made him look wilder than she remembered.

Noticing her reaction, Dad had said, 'What's wrong?'

'Excuse me,' said Daniel loudly outside. 'I want to speak to my wife!'

Dad, bless him, had risen to the occasion like a hero.

He immediately turned and blocked the doorway with his body. Speaking over his shoulder, he said, 'Molly, do you want to speak to this man?'

'This *man?*' Daniel spluttered. 'I'm her husband! Move out of my way.'

'That isn't very polite, is it?' Dad retorted calmly. 'If I wanted you inside my house I would invite you in.' He turned to her. 'Molly?'

She swallowed, the sight of Daniel bringing back her fear of him.

Should she speak to him?

Somehow, it seemed only fair, considering she'd left without any warning. She hadn't even written him a note.

Then Daniel said, glaring at her, 'I *demand* to speak to you! You have no right to treat me like this. Tell your father to let me in. How *dare* you leave me standing out here.'

His angry tone, which had become deeply, painfully familiar, triggered a modicum of courage to rise up in her. She couldn't spend the rest of her life listening to his haranguing and hectoring. She had to stand up to him or accept she would never be free or happy.

'I don't want to talk to you,' she said, her pulse thudding. 'I'm sorry, but it's over.' She swallowed. 'I want a divorce.'

'No, it *isn't* over,' Daniel asserted forcefully. 'You don't get to make that decision.'

'Right,' said Dad. 'I've heard quite enough. Leave now, young man, or I'll call the police.'

Daniel turned his glare to her father.

'Leave. Now,' Dad repeated.

The quiet menace in her father's tone was something Molly had never heard before. It struck a chill through her, and she wasn't even the object of it.

Daniel took a step backwards and passed a hand over his forehead. 'I'm sorry for losing my temper, Mr Terrell.'

She knew what was coming next. He was so predictable, like the seasons of the year. He'd gone from winter to spring, anger to gentleness. It was all an act.

'You have to understand, I had no idea what was going on,' Daniel continued. 'I returned from a business trip to an empty home. No note, nothing. Molly,' he stepped closer to the door, 'you broke my heart leaving me like that. Let's talk about it. This doesn't have to be the end.'

'My daughter doesn't wish to speak with you at this time. Go away.'

'Not yet,' said Daniel. 'Just a few words. Come on, darling. You owe me that.'

Feeling even bolder now she had her father's support, Molly replied, 'I don't owe you anything. Go home. I'm speaking to a solicitor today.'

Her husband's face darkened again, but, glancing at her father, he controlled himself. 'There's no need for us to go through lawyers. We can sort this out between ourselves. If you really want a divorce, I won't fight it. But I don't think we're at that stage yet.'

She had heard this refrain so many times before. It washed over her, leaving no trace. 'Yes, we are, Daniel. *I* am.'

Dad had slammed the door in his face.

She had almost collapsed in relief. The part about her having an appointment to see a solicitor had been a lie, intended to convince him she was determined to go through with the divorce.

She *was* determined, though the idea terrified as well as delighted her. She just hadn't contacted anyone about it yet. She would look for a local family law solicitor on the internet after breakfast. Maybe she would find someone who could see her today.

'Breakfast's ready,' Dad called from the kitchen.

———

By early afternoon, she was full of nervous energy, the encounter with her soon-to-be ex-husband playing on her mind and sending ripples of angst through her. The prospect of taking the first step to move on with her life felt dream-like and unreal, as if it couldn't be happening, as if *she* couldn't be doing anything so bold. Though her solicitor's appointment wasn't until 3.30, she wanted to get out of the house now.

She decided to go somewhere her parents had taken her as a child, before Becky came along and things got complicated and difficult.

Dad had gone out, so she locked the back door before putting on her coat, grabbing the spare key, and stepping outside. As she pulled the door closed and the lock snicked shut, a sudden fear hit her.

She paused, prickles tickling her back.

Slowly, she turned around and scanned the driveway and road.

They were empty.

She exhaled.

It hadn't occurred to her until she was outside that Daniel might be lying in wait, hoping he could resume his pleas for them to talk. She knew from long experience what 'talking' meant.

But he was nowhere to be seen.

She fastened her coat and set off.

CHAPTER FIFTEEN

As Shauna walked across the lobby of Cambridge Central with Phillipa Edwards, the desk sergeant, Beth, beckoned her. She told Will to take Edwards to the interview room.

'A handbag was brought in,' the sergeant said. 'I was busy dealing with an enquiry—typical morning rush...' she rolled her eyes '...when a man dumped it on the counter and left, saying he'd found it in the street and he didn't have time to wait around. I tried to stop him, but he walked off. It wasn't until I got the chance to look inside the bag I realised...Well, I gave it to Forensics.'

'It's Phillipa Edwards' bag?'

'You'd better talk to them, but I think so.'

'Did the man say where he'd found it?'

Beth winced. 'No, sorry.'

'Damn.'

'The security cameras will have recorded him. Maybe we can make a public announcement asking him to come forward.'

'Yeah,' Shauna replied. 'I'll run it past Bryant.'

Not that the DCI had been particularly helpful so far.

She joined Will and Edwards in the interview room. Will had settled Edwards in with some of the station's terrible coffee from a machine. She looked tired and stressed, understandably in the circumstances.

'We were expecting to speak to you at the hospital today,' said Shauna.

Edwards shuddered. 'I couldn't stay there any longer, and as the police officer outside my room had disappeared, I assumed I was free to go. I hope I didn't cause any confusion.'

'Only a little,' said Shauna. 'I want you to understand this isn't a formal interview. You haven't been cautioned, but—'

'Why on Earth would you caution me?'

'It's just a chat. A fact-finding mission. We would like to form a picture of your husband, his life at home and work, his friends and acquaintances, that kind of thing.'

'Do you think he was murdered by someone he knew?'

'It's too early to draw any firm conclusions. Has the coroner's office been in touch with you yet?'

'No. Why would they?'

'They'll need someone to formally identify your husband's body.'

'Oh.' She sniffed, took a tissue from the box on the table and dabbed her eyes. 'I think I would like to see him.'

'Phillipa,' said Shauna, 'now you've had time to think about it some more, do you have any idea who might have done this? Did Thomas ever mention anyone with a grudge? Perhaps a client or someone from his past.'

'No. I've been over it in my mind again and again. As far as I knew, he got along with everyone.'

'Might he have had business dealings he didn't tell you about?'

'He wasn't like that. He was a very honest person.'

Shauna sat back in her chair, frowning.

'I'm sorry,' said Edwards. 'I wish I could help.'

'Solicitors living in leafy suburbs generally aren't murdered in their own homes,' said Shauna. 'Are you sure there isn't something you aren't telling us? Something a bit embarrassing, maybe, that you think isn't important to the investigation.'

'No,' Edwards replied firmly. 'Nothing.'

Shauna paused again, studying the woman's face. Edwards met her gaze, teary-eyed.

'I understand this might be painful for you,' Will said, 'but maybe could you tell us about Thomas?'

'What would you like to know?'

'His personality, habits, relationships. Whatever springs to mind.'

'He was a good man. Friendly when he needed to be, but he kept to himself most of the time. It was just us two. We live...we lived...quietly, which was how both of us liked it. We weren't hermits, but we didn't have people over. Thomas was very ordinary, really, but he was kind and good and...and I loved him.' She grabbed more tissues and wiped her eyes then blew her nose.

'He'd changed jobs fairly recently,' said Shauna. 'Why? Was he having problems at his previous place of work? Colleagues he didn't get along with?'

'He'd been at his old place of work for over ten years, and he felt it was time to move on. He practised family law. Divorces, mostly.'

'Did he talk about his work much?' asked Shauna.

'Hardly at all.'

'He didn't enjoy it?'

'No, he liked his job. He just preferred to keep his work and home lives separate. We both did. Well, in my profession, it's required.'

Shauna gave Will the nod and he left.

'We talked to members of your team at the prison,' Shauna said. 'A couple of them mentioned your father-in-law dying recently. That must have been hard.'

'Yes. He was in remission from prostate cancer, but then he developed leukaemia just last year. He went downhill very fast. Thomas was devastated.'

'His father had left him a large inheritance, we heard. Yet he chose to continue working.'

'As I said, he enjoyed his work.'

'Aside from yourself, would anyone else benefit financially from Thomas's death?'

'No.' A fraction of a pause. 'My husband and I shared our finances equally. The legacy went into joint accounts, and I had full access to the money. Thomas had often suggested that I took early retirement, but I also like my job. So, I'm not deriving any financial benefit from his death.'

Shauna made a mental note of Edwards' defensiveness. The woman had clearly understood the implication of the line of questioning. She was attempting to close off the avenue of suspicion—not unreasonably.

'How would you describe your marriage?' Shauna asked.

'Thomas and I have...had... been happily married for seven years.'

'Only seven?' Shauna had assumed the couple had been married longer. According to their information, Phillipa Edwards was forty-four and Thomas had been forty-eight when he died. Their ages had made her assume a lengthier marriage.

'It would have been eight years in June,' said Phillipa tightly.

'Have you been married or in any long-term relationships before marrying Thomas?'

'I've only been married once. None of my previous relationships were what you would call serious.'

'So it's unlikely a former boyfriend was jealous of your husband?'

'Extremely unlikely.'

Will returned carrying an evidence bag. He put it on the table and sat down.

Edwards' eyebrows rose. 'What's that?'

The handkerchief sat between them, grey and unprepossessing under transparent plastic.

'Do you recognise this?' asked Shauna.

'No, I don't.'

'We found it beneath your sofa.'

'I don't believe it. That's ridiculous. Thomas never used handkerchiefs. If he needed to blow his nose, he used a tissue.'

'Do you employ a cleaning service?' Shauna asked.

'No. With only two of us at home we never saw the need for one.'

'Can you think of any other explanation for why it would be there?'

'None at all. Unless your team has made a mistake and this is from another investigation.'

Shauna replied coolly, 'I can assure you that isn't the case.'

She left the handkerchief where it was.

'Let's move on to the night of the murder,' she said. 'What do you remember?'

'I would love to tell you. Believe me, I spent last night trying to recall what happened, racking my brains, but my memory remains a blank.'

'Well, do you remember what happened that day?'

'Yes, it's only the late evening I can't bring to mind.'

'Right. Could you tell us what you did before then?'

Phillipa's eyes shifted left and up. 'I completed three assessments in the afternoon, wrote up the reports, and then I left work at my usual time, about six o'clock. I arrived home about six thirty and made some pasta while waiting for Thomas. He got back at seven.'

'Do you remember eating dinner with your husband, Phillipa?' Shauna asked.

She thought for a bit before answering, 'Yes.'

'Did you have a drink with your dinner or afterwards?' asked Will.

Maybe her memory loss wasn't due to psychological trauma. Maybe she'd been blackout drunk.

'Just a glass of wine,' Edwards answered, adding, 'I think the rest of the bottle's still in the fridge. Then we watched television. The next thing I recall is someone approaching me in the supermarket car park, asking me if I was okay. I have no idea what happened in between.'

'So you don't know where you went that night?' asked Shauna.

'Not a clue.'

'Is it possible you spent the night at home?'

'I really have no idea.' She chewed her lower lip for a moment, then said, 'Self-diagnosis is often unwise, but I believe I'm suffering from psychic shock. If I am, my memory may return over the next few days, or I may never be able to recall the evening's events. To be perfectly honest with you, much as I would like to help bring my husband's killer to justice, I'd prefer to remain ignorant of his last moments.'

'Understandable,' said Will gently.

It was time to try a new line of questioning.

'Given your job,' Shauna said, 'is it possible one of your former patients may have murdered Thomas?'

'I've received the occasional veiled and not-so veiled threat over the years, but nothing in recent memory.'

Shauna asked, 'Can you remember who made these threats?'

'I'll check my reports, but, to be honest, threats are par for the course in my profession.'

'Your supervisor, Dr Terrell, provided a list of offenders you've treated who were recently released. We're checking those leads.'

Shauna leaned back in her seat. 'Unless DS Fiske has any questions...?'

Will shook his head.

'Then I think that'll do for now. If anything does occur to you—'

There was a knock on the door and it immediately opened.

It was Connor, wearing latex gloves and holding an evidence bag. Inside the transparent envelope sat a brown leather hand-bag. 'I thought you might want a positive ID on—'

'That's my bag!' Edwards exclaimed. 'Where did you get it?'

'A member of the public handed it in this morning,' Shauna replied.

'Can I have it back?'

'Not yet, I'm afraid,' said Will.

'Not for a while,' said Shauna. 'Can you remember what was in it?'

'Just the usual. If you let me see inside I can tell you if anything's missing.'

'That won't be possible,' said Shauna. It felt pedantic to refuse, but allowing potential suspects access to evidence was a big no-no. 'Could you write a list of the contents as well as you can remember them?'

Will tore off a sheet of plain paper from a pad and gave it to Edwards along with a pen. The woman hesitated before taking them, a frown of annoyance creasing her brow.

'Will you be staying at Dr Terrell's house for now?' asked Shauna.

'I expect I'll be there for a few days at least.'

'I'm sure the support is welcome,' said Will.

Shauna left Will to finish up with Edwards. Returning to the office, she sat at her desk. Something compelled her to take her own handbag out of her desk drawer. Her purse had sunk to the bottom as always, buried in everyday detritus. It was old, worn and overstuffed with bank cards, store loyalty cards, change, sentimental items and a couple of tenners.

She fished around in it, pulling out her photographs. They were dog-eared and faded. One photo was of Liam as a baby. Another was of Charlotte at her first school fair. The third showed Naomi at a birthday party, blowing out candles.

CHAPTER SIXTEEN

The halfway house for recently released prisoners was surprisingly close to Cambridge town centre. As Ruth navigated towards it, following the map on her phone, she wondered how vexed local property developers were about the million-pound real estate housing a charity to help ex-convicts transition back into society.

The shopping precinct was busy despite the bitter weather. Winter seemed to be hanging around forever, digging its claws into every nook and cranny, refusing to allow even a ray of warm sunshine to break through the ever-present blanket of grey cloud. She pulled her scarf up over her cold nose.

A tourist stepped backwards into her path, preparing to take a selfie in front of King's College Chapel. Ruth had to quickly dodge her.

'Sorry!' the woman exclaimed in a foreign accent.

Ruth smiled politely and was about to continue on her way when she changed her mind.

'Would you like me to take it?' she asked the young woman, who seemed to be alone.

'Yes, thank you very much,' the tourist carefully enunciated.

Accepting the offered smartphone and sliding her own into

her pocket, Ruth checked behind herself and then backed up a short distance.

She took care to get all of the college into the frame. The tourist posed like a professional, tilting her head to smile winningly at the camera, but Ruth was more struck by the building behind her. How many times had she walked past the ancient, beautiful edifice? It had to be thousands over the course of her lifetime. These days, she barely noticed it.

She snapped the shot and paused a moment, appreciating the forgotten pleasure of the sight, before handing the phone back.

'Oooh, thank you!' said the tourist, gazing happily at the screen.

The crowds were continuing to thicken. Ruth skirted a family of shoppers who had spread themselves annoyingly wide, impeding everyone in the vicinity, and set off down narrow Trinity Street. She was still ten minutes' walk from her destination yet her heart was beginning to race.

What she was doing was madness, but she couldn't forget the state Phillipa had been in when she'd returned from her police interview. At first, she'd said it had gone well, but then she'd collapsed in tears. She was a mess, and Ruth felt compelled to help her. The local media was going to town on the murder and the pressure on the police to solve it would be intense. If she could find out something useful to tell them, they would leave her friend alone.

The only contact information on file for Derek Abelton was the address of the halfway house. She was taking a chance he'd be home and that he would agree to speak to her. She was also taking a chance he wouldn't react aggressively. He had borderline personality disorder. His behaviour would be unpredictable, but she doubted he would do anything in front of witnesses. She only wanted to talk to him and gauge his reaction to the mention of the murder.

The dot on her mobile at the end of her route turned out to be a rundown Victorian town house. An intercom with worn metal buttons and numbers was fixed to the wall next to a weather-worn blue door, the previous coating of red paint visible through the chips.

She hesitated. The address she had didn't state any room numbers. Then she saw at the bottom of the list one label bearing the word Office.

Whoever was in the office took their sweet time in answering her buzz. She stamped her feet as she waited, wondering if she should try one of the rooms instead, or all of them, when the intercom came to life, broadcasting background noise of crockery and cutlery clashing. A desultory male voice said, 'Yes?'

'I'm here to see Derek Ableton.'

'Visitors aren't allowed.'

The intercom went silent.

'Could you please tell him...'

No one was listening to her.

She pressed the button again, keeping her thumb on it for long seconds until, suddenly, the door was yanked open.

A long-haired man in faded jeans and a brown cardigan, smelling of cigarette smoke, glared at her as he took in her appearance. His belligerence faded a few notches.

'Visitors aren't allowed here.'

'I understand. Could you possibly ask Derek to step outside?'

The man gave her a second visual once-over, and Ruth became acutely aware she didn't look anything like the kind of person Ableton would know.

'Are you his probation officer?'

'No. I'm a...a friend.'

The man's eyes narrowed. He was clearly responsible for managing the place and keeping his clients on the straight and narrow. If they broke the conditions of their licence, it would reflect on him.

If she hadn't been who she was—a middle-aged, respectably dressed woman—he would have told her to piss off, no doubt. As it was, he only gave her a final, distrustful glance before disappearing into the building, leaving the door open.

She peeked into the dark, musty hall.

What a dreary, horrible place.

A nasty smell of overcooked cabbage floated out into the chilly air, and she was reminded of school dinners at her boarding school. It was no wonder career criminals ended up inside over and over again if this was their reintroduction to society.

The clump, clump, clump of heavy footsteps approached, and the silhouette of a tall, bulky man came into view.

Derek Ableton emerged into the light.

As soon as she saw him, Ruth was confident she'd never treated him. His fleshy face was crushed in around and above his right eye, due to some old injury. She definitely would have remembered him.

'I don't know you,' he said accusingly.

He turned.

'Wait,' Ruth blurted. 'I have something for you.'

'What?' He frowned at her, disbelieving.

She dug into her coat pockets and pulled out three packets of cigarettes. Smoking wasn't allowed in the prison system anymore, though prisoners were allowed to vape in their cells. But most prisoners were smokers before they were incarcerated.

She'd been surprised how expensive the packets were.

'Uh, thanks.' Ableton held out his hand.

He couldn't know why she was there, but that wasn't going to stop him from taking advantage of the crazy old woman who'd turned up to see him.

Ruth stepped away, moving the packets out of his reach. '...In exchange for a few minutes of your time. Perhaps we could go for a walk?'

Ableton's frown deepened, but then he shrugged and sighed and retreated into the building.

She thought he was going to close the door on her, but he returned carrying an old woollen coat. 'Five minutes, all right?'

'That's as long as it'll take, I'm sure.'

She set off, retracing her steps towards the town centre, where there were plenty of people about. Ableton had served two sentences for grievous bodily harm. She didn't want to become the reason for his third conviction for the crime.

Once more, the sheer recklessness of what she was doing hit her. She couldn't really explain it, except she felt compelled to help Phillipa. If there was a quick conclusion to the investigation, perhaps her friend could begin to heal.

Ruth had prepared a few questions, but now she was in the presence of this large man they'd flown from her mind.

'Is this about the murder?' Ableton asked.

After a moment of surprise, Ruth replied, 'Yes, it is about a murder. Have the police already spoken to you?'

'Nah. Not yet. It's only a matter of time, though. It was my shrink's husband, wasn't it?'

'That's right. How did you know?'

Another shrug. 'I couldn't have one of them fags now, could I?'

Ruth took out one of the cigarette packets. She was about to open it and give one to him, but he snatched it from her hand.

'Hey!'

Ableton grinned like a cheeky child as he removed the plastic packaging. He flipped up the top of the packet, drew out a cigarette, put it to his lips, and then lit it with a lighter from his pocket. He drew in a deep lungful of smoke and halted to lean on an old brick wall. Bending one knee, he rested the sole of his foot on the wall and said, 'This is far enough. I'll give you until I finish this.' He lifted the lit cigarette he held between two fingers.

'I'm a-a friend of your psychologist,' said Ruth. 'Obviously, she's devastated.'

'Obviously,' Ableton mimicked sarcastically. He took another long drag of his cigarette. The tip noticeably shrank.

If he *had* killed Thomas, he wouldn't admit it, naturally. All she could do was to watch and listen for signs he was uncomfortable discussing it. If her professional life had taught her anything, it was to perceive suppressed emotions. She doubted he would feel any guilt, but he would be concerned about suspicion falling on him.

'It's strange you know so much about the murder,' Ruth pressed. 'Why is that?'

'It's funny you know Edwards was my shrink.' He pulled on the cigarette again, fixing his lopsided gaze on her through the smoke. 'Who are you *really*?'

Before she could answer, he continued, 'You're another one, right? You work in the Mental Health Unit.'

He was shifting the power dynamic. They were not in a comfortable assessment room, a prison officer standing outside the door. If Ableton wanted to hurt her there wouldn't be anything she could do about it. She decided to not fight the assertion of control, to not antagonise him. Perhaps over-confidence might make him less cautious, too.

His cigarette was more than half smoked to ash.

'I am,' Ruth replied. 'I'm trying to help Dr Edwards.'

'Help *her*?'

'Yes, of course.'

He exhaled a great cloud of smoke into her face, and then watched, bemused, as he registered her distaste.

'Mr. Ableton, whoever committed the murder will be caught, and they will go to prison for a long time. If you know anything about what happened, you would be wise to go to the police immediately and tell them. The longer you wait, the worse the outcome will be for you.'

He suddenly leaned towards her, thrusting out his neck and putting his face close to hers. 'What are you accusing me of? You trying to say I did it?'

Though her heart thudded, Ruth stood her ground. 'I'm just saying—'

He threw down the remains of his cigarette.

'*Fuck* what you're saying.' He shoved a hand into each of her coat pockets and grabbed the packets of cigarettes.

She stood helpless as he took them from her, mentally recoiling but physically unable to move.

Clutching three packets in one of his large hands, Ableton strode away, calling out over his shoulder, 'If you want to know who killed Edwards' husband, talk to Baram Scott.'

CHAPTER SEVENTEEN

Molly had hoped the walk to the Botanic Garden would help take her mind off things, but instead she found herself becoming more anxious. She couldn't stop going over Daniel's sudden appearance yesterday. Looking back, aside from the horrible shock he'd given her and tension of the confrontation, she was appalled by his attitude towards her father.

Until her father had arrived home and Daniel tried to force his way past him into the house, the two had never met. She didn't think her husband had even seen a photo of her parents. He'd certainly never shown any interest in seeing one, or a photo of Becky.

Yet he'd turned up to harass her at her parents' home, and when he'd encountered Dad for the first time he hadn't said hello, introduced himself, or done anything a normal person would do when meeting their spouse's father.

The circumstances hadn't been exactly conducive to social platitudes, but Daniel needn't have been so rude. She felt aggrieved on her father's behalf. If Daniel's intent had been to bully her into returning to him, he'd had the opposite effect. Her family wasn't perfect, but she'd never felt a greater sense of belonging.

Her soon-to-be ex-husband was a terrible person. How had it taken her so long to see it?

She turned a corner and stepped out onto Hills Road, busy with traffic even though it wasn't the rush hour. The noise of the cars, lorries and buses ruffled her already fragile emotions. As she continued her journey, unwanted memories of her marriage resurfaced.

Everything had seemed fine between them at first. She hadn't thought anything of it when Daniel suggested they move away as soon as they were married. He loved the isolation of the Highlands, he'd said, and he wasn't a people person. He was sensitive, a loner. He wanted them to be alone too, with plenty of time together. It explained his standoffishness with her friends. It had seemed to make sense.

She'd thought it would be romantic.

She'd been an idiot.

There had been plenty of warning signs, but she'd missed them or excused them, telling herself he was tired, or depressed, or stressed.

From the moment they'd met, in the final semester of the second year of her Fine Arts degree, he'd criticised her friends behind their backs, telling her they weren't as nice as she thought, that they were using her, or looked down upon her. He'd also been antagonistic towards the other bartenders in the Student Union where she'd worked, and he'd even had disparaging things to say about her fellow students in her classes, though he didn't know them.

Daniel disliked anyone she knew, and his hatred increased in line with the closeness of her relationships, so his acrimony was greatest against her family.

In the early weeks after they'd got together, he'd quickly picked up on her unhappiness regarding her parents and built on it, implying they'd put her aside when Becky was diagnosed and they would probably be secretly glad if she disappeared from their lives. At first, she'd thought things weren't as bad as he intimated, but she also knew there was a kernel of truth to what he was saying. She'd begun to contact her mother and father less and less, telling herself her phone calls and emails were most likely a chore for them to answer.

She'd been so easy to manipulate. She'd fallen in love with him because he'd discovered her inner pain and affirmed her fears and because he'd showered her with attention. She'd been flattered and amazed he was so into her. Then her love had blinded her to his faults.

Daniel had suggested that they spent their first summer together in the Scottish Highlands. When the semester was over and he'd graduated, they'd packed their suitcases and taken two trains and a bus to reach the tiny, one-bedroom, renovated crofters cottage. Those first months of their relationship had been wonderful. They'd spent their days walking the hills among seas of heather and gorse, watching the sun's rays glinting on the water of the loch, and their evenings were spent planning their future.

He'd encouraged her to put off completing her degree for a year so they could get married and 'cement their partnership' in their remote cottage, isolated from the influence of society, friends and relatives. His parents had died while he was a child, leaving enough of a legacy to supply him with a small income for the rest of his life. It wasn't much, but it would be enough to pay the rent and daily expenses if they were frugal. And who needed a car or lots of clothes or expensive food when they had each other? At the time, it had all seemed incredibly exciting.

She'd readily agreed. She could return to uni and finish her degree later—the course structure allowed it—and what was education compared to the great adventures of life and love?

She would spend her days painting the breathtakingly beautiful, ethereal highland landscapes, and Daniel would start up as a software consultant. Even then, when she'd been in the throes of her infatuation, she'd wondered how her soon-to-be husband could become a consultant before he had any real work experience, but her misgiving had seemed minor compared to the grand sweep of her vision of the future. If Daniel's business was unsuccessful, she might be able to sell her paintings—yes, she'd been *that* naive—or, at the very least, when the year was up they could return to civilization and get entry level jobs, secure in the knowledge they'd each found *the one*, and nothing that life threw at them could change the fact.

The new semester had begun, but, after a quick register office wedding, she and her new husband remained at their cottage, signing a lease for a year. A flurry of emails, texts and calls from her parents—which Daniel advised her not to open or answer—dried up after three or four months to an occasional effort every month or so, and then, eventually, nothing. Daniel asserted his judgement that her mother and father didn't care about her had proved correct.

And then, over the course of the following five years, everything had gradually fallen apart.

Her memories faded. She reached the gardens. As she walked through the gates, she wondered how she could have been so foolish and weak.

The assistant in the booth gave her a strange look when she paid the entrance fee. Understanding she must be wearing her worries on her face, she managed a smile, and the young man smiled back sympathetically.

She took the nearest path and allowed the green landscape and peacefulness to wash over her, easing her mind. When she reached the Scented Garden, she sat in the empty arbour. The time of year meant few of the plants were in bloom, but faint aromas still reached her nostrils. Hardly anyone was around. Resting her head on the wooden frame, she closed her eyes.

Her marriage had been a disastrous mistake, but it was nearly over now. She would speak to the solicitor soon and start the divorce process. With luck, she would never have to set eyes on Daniel again. She could move on with her life. She was still comparatively young.

Sensing someone sit down beside her, she opened her eyes.

She glanced over and jerked with shock, her heart suddenly thudding.

Daniel.

He turned to face her, grinning maliciously. 'You were completely away with the fairies for a while there, weren't you? I was wondering when I would get your attention. But then you never were the most attentive wife, were you?'

Molly was too shocked to speak. Her sense of peace had been shorn away.

'What's wrong?' he asked. 'Too overwhelmed with joy at my sudden appearance? Or perhaps you're amazed, wondering how I found you? It saddens me to say it's probably the latter. I'll put your curiosity to rest. At the beginning of our relationship, when you were still unconvinced about your parents' neglect, you would tell me how your mother would often bring you here. She would paint the flowers, you said, which was where you got your love of art. It was quite a sweet tale. So I thought, now you're deluding yourself that your parents actually care about you—that they care about you more than *I* do—you would probably come back here.'

He stretched out his arms and lay them across the back of the seat, his left arm coming uncomfortably close to Molly's back. She shrank into the corner.

'I have to admit, it is quite pleasant, if you like this kind of thing,' Daniel said, returning his attention to the scenery.

She was fighting an internal battle. Faced with her husband's presence, and alone, out of reach of her parents or anyone else who might help her, her resolve to stand up to him began to melt. Before it dissolved entirely, she stood up, preparing to leave without saying a word to him.

But his hand fastened around her arm, and he pulled her down to the seat.

She gasped and looked around for other visitors to the garden, unsure if she was hoping for help or if she was ashamed. But the place appeared deserted apart from the two of them.

Maintaining a tight grip on her arm, Daniel leaned close to her ear and whispered, 'You're not getting away from me so easily. You might think you know me, Molly, but you don't. You have no idea what I'm capable of.'

CHAPTER EIGHTEEN

'What was *that* about?' Shauna asked Will.

They had just finished talking to Derek Ableton, quizzing him about his whereabouts on the night of the murder, and were on their way back to their car.

'You mean *the look*?' Will asked.

'That's exactly what I mean,' she replied, glad she hadn't been imagining it.

The entire time they'd talked to Ableton, he'd been smirking. At first, she'd thought he was just an arrogant sod. But then she got the feeling there was more to his attitude than a personality defect.

'Yeah,' Will agreed. 'He knows something we don't. I'd put money on it.'

'I wonder what.' She gave a sigh of frustration. 'His alibi is pretty solid.'

The manager at the halfway house had confirmed Ableton's story he'd been watching television in the shared lounge until one AM the night of the murder. The timing of the glass breaking and the estimated time of death, plus the distance from the halfway house to Maiden Close made it impossible for Ableton to be the murderer.

'If we don't turn up a lead soon,' Shauna went on, 'I'll bring him in for questioning anyway.'

Next stop was Royston, home town of Joshua Drake, fifteen miles south-west of Cambridge. This time, she drove.

'Remind me what we have on Drake?' she asked.

'He did eight years for corporate fraud and was released last month,' Will replied. 'The only other thing on is record is a caution for domestic violence.'

'Eight years?' Shauna asked. 'What did he do? Rob the Royal Mint?'

'He would have been done for theft then, wouldn't he?'

'You know what I mean. Eight years is a long time.'

'You can beat up old ladies until the cows come home,' said Will, 'but judges don't like it when you steal from the rich.'

'Judges don't like it when you steal from their friends.'

'Now then. Let's not get cynical.'

They progressed in silence for a few minutes, then Shauna asked, 'What company did he embezzle from?'

'Some multi-national. An oil company. He was ordering fake services for a non-existent department, but it was only after he'd left the job a new manager noticed the discrepancy. He was out of the country by then. He'd stolen over a million, but he had nothing to show for it. Gambler.'

'So how did we get him? Was he extradited?'

Will made a *pfft* sound, signalling amusement. 'He wasn't important enough.'

'So how was he caught?'

'Guess.'

Shauna tapped the steering wheel.

'How do most of them get caught?' Will prompted.

In her years in the police service, Shauna had been involved in the apprehension of hundreds of criminals in one way or another. It hadn't taken her long to notice the common denominator between them: stupidity.

Police officers did a difficult and sometimes dangerous job, but the truth was, if those who broke the law were smarter, the work of the police service would be a whole lot harder. Whether it was through leaving clear evidence like fingerprints, DNA, or actual ID, being captured on CCTV cameras or bragging to their friends, trying to sell stolen goods to undercover officers or simply being caught in the act, most offenders virtually gave themselves up.

'I know,' she said. 'He came back to the UK.'

'Got it in one. The officers were waiting for him as he got off the plane at Heathrow.'

She smiled. 'Well, Mr Drake doesn't sound like a psychopathic murderer.'

'No. But the caution gives him a history of violence.'

They'd left the city and were travelling through open countryside. All around, Cambridgeshire's flat landscape of farmland and hedgerows stretched to a pale grey horizon. Warming temperatures had melted the overnight frost, and the parks were looking green and fresh, though the trees remained bare, their black, netted branches reaching up into the overhanging blanket of cloud.

Will's phone pinged in his pocket. He took it out and thumbed the screen. 'Phillipa Edwards' medical history has come through.'

Shauna had requested it almost on a whim, wondering if the woman had experienced amnesia before or if her current bout was solely related to the murder.

'Anything interesting?' she asked.

'Not much here. Nothing psychological.' Will's thumb paused in its scrolling as he seemed to find something worthy of reading more closely.

Shauna tried to peer sideways at the screen but was forced to return her attention to the road. 'What have you found?'

'Probably not relevant, but she had a baby when she was...' He appeared to do a mental calculation. 'Fourteen.'

'*Fourteen*?! You're joking.' Shauna's mind flew to her most recent memory of the prim, middle-aged, middle-class woman, sitting in the interview room at the station. She couldn't imagine anyone less likely to have been a teenage mother, except perhaps the Queen.

'Says here she gave the baby up for adoption,' Will added.

'Jesus. Fourteen.'

'Just shows,' Will said, sliding his phone back into his jacket's inner pocket, 'you can't judge by appearances.'

'I suppose it makes sense in a way.'

'What do you mean?'

'Giving the kid up. If Edwards had grown up on a council estate, she would have kept the baby. There wouldn't have been much shame in it, even back then. Unless you were from a posh family and your parents had *expectations*.'

'Yeah, I suppose so.'

'Shit,' said Shauna, noticing a red line appear on the satnav. 'Missed it.'

They'd reached the outskirts of Royston and had just passed the entrance to the housing estate where Joshua Drake lived. She looked for somewhere to turn around and saw a bus lay-by, where she pulled in and waited for a break in the traffic. In another few minutes they were parked in front of Drake's house —a modern semi-detached, identical to all the others in the road.

Here we go again, thought Shauna as they walked up to the door, remembering their house call to Baram Scott. Their welcome wasn't likely to be any friendlier here.

She rang the doorbell, and immediately a dog began to bark inside. The animal could also be heard scratching and sniffing at the door. A young woman wearing pink jersey leisure trousers and a matching top opened it. Her hair was the kind of blonde that came from a box and she was fully made up even though she appeared to be spending the day at home.

'Yes?' she said, one hand on the door and the other holding the collar of a golden Labrador, which was lunging at them, though not in an aggressive way. The dog looked intent on licking them to death.

Shauna asked to speak to Joshua Drake, explaining who they were. As she spoke the woman's expression changed from bland curiosity to annoyance.

'You'd better come in,' she said resignedly, adding, as she opened the door wider, 'You don't mind dogs, do you?'

'Absolutely not,' said Will, reaching out to ruffle the animal's neck. 'Are you Mrs Drake?'

'I'm not *married* to him,' she replied, her tone implying that would be a very stupid thing to do.

They stepped into the hall. The dog quickly investigated their genitals before deciding they were definitely friends, and wagged its tail enthusiastically in response to Will's pats.

Footsteps sounded on the stairs.

'It's the police,' the woman called out with a note of irritation.

The footsteps halted abruptly. Shauna could see a pair of male legs wearing blue jeans. The man slowly walked down a few more steps.

'Mr Drake?' she said firmly. 'We'd like to ask you some questions.'

Drake descended the rest of the way. He was tall and skinny, and he looked as though he'd only just got up, though it was the early afternoon. His dark brown hair was in need of a haircut and he hadn't shaved for several days.

'I'll make some tea,' said not-Mrs-Drake.

'That's very kind of you,' said Will as they went into the living room, 'but there's no need.'

It *was* very kind of her, Shauna reflected. She'd rarely met such a warm reception at the home of a potential suspect.

The woman disappeared, presumably to make some tea anyway.

Drake sat down, the knees of his long legs rising high as he perched on the low sofa. Will took the only other seat in the cramped space, a matching armchair. Shauna remained standing.

Before anyone had said anything, Drake's gaze shifted towards the view through the window and he rubbed his hands together.

What was he so nervous about?

Shauna allowed the awkward silence to play out.

'What do you want to talk to me about?' he asked.

'Can you tell us your whereabouts on the evening of the third of February?'

'Why?' he asked. Before Shauna could reply, he added, reflexively, 'I was at home. You can ask Sandra.'

Sandra had appeared as he spoke, carrying a tray filled with steaming mugs with tea bag tags hanging over their edges. Drake gave her a *What the fuck are you doing?* look.

'Yeah, he was with me,' she said wearily.

'What were you doing?' asked Will.

'The same as we always do,' Drake replied. 'We were watching telly.'

'Do you remember what programmes you watched?'

Sandra had given Drake an alibi, albeit a reluctant one. Shauna wondered what Will was doing. Drake was nervous, but she didn't think it was about the murder. He was worried about something outside. His attention continued to flick to the window. She realised Will was playing for time.

Drake threw yet another glance at the street. 'The usual. I don't remember. What did we watch, Sandra?'

'What day was the third?'

Drake started and his eyes snapped wide.

Shauna leaned over to get a better view of the street. A man in black, casual trousers, torn at one knee, and a black bomber jacket was striding in the direction of the house.

Drake swept his gaze firmly forwards, his facial muscles rigid and the colour of his skin visibly paling.

'Expecting a visitor?' Will asked innocently.

'No.'

Sandra, who had sat down on the sofa, relaxed into the cushions and rolled her eyes.

An uncomfortable silence fell, which Drake tried to dispel with a cough. 'Is that all you—'

The doorbell rang.

No one moved.

'Aren't you going to answer your door?' asked Shauna.

'You answer it,' Drake told Sandra. 'Tell him I'm busy and to come back later.'

She considered his request for a couple of seconds, twirling one finger in the fringe at the edge of a cushion. Apparently relenting, she began to rise.

'You can answer it, Joshua,' said Shauna. 'We'll wait. We don't have any urgent appointments, do we, DS Fiske?'

'Nope,' he replied.

Drake looked at Sandra in a panic, but she ignored him. He dragged himself upright and went on leaden feet out of the living room and into the hall. Will followed him and leaned on the door jamb, watching their suspect as he opened his front door.

Shauna listened.

The stranger said, 'I've come for the—'

'Now's a bad time,' Drake interrupted, 'The p—'

'Come on,' the visitor whined, 'I really need it. Here's the money. Give it to me.'

'No,' said Drake. Then he whispered something.

'*Fuck!*' the man exclaimed.

Shauna heard the sound of panicked feet pounding asphalt as the visitor sprinted away.

'Joshua Drake,' said Will. 'Please empty out your pockets… ah, shit.'

He ran out.

Shauna was two steps behind him as she entered the hall. In another second they were both speeding after their absconding suspect.

When she'd been at school, Shauna had been terrible at sports. She couldn't play in a team or catch a ball to save her life. But there was one thing she'd excelled at: the hundred metres.

She passed Will. Drake's feet, clad only in socks, flashed up muddily in front of her. He was running over the front lawns and was only a few houses from the corner and the main road, but she was gaining on him. He looked over his shoulder and jerked in surprise when he saw her. His fear lent him another spurt of speed.

It wasn't enough.

She launched herself at him in a rugby tackle, wrapping her arms around Drake's thighs. The two of them hit the ground heavily, but the recently thawed earth softened the landing.

She scrambled onto him, pulled his arm behind his back and twisted it upwards.

'Owwww! All right, all right! I'm not resisting. I'm not resisting!'

Will arrived, puffing.

The dog also appeared and began gambolling around the group, happy to join in the game.

'Stand up,' Shauna ordered, easing the pressure on Drake's arm. He climbed awkwardly to his feet.

'Right,' Will said between pants. 'I'm gonna ask you again. Turn out your pockets.'

Drake was also out of breath, but the sigh he heaved next sounded emotionally painful. With his free hand he reached into one of his pockets and pulled out an empty inner.

'Other side,' said Shauna.

He pulled out the other front pocket of his jeans, where a lump distorted the surface. In his hand was a small, clear, plastic bag filled with white powder.

Shauna had to bite her cheek to prevent herself from laughing. Their suspect might not be a murderer, but he'd been dealing drugs within weeks of his release. No wonder Sandra was pissed off at him. And what appallingly bad luck to have one of his customers arrive while two detectives were sitting in his living room.

As Will took the bag, Shauna applied a tad more pressure to Drake's arm, just in case he was getting any stupid ideas. He mumbled something about police brutality.

Will was peering into the bag.

'Joshua Drake,' he said, 'I am arresting you on suspicion of supplying a controlled drug. You do not have to say anything...'

In the distance, Sandra could be heard calling, 'Billy! Billy! Come here! Come on! There's a good boy. Good boy, Billy.'

The labrador had bounded back to her. She stepped back to let him inside and closed the front door.

CHAPTER NINETEEN

Late afternoon had turned into evening and the grey light filtering in at the incident room windows had darkened. Only Shauna and Will remained at work.

Photographs of Thomas Edwards' corpse, taken at a range of angles, formed a grotesque display on one wall. On another wall hung a map of Cambridge and its surroundings. Connor had helpfully marked number 23 Maiden Close and the car park where Phillipa Edwards had reappeared after her night at an unknown location.

Shauna had sent him, Alfie and Jas home. They'd done sterling work over the last couple of days, providing detailed reports on what the neighbours living near the crime scene had heard or seen, what was contained in the files Belinda had sent from Barker and Partners (nothing of interest) and myriad other tasks that had turned up pitifully little helpful information. The announcement asking the man who had brought in Phillipa Edwards' handbag to return to the station had yielded no response.

They were stuck. They hadn't been able to discover anyone who might have had a grudge against the victim, and their other possible leads—the criminals Phillipa Edwards had treated—had alibis. Even Edwards' handbag seemed to be a dead end because they didn't know where it had been found. No suspicious searches or unusual activity had been discovered on either of the couple's personal laptops.

'What if we look at prisoners who were released earlier than those three?' Will suggested.

'We could,' Shauna replied, 'but it doesn't seem likely someone would wait a few months before taking out their revenge on their psychologist, though, does it?'

'I suppose so,' he conceded.

'Unless they were triggered in some way.'

'Are we sure Scott has an alibi? We didn't actually speak to him.'

'I forgot to say, he left me a voicemail. He must have found my card. His mum vouched for him, so...'

'What was in the message?'

'He said he'll be home all day Monday if we want to talk to him then.'

'As easy as that? Twenty years for a crime he supposedly didn't commit, and he's happy to help?'

'Maybe he's keen to be eliminated from the investigation. We'll go and see him. Better to cross the Is and dot the Ts.'

'Cross the Ts and dot the Is.'

'What? Oh, yeah.' She yawned. 'All we have is Phillipa Edwards. She might not remember the events of that night, but it's clear from everything else she says she was at the house. If she did it, she either remembers and she's lying, or she had some kind of psychotic break and has genuinely blanked it from her mind.'

Will nodded. 'But where did she go afterwards?'

'She definitely spent the night somewhere indoors. I'll ask the team to contact all the hotels and B&Bs in the local area.'

'All right. It's getting late. Should we wrap up?'

'Yeah, okay.' The lack of progress was frustrating. Shauna hoped Forensics might turn up something. Traces of Thomas

Edwards' blood on his wife's clothes would be nice, but for some reason she strongly doubted they would find any.

Will was concentrating on something on his computer.

She was still unsure what to make of the younger detective. Her first impression had been he was cocky and superficial, but since then he'd played 'good cop' at Phillipa Edwards' interview convincingly, demonstrating compassion and understanding. Earning the suspect's trust by pretending you were on their side was a well-known interview tactic, but Will Fiske was either a very good actor or surprisingly empathetic.

'Right, that's me done for today,' he said, suddenly looking up and catching her watching him.

She quickly switched her attention to her screen, and then inwardly cringed in embarrassment. He must have noticed. It would have been better not to turn away.

When she looked at him again, Will's small smile told her all she needed to know, and she fought to stop herself from blushing.

'I don't know if you heard,' he said, 'but a few of us are meeting for a quick after-work drink. Want to come along?'

'Oh, no. Thanks, but I'd better head home.'

Will turned off his computer and the bright reflection from the monitor on his face disappeared. 'You sure? It's been a long day. It'd be good to relax a bit, chat about something other than work for a change. You can get to know people better after a couple of drinks.'

She knew exactly what he meant—he was leading the effort from the rest of the department to find out about the new detective inspector. She also knew she was driving their curiosity by being secretive. If she'd simply told them a bit about herself, they probably would have left her alone. But she wasn't ready yet.

'Yeah, we spend too much time here, right? It's hard on part-ners and kids,' said Will. He was too much of a detective not to have noticed the indentation on her finger where her wedding ring used to be. He was fishing again.

Shauna decided to turn the tables. 'It is. I take it your girlfriend doesn't mind you going out drinking with your workmates?'

He smiled knowingly. 'She used to. It was one of the many things that broke us up.'

He was good.

Now she was feeling guilty. After rebuffing his attempts to dig into her background, when she'd done the same to him, he'd been frank and honest.

Shauna thought of the tiny terraced house she was renting until she could find something to buy, which, given Cambridge house prices, might be never. She thought of unlocking her front door and going into the cold, dark, empty place, immediately turning on the television just to fill the silence, and then eating pizza for dinner with a glass of wine for company.

'Okay, I'll come for a drink. Just one. Then I'll have to go. I can hardly keep my eyes open.'

'I know the feeling.' He stood up and took his coat off the back of his chair. 'Ready when you are.'

———

She stepped from the freezing late winter night into the warmth, light, and noise of the pub and immediately regretted her decision to accept Will's invitation.

The 'few of us' he'd mentioned turned out to be half the staff. They were filling most of the pub, and they'd all turned their gazes on her. Unfortunately, among the sea of faces, she couldn't spot Jas, Alfie or Connor, the only people she knew a little and would feel comfortable around.

Dread and loathing at being the centre of attention almost made her reverse direction and walk right out again, but Will was right behind her, blocking her escape.

'What can I get you?' he asked.

It looked like she was doomed to stay, at least for fifteen or twenty minutes.

'A glass of white would be great, thanks.'

He left her to join the crush at the bar, and Shauna stood awkwardly alone for a few moments until a woman she didn't immediately recognise walked over. As the woman got closer, she recognised Beth, one of the desk sergeants.

'Glad you could make it. Not everyone has had a chance to meet you yet. If you come with me, I'll introduce you.'

'Thanks,' Shauna replied, trying to sound like she meant it.

She followed the sergeant to a mixed group sitting around a circular table, some crammed into the bench seats and others perched on old wooden chairs. The empty glasses at the centre of the table and their relaxed, rosy faces told her they'd already been there a while.

There was nowhere for her to sit, so one of the men stood up to give her his chair. She didn't want to take it, mostly because if she did, she would be trapped among these people she barely knew. The man and she argued politely back and forth until out of sheer emotional discomfort she was forced to relent and sit down.

The man stood behind her, out of her immediate view, though she could feel his presence looming.

She looked for Will as an unexpected port in this storm of awkwardness. He was still at the bar, waiting to be served.

Beth introduced her to the crowd, and then introduced everyone to her, one by one.

Shauna knew she would never remember all the names and, come Monday morning, she would be struggling to greet them. The conversation they'd been having when she turned up resumed. They were talking about a television programme she'd never heard of.

She felt ignored and yet, at the same time, under deep scrutiny. Her empty, cold, quiet house seemed inviting now. Ever since Will had caught her watching him at his desk, the evening had turned into one big embarrassment fest.

'Here you go.' He appeared as if from nowhere, pulled a coaster across the table and placed a full glass of wine on it.

'Thanks.' Shauna wondered how quickly she could finish her drink and leave without being rude.

'I have to confess,' said Beth, who was sitting next to her, 'something's been bothering me for ages. Do you mind if I ask—'

Here it was. Shauna braced herself for the prying question. *Was she married? Did she have any kids?*

'—when I notified you about the Edwards' murder case, what on Earth were you doing at Wicken Fen?'

'*Oh*, that.' Shauna relaxed a little. 'Actually, I know this must sound odd, but I was trying to get a photo of a short-eared owl. Early morning is the best time to catch them.'

'You're a twitcher!' the man standing behind her announced.

'I suppose you could say that, but, honestly, I'm not very knowledgeable. I just do it for fun.'

'My husband's a twitcher,' said a woman on the other side of the table. She rolled her eyes. 'Always going on about bloody birds. It's an obsession.' Then she looked at Shauna in a mild panic. 'I didn't mean...'

'No, it's okay. It *can* get obsessive. I mean, why else would you lie around in a muddy field at the crack of dawn?'

Chuckles from the rest of the table lowered Shauna's tension another notch. She took a drink of wine. Perhaps the evening wouldn't be so awful after all.

After a short discussion on birdwatching, the conversation turned to other topics. A short while later, when her glass was nearly empty and she was feeling warm and tranquil, Will told the table about that day's arrest of Joshua Drake. He spun the event into a hilarious tale, likening her chase and capture of Drake to Usain Bolt winning gold at the Olympics.

Though his anecdote put the attention back on her, Shauna found she didn't mind. By the time he finished, she was listening as if he was talking about someone else and crying with laughter.

She noticed the pint glass he was holding was empty, so she drank the last of her wine, got to her feet, and offered to buy the next round. Only Will accepted her offer. He accompanied her to the bar.

'You tell quite a story,' she said as they waited.

He shrugged. 'One of my many talents.'

'I'm sure,' she replied—and instantly regretted it. She'd only meant to pay him a compliment, but she realised her response could have sounded flirtatious.

It was too late.

A light seemed to come on behind his eyes, and the knowing smile from earlier returned.

Shit.

The wine had gone to her head.

The barman stepped over to them. 'What can I get you?'

'A St. Clements,' she replied. Better to stay off alcohol for the rest of the night. 'Will?'

He ordered another pint of bitter.

They waited for the drinks, and Shauna remained silent, wondering how to retreat from this unprofessional, overly familiar situation she found herself in with her detective sergeant.

The barman placed her orange juice and lemonade and Will's beer on the bar, and she paid with her credit card.

'Someone's taken your seat,' said Will. 'Shall we find a quiet corner to talk about the case?'

No.

Absolutely not.

No way.

'Uh, okay.'

What possible reason could she give to refuse?

Misgivings flooded her. At best, her subordinate thought she fancied him. At worst, if they spent the evening in private conversation, so would everyone else.

She would have to down her drink in record time, make her excuses and bolt like the famous athlete.

A couple at a small table in the corner were leaving, and they took their still-warm seats. The pub was filling to capacity, the new, non-police patrons driven in by falling sleet and icy pavements. Will leaned towards her and raised his voice over the hubbub.

'How are you finding Cambridge?'

She bit back her instinctive reply, *I thought we were going to talk about the case.* Then she suppressed a sarcastic *I turn right at Bedford.* 'It's nice. I like it.'

He leaned closer. 'If you ever want someone to show you around, just let me know.'

'Thanks for the offer, but I prefer to explore on my own.'

Leaning back in his seat, Will studied her for a few beats before taking a drink of beer. 'Well,' he said, leaning in again, 'if you ever change your mind...'

He winked.

What?! She raised her eyebrows. 'Detective Sergeant, you seem to have the wrong idea about our relationship.'

'Have I?' He took another drink of beer.

Arrogant twat.

'Yes, you have,' Shauna replied, her tone icier than the road outside.

She stood up, and Will's confident expression faltered as he appeared to finally understand he'd overstepped the mark. She hadn't touched her drink, but it was past time to leave.

As she walked away from him without another word, she felt her phone vibrating in her pocket. She took it out and looked at the screen. Someone was calling from a private number. It was too late in the evening for a social call. Was it an emergency? Something to do with her kids? Mindful of the noise in the bar, she put a finger to one ear as she answered, continuing her march to the exit.

'DI Holt?' said a voice that was strangely distorted. It sounded as though it was being fed through a computer program to ensure anonymity.

'Yes. Who is this?'

'Your nemesis.'

'My what?' Shauna had to push through a knot of people who had inconveniently gathered right next to the door.

Had the caller really said they were a *nemesis*?

She opened the door.

'Think you're so smart,' said the odd voice, 'working on a famous case? Leave it alone. Resign, or you'll regret it.'

The chill night air burst on her skin as she made it out of the pub. The ambient noise level plummeted, and she could hear breathing at the other end of the call.

'Why?' she asked, hoping to tease out more information, anything that might give her a clue about the caller and their connection to the murder.

But the line went dead.

CHAPTER TWENTY

Ruth tried to open the front door quietly, but Molly immediately came out to the hallway.

'Where are you going?'

'Nowhere special,' Ruth had replied, trying to keep her tone light.

'Do you have a doctor's appointment? Are you all right?' Her daughter's expression became full of concern.

Ruth had seen that look directed at her several times since Molly's return and it made her feel guilty. *She* should be the one who was concerned about her daughter, but the situation with Phillipa had eclipsed everything.

'No, nothing like that. I...' She looked up the stairs, her stomach clenching with anxiety. She had to get out of the house without alerting her friend. She'd taken a day's holiday and she might not get another opportunity. Anders had volunteered to cover for her, but she couldn't impose on him again. She felt guilty slipping away and leaving Dom to deal with Becky, who was home from school with a bad cold.

'It's something to do with Phillipa?' asked Molly.

Ruth gave up. Continuing the subterfuge would only delay her. She nodded, feeling a flush creep up her neck.

'What is it?' Molly pressed. 'Where are you going?'

'I'm sorry, but I'd rather not say.'

'Mum, tell me where you're going!'

'I-I'm going to speak to someone, but I don't want Phillipa to know about it.'

'I won't say anything to her. You can tell me who it is.'

'I'm going to talk to a former patient, that's all.'

Ruth saw understanding dawn in her daughter's eyes.

'Mum! You're *not* going to talk to one of the suspects! Tell me you aren't.' She rushed into the open doorway.

Ruth struggled to answer. She was a terrible liar. It was better to simply not reply. She side-stepped her daughter, trying to get out of the house.

'You are!' Molly exclaimed, moving again to bar her way. 'You're going to see one of the people the police think might have murdered Phillipa's husband.'

'*Shhhh*! She'll hear. She wouldn't want me to approach them.'

Ruth peered up the stairs for a second time. Her friend still wasn't up, though it was past eight-thirty.

She motioned Molly to move outside, then followed her and pulled the door almost closed. 'Please keep your voice down. Phillipa will be up soon and if she finds out what I'm doing she'll try to stop me.'

'Of course she doesn't want you to talk to a potential murderer!'

'I talk to *actual* murderers all day, dear. It's my job.'

'But in prison you have security. You have guards there in case something happens. You don't go into their *homes*. This is different.'

'I'm just going to...Look, we can't stand on the doorstep and talk about this.'

'Mum, you can't—'

'Molly, you may be twenty-five, but I am still your mother. You can't tell me what I can and can't do.'

'Well then, I'm coming with you.'

'No. You have to stay here.'

'Why?'

'To look after Phillipa.'

Annoyance flashed into Molly's features. 'She's a grown woman!' Then she grew calmer and went on, 'I know she's been through a lot, but she can still make her own breakfast and turn the television on. I'm coming, too. Have you got your keys?'

'Yes, but—'

Molly pulled the door closed, locking it. 'I don't care what you say, I'm not letting you go and visit this man all by yourself. It isn't safe, and you know it isn't. And if you don't let me come, I'll tell Dad what you're doing. He doesn't know, does he?'

Ruth shook her head. She hadn't dared tell Dom about her excursion to talk to Derek Ableton the other day either. He would have been furious.

'So don't argue,' said Molly emphatically.

Ruth stared at her daughter. She was seeing a new side to her. Molly had always been so gentle and amenable.

There seemed to be no option other than to agree. 'All right. If you insist. But you have to wait in the car.'

Molly asked her the address and said she would drive. They left Maiden Close and drove down Queen Edith's Way before heading towards the north of the city.

'You haven't said why you want to see this suspect,' said Molly. 'Isn't that the detectives' job?'

'I'm not even sure they've spoken to him yet...If I tell you something, will you promise you won't tell Phillipa?'

'We've barely spoken two words to each other, Mum, but I promise.'

'The police seem to think she did it.'

Perhaps that was somewhat of a leap, based only on what the detectives had implied that day they'd come to the prison and the state Phillipa had been in when she'd returned from the police station, but Ruth felt it was true in essence.

'Do they?' Molly took her gaze from the road to glance at her mother, as if checking she was serious. 'Why would they think that?'

'It doesn't make any sense, does it? But that's the impression I got when the detectives spoke to me. They talked a lot about Thomas's legacy and how she would get it all. It *is* true that most murder victims know their killers, but the police are obviously barking up the wrong tree in this case. After five years of working with her, I know Phillipa very well and I can't think of anyone less likely to be a murderer.'

She paused before adding, 'The detectives asked for a list of recently released prisoners she'd treated, but I don't think they're taking that possibility seriously. What if they're only looking for evidence that points to her? So I thought if I spoke to the suspects myself, I might be able to tease out some information. I'm used to speaking to these people. I could give the detectives something concrete to go on.'

'I really don't think Phillipa's a murderer,' Molly said, 'but I'm sure the police won't arrest her unless they have some evidence.'

'Well, if you believed what all the prisoners say, everyone behind bars is innocent, but there have been some genuine miscarriages of justice, usually when the police investigation targets a particular person regardless of what the evidence indicates. In an ideal world, it wouldn't happen. Unfortunately, our world is far from ideal.'

'But if the murderer is a prisoner Phillipa treated,' said Molly, 'you're going face to face with someone who wants to murder psychiatrists.'

'Not quite. Phillipa is a psychologist, and it was Thomas who was killed.'

'Does it make a difference?!'

'I know it's risky, but if I don't do something, who will? And I'm already getting results. I spoke to one of them last week. Although it didn't go as well as I'd hoped, I think I learned something significant.'

'You've already met one?' Molly's grip on the steering wheel tightened. 'Mum, have you been feeling all right lately?'

Ruth reached over to pat Molly's knee. 'Please try not to worry. I know what I'm doing.'

'I'm not sure you do.'

———

They pulled up outside a shabby house.

'I wish you would think twice about this, Mum.'

'I have to help Phillipa. She doesn't have anyone else.'

'Doesn't she? Doesn't she have any other friends, or any relations? I wondered why she was staying with us.'

'She's never mentioned anyone. I got the impression her family was a sore subject, and I didn't want to pry. I think they might all be dead. And as for friends, she hasn't been living in Cambridge very long.'

'I thought she'd been here a few years.'

'Yes, but it's hard to make friends in a new place, especially when you work full time.'

Molly said, 'Okay, whatever. But if you insist on doing this, I'm coming in with you.'

'No! You have to stay in the car. This man could become hostile.'

'That's exactly *my* point!' Molly exclaimed. 'I don't want you to get hurt. If there are two of us, he'll be less likely to do anything.'

'You're my daughter, dear. I'm not taking you into danger. What would your father say if he knew?'

'And I'm not letting you do this alone. Seriously, I won't let you out of the car.'

There was that determined, assertive look again. Ruth buckled. 'Oh, all right! Come on then. But when I'm talking to him I don't want you to say anything. Nothing at all.'

'Okay, I'll be quiet. But if I say it's time to leave, we go.'

Deliberately not agreeing to the condition, Ruth exited the car. Together, they walked to the ex-prisoner's front door.

She rang the bell.

A man's voice called out from the side of the house, 'Round the back.'

When they arrived Scott was waiting at the side door. Ruth recognised him from the photo on his file. He was unshaven but his blue jeans and jumper were clean, if rather old. For a man in his forties who had spent most of his adult life in prison, he looked in good shape. His eyebrows drew together in confusion as he looked them up and down.

'Mr Scott? My name's Ruth Terrell. I'd like to talk to you about something important, if it's convenient.'

'Terrell? Do I know you? The name rings a bell.'

'You might have heard me mentioned—'

'Oh yeah. Terrell. Dr Terrell, right? Sorry, I didn't mean to be rude. I was expecting someone else. You'd better come in.'

'Chocolate lime?' Will asked, holding out the bag of sweets over the shared desk like a peace offering.

Neither of them had spoken about the incident at the pub since returning to work on Monday. Shauna had considered giving her detective sergeant a dressing down, but he appeared to be embarrassed and contrite, never meeting her gaze or mentioning anything not work-related. She'd decided that drawing attention to what had happened would only make things more awkward.

'Thanks.'

She reached out and took a sweet. As she untwisted and peeled off the cellophane, Will cast a glance around the incident room. Connor had gone out with lunch orders for the local burger place, Jas was on the phone with a B&B and Alfie was digging into Phillipa Edwards' background. Will leaned closer and said softly, 'Look, about the other night—'

'Don't worry about it,' Shauna swiftly interrupted. 'If you've finished what you were doing, let's go over the forensics report.'

Will's gaze rested on her a moment before he said, 'All right. I've read the whole thing but I can't see any leads.'

Neither could Shauna. No fingerprints had been found on

the murder weapon and only Phillipa and Thomas Edwards' prints had been found in the house. Though it had been raining that evening, no footprints had been found in the garden. No blood had been found on Phillipa, and no fibres from Thomas's clothing had been on her clothes. Not that it would have meant much if they had, given that the two of them lived together. No blood other than the victim's had been found at the crime scene.

Shauna said, 'Yeah, a big pile of nothing.'

The post-mortem report had arrived, too. The victim had bled to death within a couple of minutes from a single stab wound. A toxicology screen of his blood had come up negative except for a low level of blood alcohol. The only other thing of note James had discovered was the early stages of heart disease.

'The clothes thing doesn't add up.' Will frowned at his screen. 'How did she murder him and not get any of his blood on her?'

CCTV footage from the prison had shown the clothes Phillipa Edwards had worn at work the day of the murder were the same as she'd been wearing when she'd re-surfaced.

'I thought about that,' Shauna replied. 'She could have bought two sets of identical clothing, knowing there would be a recording of what she was wearing. After the murder, she went to wherever she'd stashed the second set, washed off all the evidence, and wore the new clothes the next day.'

'Pretty cunning,' Will remarked.

'She's a smart woman. She could have had it all planned out to the last detail.'

'So where did she go that night?'

'That's the question.'

None of the neighbours had security cameras, let alone cameras facing the street, to record Phillipa Edwards leaving her home, and no one recalled seeing her.

'Maybe Jas will turn up something,' said Will.

Hearing her name spoken, the young DC flashed them a

friendly smile as she was giving a description of Edwards' appearance over the phone.

That uncomfortable feeling of coming up against a dead end was hitting Shauna in the face again.

'I told Scott we would talk to him today,' she said. 'We might as well cross him off our list.'

'Okay, but I hope his mum isn't home. I've got a feeling she won't be pleased to see us.'

'Not everyone's going to fall for your charms, Will.'

'That's clear as day.' He grinned sheepishly.

———

Will did the driving, though Shauna was now becoming familiar with the layout of Cambridge.

She'd been truthful that night at the pub when she'd told Will she liked the city. Leaving the Met and relocating from London had been an upheaval, especially so soon after her divorce, but living in Cambridge had made things easier. It had a different atmosphere from a big metropolis, a gentler, more personal feel. Although it wasn't home, she could imagine it becoming so at some point.

The realisation was bitter sweet. Her kids would have been happy growing up here.

'Everything okay?' Will asked, jerking her back to reality.

She blinked. 'Yeah, fine.' The whirr of the car's fan, plastic smell of the interior and warm airflow on her face surged in.

He glanced at her again. 'Look, I really want to talk to you about the other night.'

'There's no need. Let's pretend it never happened, okay?'

'No, it's not okay.'

Shauna grimaced and looked out the side window. She was reluctant to pull rank on her DS to make him shut up, but she also didn't want to hear his half-hearted apology or excuses. 'If you're worried it's going to affect your promotion prospects, don't be. I'm not going to write you up, and I'm not going to mention it to Bryant or anyone else. As far as I'm concerned, it's in the past and that's where it's staying. Now, can we move on?'

He gave a sigh of exasperation. With a pained look, he said, 'I can see why you'd think I'm only worried about my job, but I just want to set things straight between us. Honestly, if you did write me up, I'd feel better. I deserve it. I can't stop kicking myself for being such an idiot.'

Shauna watched him for a moment before replying. His feeling seemed genuine.

'To be fair,' she said, 'I don't think flirting with your DI is against the code of conduct. If I were to report you, I'm not sure what I'd say. *Detective Sergeant Fiske insinuated I was attracted to him.* Doesn't sound like an actionable offence.'

'I don't know. I have exes who could argue a good case.'

She gave a short laugh.

After a pause, he said, 'I really am sorry.'

'All right, apology accepted. Now, can we *please* put it behind us and focus on work? Let's get this interview with Scott over with.'

'Sounds good.' Will flipped the indicator and turned the steering wheel, taking them into Donne Crescent.

Baram Scott's house looked just as forlorn and neglected as it had before. The driveway was empty, but a car was parked on the street in front of the house. Will pulled up on the opposite side of the road. He turned off the engine and asked, 'Did you hear any more about that phone call you got when you left the pub? Have they traced the number?'

'Not yet, but I don't think it's important. A murder case always attracts cranks, and my mobile number isn't that hard to get a hold of.'

'Isn't it?'

'I give my card to everyone I talk to on a case. You never know when someone might suddenly remember something relevant.'

'But you haven't been in Cambridge long. You can't have given your card to many people yet.'

'Hm, true.'

'What did he say exactly?'

'I don't know if it *was* a man. The distortion was very strong. It could have been a deep-voiced woman. I could only just make out what they were saying, something about them being my nemesis and warning me to stay off the case. Like I said, it was just some crank, probably drunk, lonely and bored.'

'If they used the word nemesis, that implies someone with higher than average education.'

'Does it? Isn't that how the arch-villain is sometimes described in comic-books? The caller wouldn't have to know exactly what the word means to use it correctly.'

'Okay, but he or she did manage to find your number, like the murderer found out Thomas and Phillipa Edwards' address.'

'Yeah, but...'

The wail of a siren distracted Shauna. She looked over her shoulder in the direction of the sound, which was coming from the bottom of the road. A beat later, flashing lights came into view. As she watched, a patrol car raced up the street.

It abruptly stopped at the bottom of Baram Scott's driveway.

Shauna and Will shared a look of surprise before she jerked her door open and leapt out.

A second wail was already following the first, and as she ran over the road, an ambulance swept around the corner.

CHAPTER TWENTY-TWO

Molly wasn't sure what she was expecting to see inside the ex-offender's home, but everything looked normal. At first glance, it was cleaner and less cluttered than her parents' house. Money was clearly tight, judging from the aged kitchen cabinets and worn lino flooring, but that was only to be expected. As Mum often remarked, poverty and deprivation frequently went hand in hand with criminal behaviour.

What on Earth was she thinking of, visiting this man? Why couldn't she just let the police do their job?

Was she going senile?

The man, Scott, who her mother had come to see, had given Molly one or two curious glances, no doubt wondering who she was. Mum hadn't introduced her and the idea of introducing herself felt silly.

Hi, I'm Molly, Dr Terrell's daughter, and I'm here to make sure you don't kill her.

'Would you like some tea?' Scott asked.

'That's very kind of you,' Mum replied, 'but we won't be staying long. I appreciate you taking the time to talk to me.'

'No problem. Is it something to do with my treatment?'

'Your...? Oh, no, not at all, sorry.'

'Right.' His curious frown grew deeper. 'Come through to the living room. It's a bit cramped in here.'

Scott's allusion to the living room being less cramped had been ambitious. The three-seater sofa was empty but the other seat, a low armchair, was occupied. An old woman was curled into it, her knees raised higher than her hips. Thick support bandages swathed her legs where they stuck out from the bottoms of soft baggy jeans. At the end of her sausage limbs, her feet disappeared into large slippers that had once been pink and fluffy but were now grey and flat.

'We've got visitors, Mum,' said Scott, his tone implying she should leave.

'Oh, really,' said Molly, 'there isn't any need. I can stand.'

Scott began to explain, 'If it's prison stuff—'

'Who are you?' the old woman barked. 'Are you the police?' She squinted at Molly and her mother. 'I told you once to piss off. Baram didn't have nothing to do with—'

'Mum! Why don't you go and have a lie down?' he suggested.

Her face creased into a deep scowl, but she began rising slowly to her feet, gripping the armrests of her chair like her life depended on them.

Molly moved to take her elbow. 'Can I help you?'

'Get away from me, bitch!'

'Cut it out!' Scott admonished. Addressing Molly and her mother, he went on, 'Sorry, she's in a lot of pain, and...'

'We understand,' said Mum.

The old woman had made it to a standing position. She hobbled out of the room.

'She's still angry about my sentence,' Scott said softly, his gaze on his mother as she climbed the stairs in the hall, placing both feet in succession on each step. 'I don't think she'll ever let it go. I didn't do it, you see.' He turned to Mum. 'I bet all your patients say that.'

'To be frank, yes they do. I reserve judgement. It is healthy move on from anger and resentment over perceived injustices, however, if you can manage it.'

'*I* can. Mum's the one who can't. She'd always wanted grand-kids. My girlfriend broke up with me when it all went down, not that I blame her. Now, I'm a bit old for kids and not many women want to date an ex-con. But you're not here to listen to my problems. You can sit down.'

He took one end of the settee while Mum took the other. Molly remained standing, feeling foolish. When Mum had said she was going to speak to a murder suspect, she'd imagined someone out of Dickens; someone gruff, surly and menacing, like Bill Sykes. Scott appeared as ordinary as they came. She wouldn't have looked twice at him if she'd passed him in the street.

Mum said, 'I'd like to ask you a few questions about the psychologist who treated you—Dr Edwards.'

'Oh, her.' He settled back in his seat. 'All right. What do you want to know? I saw her a few times. Thought she was pretty good.'

'Are you aware her husband was murdered?'

His expression darkened. 'I do watch the news, yeah.' A harsh edge had crept into his voice.

Most people would have expressed sadness or concern about the tragic event. Scott didn't. The atmosphere in the room had changed.

'I was wondering...' Mum seemed at a loss for how to go on.

'If *I* know anything about it?' he asked.

Molly cringed, vicariously embarrassed.

'Don't turn this into something it isn't, Mr Scott,' replied Mum crisply. 'I'm here because you knew Dr Edwards, and you were at Shelby a long time. You have a better understanding of what went on than myself or the prison officers, an insider's understanding. We don't know the half of it, of that I'm sure.'

Her flattery seemed to mollify him a little.

'Yeah, but I still don't get it,' he said. 'Why are *you* asking me about this murder? Isn't this something for the police to handle?'

'The police investigation is ongoing, but I'm also helping Dr Edwards by reaching out to her former patients. Anything you might be able to tell me could help.'

'Like what? Where I was that night?' he asked sarcastically. 'I was here, as it happens. Enjoying my freedom, keeping my nose clean.' He rubbed his forehead with his palm. 'I'm not doing time again. No way.'

'Let me help you. It seems the police have already been in contact. If you *do* know anything, tell me and I can pass the information on. I could tell the police I had a tip off from a prisoner. It would sound better coming from me. Once they have a firm suspect, that takes the pressure off you, and the real killer will be brought to justice.'

'What makes you think I know who did it? Oh, wait, I have an *insider's understanding*.'

Mum didn't reply. Molly guessed she was using silence to tease out a meaningful response.

She'd never seen her mother 'at work' before. Mum generally never discussed the details of her job and although Molly had naturally always known what her mother did, she hadn't really given it much thought. She'd only felt a vague but constant apprehension that one of the prisoners might hurt Mum one day. It was interesting to see this other side of her. It turned out her mother could be quite manipulative.

'Maybe I do know something,' Scott said grudgingly, 'but...it mustn't get out that it came from me.'

'I won't tell anyone. But if you have any information that could give the detectives a nudge in the right direction...'

'Okay. A few of the prisoners had a real thing for Edwards. You know what I mean? They'd talk a lot about what they wanted to do to her. Used to fake breakdowns to get an appointment to see her.' His gaze flicked to Molly.

'So you're saying someone could have murdered her husband because they were jealous of him?' Mum asked.

Scott shrugged. 'You asked me what I know, and I told you.

One of the blokes who fancied Edwards got out a week before me. His name's Ableton. He was in for GBH.'

Mum's shoulders slumped a fraction.

'Ableton,' she said. 'I see. Is there anything else you can tell me?'

'Hey, I gave you a name, didn't I? Don't push it.'

The sound of a heavy, soft object hitting the floor came from overhead. Scott's head jerked up and he stared at the ceiling. Without a word, he jumped to his feet and ran upstairs, his feet thudding on the treads.

'What was that?' asked Molly.

'It sounded like—'

Anguished yelling sounded through the floorboards. Molly couldn't quite make out what he was saying.

'I think we'd better see what's happened,' said Mum.

Molly followed her mother up the stairs to the landing. The yelling was coming from an open doorway, but the bedroom inside was so dark she could only make out the edge of a bed.

'Mum!' Scott shouted. 'Get up! What's wrong with you?'

'Call an ambulance,' Mum said, peering inside.

She moved towards the bedroom, but Molly touched her arm. 'Do you really think you should?'

'Call an ambulance,' Mum repeated, stepping into the room.

Molly searched her bag for her phone.

'Get out!' Scott roared. 'This is none of your business.'

Mum replied calmly, 'Mr Scott, please move out of the way so I can help your mother.'

Molly scrabbled around in her bag among old envelopes, her brush, her purse, a fold-up umbrella and reusable carrier bags. Where had her phone gone? It always managed to slip underneath everything else. Had she forgotten it?

'Leave us alone!' Scott exclaimed. 'Fuck off.'

'Please, I can help. If you would just...'

Molly found her mobile and pulled it out.

There were sounds of struggling coming from the bedroom. Molly heard a soft *Oh*!

She ran into the bedroom.

Daylight barely penetrated the thick curtains, throwing Scott and her mother into silhouettes. Scott was bending over something on the floor on the other side of the bed. Her mother was trying to go around him, but piles of belongings meant there was no room unless he gave up his space.

Scott threw back an elbow, hitting Mum in the chest and making her gasp. Then he turned and grabbed her.

'Stop that!' Molly cried out. 'Don't touch her!'

She jabbed the 9 on her phone three times.

CHAPTER TWENTY-THREE

Once she'd run through the open side door, the commotion coming from the upstairs of Baram Scott's house directed Shauna where to go. Will ran up the stairs after her. At the top, two uniforms could be seen in one of the bedrooms, grappling with someone she presumed to be Scott, though in the gloom it was hard to be sure.

More surprising to her was a frightened-looking young woman standing on the landing.

'Who are you?'

'Molly Markson.'

The name held no meaning for Shauna, but she didn't have time to find out what the woman was doing there. She guessed she must be a relative.

'Sir, please calm down,' said one of the uniforms in the bedroom. Grunts and gasps ensued as Scott failed to comply.

The paramedics from the ambulance appeared below.

'Shit,' Shauna said, 'there isn't room to swing a cat.' She called out to the police officers, 'I'm DI Holt. Do you have someone requiring medical attention in there?'

'Yes, there's a woman on the floor. She looks unconscious.'

'Leave my mum alone!' yelled Scott. 'No one's touching her.'

'Please move out of the way, Baram,' came a woman's voice from the bedroom. 'Come on, you don't want to be arrested, do you?'

Will raised his eyebrows at Shauna. She hadn't realised there was another person in the room either. And the voice sounded familiar, though she couldn't put a name to it yet.

'Um,' said one of the paramedics from the hall, 'is the patient up there?'

Shauna replied, 'Yes, she's—'

'This is ridiculous!' exclaimed Molly Markson before calling out, 'Mum, come out of there.'

Mum? Wasn't it the mother who needed the ambulance?

Then, from the bedroom came the sound of a man cursing.

'All right,' said an officer. 'Come along with us, sir. Let's allow the medical people to do their work.'

The uniforms were bringing Scott out. At the same time, the leading paramedic reached the landing carrying a defibrillator.

'We can't help here,' Shauna said to Will. 'We're just in the way.' They went downstairs and outside the house.

The two police officers emerged a minute later, gripping Scott's arms firmly. Shauna recognised him from the picture on his file. The next person to leave the house was the young woman they'd met on the landing. Shauna began to approach her when another figure walked out the front door: Dr Ruth Terrell.

That was who she'd heard speaking in the bedroom.

Terrell knew the names of the three ex-prisoners under suspicion. Surely she couldn't be...?

Swallowing her astonishment, Shauna altered trajectory and marched over to Terrell.

'Dr Terrell, what a surprise to see you here. I didn't know you made house calls.'

The psychiatrist looked uncomfortable.

'But, silly me, you're not that kind of doctor, are you? I'm completely confused. What *exactly* are you doing here?'

'I don't believe there's a law against visiting released inmates,' Dr Terrell retorted. 'Now, my daughter and I must be going.'

'Your daughter?' Shauna glanced at Markson and filed the fact away for future reference. 'There might not be a law against visiting released offenders, but I'd be very surprised if your code of ethics doesn't prohibit you from socialising with them. And I can assure you there's definitely a law against interfering with a police investigation, and another one called perverting the course of justice.'

Dr Terrell reddened. 'I was not socialising with Mr Scott.'

'Just interfering in the investigation, then?' The more the surprise of discovering Terrell in Scott's house wore off, the angrier Shauna grew. What had the psychiatrist said to Scott, and what had he told her? The stupid woman could have jeopardised the entire case.

'Do you realise you could have ruined our chances of convicting the murderer? The case might not even get to trial after this.'

'Well it isn't as if you were getting anywhere, is it?' Terrell snapped. Then she sagged a little and passed a hand over her eyes.

'*Mum!*' her daughter, who had joined them, demurred.

'Not getting anywhere?' Shauna asked. 'You have no idea where we are.'

'But what have you done?' asked Terrell. 'I've been following the case in the media. There haven't been any arrests and no one even taken in for questioning except Phillipa, who wouldn't hurt a fly. The poor woman is devastated and you're determined to prove it was her just because she was his wife.'

'Dr Terrell,' said Shauna, speaking quietly lest her rage boiled over. 'I am *not* about to keep you informed about the progress of our investigation. If you have a complaint about my or DS Fiske's professional behaviour I'm sure you can figure out where to send it.'

'*Mum*,' pleaded the daughter, 'let's go.'

A paramedic carrying one end of a gurney walked backwards out of Scott's front door. The patient, an old woman, lay on it covered in a blanket, an oxygen mask over her face. Her skin was grey and she looked barely alive. When the second paramedic appeared holding the other end of the gurney, they dropped its legs and began rolling it down the garden path.

'I want to go with her,' shouted Scott from the back of the police car.

One of the uniforms in the front replied, but Shauna didn't catch what he said.

'I'm all right now,' Scott protested. 'I've calmed down. She's my mum. I don't want...' His words trailed off.

A constable climbed out of the car and walked over to Shauna. 'I take it you were here to speak to him. What do you want us to do?'

'See what the paramedics say,' Shauna replied. 'If they're okay with it, he can go. We weren't going to arrest him, unless you...'

'No,' said the officer, 'the lady has told us she doesn't want to press charges.' He glanced at Terrell. 'He was just upset about his mother. He seems better now.'

The ambulance crew were in the process of lifting Scott's mother into the vehicle. Along the street, neighbours were watching from their windows and standing at open front doors. Shauna was reminded of the woman's comment the first time she'd been to her home, about giving them something to gossip about. Scott climbed into the back of the ambulance.

'We need to leave too,' urged Dr Terrell's daughter.

'Wait,' Shauna said. 'I want to know why you were here.'

'I would rather not say.' Terrell took her daughter's elbow, and the two women walked away.

Shauna stared after them. Without arresting her, she couldn't compel the psychiatrist to explain her presence in Scott's house, but from what she'd said it seemed obvious she distrusted them and had decided to do some investigating of her own. Terrell was friends with Edwards, but her behaviour still seemed bizarre, especially for someone in her position.

'What was *that* about?' Will asked as they returned to their car.

'It was about Terrell sticking her oar in.' She sighed. 'It looks like Scott won't be available for the rest of the day. It's time we talked to Edwards again. See if we can winkle something useful out of her. She might be getting her memory back.'

'Okay, but Dr Terrell isn't going to like it.'

'Dr Terrell can take a running jump.'

CHAPTER TWENTY-FOUR

Tingles of embarrassment and anxiety ran through Ruth as she drove away from Baram Scott's house. Her palms sweaty against the steering wheel, she took deep breaths to calm herself. She felt a sense of unreality and loss of control, as if she were drunk.

Visiting Scott had been little short of a disaster. The detective's warning remained imprinted on her mind like a size-twelve boot in mud. Perverting the course of justice and interfering in a police inquiry were real crimes. She wanted to help Phillipa, but she didn't want to be arrested. She could lose her job, which would be financially catastrophic, and Molly, Dom and Becky would be dragged into the drama, too.

Molly hadn't said a thing since they'd left Scott's house. She stared ahead with her arms folded, clearly angry or upset, probably both.

'I hope that was worth it,' she suddenly muttered. 'I don't think I've *ever* been so *ashamed* in my entire life.'

'I'm sorry,' Ruth replied. 'It was awful, I know, but please don't make it worse. I feel bad enough as it is. Promise you won't tell your father about any of this?'

'I'm not promising anything! I should *never* have let you go there. The idea was insane from the start. What were you thinking, Mum?' Molly shifted around in her seat to glare at her. 'What *were* you thinking?'

'I don't know! I just wanted to help, and what I said to the detective is correct. They're making it all about Phillipa. They aren't looking at anyone else. You should have heard what they were saying when they interviewed me the day after the murder. What was her and Thomas's relationship like? Hadn't he come into some money lately? How would you describe Dr Edwards' personality? They were searching for a reason why that lovely woman would kill her husband in cold blood, anything they could use to implicate her. They just want an easy solution to the case.'

'Mum, they were asking you those questions because *that's their job.'*

The words hit Ruth like bricks. Molly was right, and yet...

'They don't know anything about Phillipa,' her daughter went on. 'They can't dismiss her as a suspect because you think she's nice and didn't do it. I can't believe I even have to point that out to you of all people. Half the time, it *is* the spouse who did it. More than half the time, probably. For all the police know, Phillipa could be the murderer. And, anyway, you say they aren't looking at any other suspects, but they were right there at that man's house. They arrived seconds after the constables. They must have already been on their way there to interview him.'

Ruth groaned. 'Yes, I'm sure you're right about why they appeared so quickly.' She frowned. 'I've gone about this all wrong.'

'Yes, you have. I'm glad you're finally starting to see that.'

'I'm such an idiot. I didn't even learn anything useful today. And I thought things were going well, better than the last time I talked to one of the suspects. I lost control of the situation then.'

'What do you mean, you lost control of the situation? What happened?' Molly demanded. 'You talked to one of those dangerous men on your own?'

'It doesn't matter now. This time round, *I* was the one in control, but I still came up with nothing.' Ruth felt calmer, thinking through the problem.

Scott had told her Ableton had a thing for Phillipa, but it didn't mean anything. It was normal for inmates to talk about staff like that. And Ableton had pointed the finger at Scott. The two clearly had some kind of feud from their prison days and were taking the opportunity to cause trouble for each other.

She tutted and said softly, 'I've been a fool. I need to do better.'

Her daughter stared at her. 'You need to stop interfering! That's what you mean, right?'

Ruth was silent as she continued to think.

'*Mum!*'

When she still didn't reply, Molly said, 'If you don't drop this right now, I'm definitely telling Dad everything.'

The warning dragged her from her musings. Speaking half to herself, she responded, 'There was never any point in me approaching the suspects face to face. Outside a therapy session, they're unlikely to tell me anything useful. Why would they? I should read Phillipa's notes, that's what I should do. Analysing the case notes could yield significant information, and that's something I can do better than the police.'

The mental health team's assessment session notebooks couldn't leave the prison premises, but she could read them at work. She was rushed off her feet there, as always—in fact, these days she'd found she was slipping further and further behind—but maybe she could make time for it somehow. All she had to do was ask Stella for the master key to the office desks. As team leader, she was allowed access to everyone's files.

'You aren't going to try to talk to any of these men again?' asked Molly.

'No,' Ruth replied, giving her daughter a small smile. 'So there's no need to mention anything to your father, agreed? Neither of us want him to worry, do we?'

'I suppose so, if you promise that's the end of trying to talk to ex-prisoners.'

'I promise I won't approach any more suspects.'

'Okay, then I won't tell Dad.'

The tension between them easing, neither spoke for a couple of minutes. Ruth drove the familiar streets on auto-pilot, her mind on the question of who would want to murder Thomas Edwards and what had happened to Phillipa in the aftermath.

Then Molly said, 'By the way, how much longer will Phillipa be staying? I am sympathetic, but sleeping on the sofa is hurting my back.'

'I'm not sure. I don't know if she can go back home yet, or if she's ready to. We haven't had many opportunities to chat with everything going on, and anything to do with the murder is a touchy subject. She avoids it, understandably. But I'll talk to her. I know she hates putting you out.'

'Thanks. I can manage for a few more nights.'

'She wants to go back to work. I've tried to discourage her, telling her to take as much time as she needs—though we're actually rushed off our feet as always—but she said she'd prefer to be working, that it would help take her mind off things.'

'I can see that. I need something to keep me busy too. I thought I would start looking for a job.'

'I'm sure you'll find something.'

'I doubt a university drop-out with A levels in Art, Art History and English will be in demand, but I'll try.'

'I'm glad you're beginning to move on, Molly. You know, I've just realised I've hardly spoken to you about what happened with Daniel.'

'Oh, it's all right. My marriage breakdown is hardly in the same league as a murder.'

'Perhaps, but you're my daughter.' She paused. 'After Becky came along—'

'I know,' Molly cut in. 'Having an autistic child hasn't been easy on you or Dad.'

'You were left to get on with things, weren't you? I hope, now you're home, I can make it up to you.' She pulled into her driveway and stopped the car, then reached out to take Molly's hand and squeezed it.

As she climbed out of the car, the front door opened. Dom stuck his head out. 'Thank goodness you're home. Where have you been?'

'Why? What's wrong?'

'Becky's having a meltdown. I don't know what's caused it. She hasn't had one like this for years.'

Her younger daughter's wailing could be heard in the background.

'Oh dear. I'm coming!'

Ruth hurried over to the house, but then she remembered Molly. She was next to the car, closing her door.

'Could you put it in the garage?' Ruth asked her. 'I don't want it iced up in the morning.' She tossed her the keys.

Molly caught them without replying. Ruth turned to go into the house, and at the same moment registered the look of sadness she'd seen on her older daughter's face.

Her conscience twinged, but there wasn't anything she could do. Becky needed her.

CHAPTER TWENTY-FIVE

It was past the end of office hours by the time Phillipa Edwards swung by the station for her second interview. The psychologist's face held a strange, blank expression when Shauna entered the room, though it quickly faded.

Working with offenders day in day out probably took its toll, Shauna supposed, though Ruth Terrell had said Edwards was enthusiastic about her job.

'Thanks for coming in,' Shauna said, holding the door open for Will.

'Did I have a choice?' Edwards responded.

Shauna took a seat, noting the woman's antagonism.

'Attending a police interview is voluntary,' she said, 'unless you're under arrest. Though this time you're under caution.'

'But if I didn't agree to it, you'd think I'm trying to hide something.'

Shauna mentally sighed. She was feeling a little antagonistic herself. Bryant had called a minute ago, demanding another update on the case even though she'd sent him a report only yesterday. He'd said he had a press conference that evening.

I need something concrete to tell them, he'd said. *'Continuing with our enquiries' won't wash any longer. The public expects results.*

And he'd ignored her question about why he'd dismissed the uniform guarding Edwards at the hospital. She should have guessed when he told her she was the most experienced DI on the team it meant he had unreasonable expectations. He must have been hoping a detective from the Met would take the pressure off him and he'd be able to coast the rest of the way to retirement. But it didn't matter how many years of experience she had, she couldn't pull a rabbit out of her arse.

She replied, 'Yes, it *would* seem odd if you were unwilling to help us find your husband's murderer.'

'Has anyone offered you a drink yet?' Will asked. 'The coffee isn't any better than the last time you were here, I'm afraid.'

'No, thanks. I'd like this to be over with as soon as possible.'

'Let's get started, then, shall we?' said Shauna.

Will got out his notebook and flipped it open.

'Have you made any progress with the investigation?' Edwards asked. 'I expected I would be kept up to date, but no one's told me anything.'

'I'll ask the Family Liaison Officer to get in touch,' replied Shauna, 'but I'm afraid there's nothing we can tell you yet. As well as DS Fiske and I making enquiries, we have officers going through Thomas's office files, his and your phones and laptops... It can take months to go over the amount of evidence we're able to gather these days. We are working as fast as we can.'

'So you still have absolutely no idea who killed him?'

'We don't have any strong suspects at the moment. As I said, it's still early days. The reason I wanted to speak to you again was to find out what else you can tell us about that evening or anything that might have occurred to you since we spoke. Sometimes the most insignificant things end up being crucial to solving a case.'

Edwards looked down and shook her head. 'I don't have anything else to tell you, I'm afraid. I wish I had. I would have been in contact if I did.'

'Really?' said Shauna. 'That's surprising.'

'Surprising I don't have any information for you?'

'It's surprising none of your memories have returned. I've interviewed other people with amnesia from a traumatic event. Often, they begin to experience small flashbacks. By themselves the flashes of memory don't seem to mean much, but they could help us. Are you sure you haven't experienced anything?'

'Quite sure,' Edwards replied, folding her hands on her lap.

'Because anything you can tell us—'

'I understand. *Sometimes the most insignificant details end up being crucial.* But everything from that time is a blank.'

Shauna paused a beat, then asked, 'Don't you think it's strange you ended up in a car park approximately twelve hours after the murder apparently none the worse for wear?'

'Extremely strange, but I can't explain it.'

Shauna held Edwards' gaze with her own. The woman stared back, unblinking.

'Perhaps it'll help if we go over what you did the day of the murder.'

'If you really must,' Edwards complained. When Shauna didn't reply, she went on, 'As I've *already* told you, I completed assessments, wrote up the reports, and then went home. Thomas wasn't due back until 7, so I made dinner. We had pasta and wine. I don't remember anything that happened afterwards until I found myself looking for my car at the supermarket.'

'Do you recall eating dinner?'

'Yes. The pasta was a bit too soft. I'm not much of a cook.' She gave a small smile, but it was directed at Will.

Will smiled back sympathetically.

'What about loading the dishwasher?' asked Shauna. 'Do you remember that?'

'No, I don't. Thomas would usually do it.'

'What did you talk about over dinner?'

'What?'

'Do you usually eat in silence?'

'No.'

'So what did you talk about?'

'I've no idea. Who remembers things like that?'

'Try.'

'I-I can't. I can't remember. I could guess, I suppose. We often discussed work—Thomas's, I can't really talk about mine—but if I told you we had a conversation about x or y, I'd be lying. I just don't know.'

'How unfortunate,' said Shauna, 'and, I have to say, remarkable. I mean, if you'd suffered a head injury, your response might make sense. But you didn't, yet you remember nothing at all, even now, after things have settled down.'

'You don't believe me.'

Shauna paused, allowing the tense seconds to play out.

Will twiddled his pen.

'You said your marriage was happy,' said Shauna, 'but all couples have their disagreements, right? What did you and Thomas disagree about?'

'Hardly anything. As I said—'

'Oh, come on, Phillipa,' Shauna said, harshening her tone. 'The perfect marriage? You can't expect us to believe that. You were arguing about something the night of the murder, weren't you? That's why you won't tell us what you talked about.'

'No.'

'But you said you don't remember. How can you be so sure?'

'Because we didn't argue. If there was a point of contention between us, we talked things out like—'

'You were arguing and things got out of hand. That's what really happened, isn't it? Did Thomas threaten you? Were you in fear for your life? Is that why you did it? Maybe he was the one who picked up the knife, you struggled and it was an accident. You didn't mean to kill him.'

'This is ridiculous,' Edwards muttered.

'A plea of self-defence might help you in court,' said Shauna, 'but only if you make a full confession.'

'I'm not confessing to something I didn't do.'

Shauna leaned over the table. 'As you keep telling us, you don't remember anything. How do you know you didn't do it?'

'I could never murder anyone, least of all the man I loved.'

Will put down his pen and said gently, 'If there's anything you should tell us, you should say it now. It will help to get it off your chest. You'll feel better.'

'I don't *have* anything to tell you,' Edwards spat.

Another tense silence ensued.

'There are some techniques for recovering suppressed memories,' said Shauna. 'Hypnosis, for example.'

Edwards hesitated for a fraction of a second. 'I'm aware of the methods. They're unreliable and can be psychologically damaging.'

'Fair enough. I can't force you, but, I have to say, I would have thought you would do everything in your power to help the investigation.'

'Emotional blackmail, detective? Rather a low blow to a murder victim's widow.'

'Just stating my opinion,' said Shauna. 'I intend to catch your husband's murderer, Dr Edwards. There are a number of things here that don't add up, and I'm going to get to the bottom of them.'

'I hope you do. I want Thomas's killer behind bars.'

'Are you staying at Dr Terrell's house for now?'

'Yes. Why?'

'I'd like to know where to find you.'

'Right. So the interview's over?'

'I don't have any more questions. DS Fiske?'

'Uh, no. I'll show you out, Dr Edwards.'

While Will was escorting the woman from the station, Shauna returned to the incident room. She opened the files on the murder and began reading the background information Alfie had uncovered on Phillipa Edwards. He'd confirmed the details in her medical history about giving a baby up for adoption at fourteen, and he'd included the name of the social worker involved in the case.

She guessed it wouldn't hurt to phone the woman and find out more, but the lead seemed tenuous. It had all happened nearly thirty years ago. Could the events really have a bearing on her husband's murder decades later?

Connor had finally dug up the names and addresses of Edwards' immediate family. Her father was deceased and her mother and sister lived in different towns in Northumberland.

Will came in.

'I don't suppose she said anything interesting on her way out?'

'Not a word. Didn't even say goodbye. I was hurt.'

'Huh.' She paused. 'She's hiding something. She's got her story off pat, like she's rehearsed it. And she's embellishing it to make it sound convincing, adding details like the pasta being too soft. If she can remember something like that, she would remember what she talked about with her husband, especially as it would have been one of the last times they spoke. You would remember those last few conversations, wouldn't you?'

I do.

'I suppose so,' said Will, then added, 'Yeah, of course she'd remember. Maybe they *did* argue and she doesn't want to tell us because it casts suspicion on her.'

'Maybe,' Shauna replied, though she felt there was more to it. 'She's a weird one. It takes all kinds, but her attitude doesn't seem right, though she could just be angry we haven't arrested anyone yet.'

'Ruth Terrell Edwards likes so much,' Will commented, 'she's willing to enter the home of a known murderer for her.'

'Yeah, that's right.' Shauna had momentarily forgotten the surprise encounter earlier.

'Scott's mum died, by the way,' said Will. 'I phoned the hospital.'

'Ah, thanks. He's going to be in a great mood when we speak to him.'

'Yep.'

A notification popped up on her computer screen: some DNA testing results from Forensics. She opened the email. The handkerchief belonged to a man, but not Thomas Edwards, and neither did the DNA match any records on file. That meant it didn't belong to any of the three ex-cons, Ableton, Scott, or Drake.

CHAPTER TWENTY-SIX

Shauna had offered to visit Baram Scott at his home again, but he'd said he would prefer to come into the station. Perhaps home was a hard place to be right now. After spending the last twenty years in prison, he had finally been able to live as part of a family once more, only for it all to be ripped from him within weeks of his release.

He would be in a delicate state, Shauna reminded herself as she waited for him. She felt a little guilty for going ahead with the interview, all things considered, but she needed to hear verbatim from him where he'd been on the night of the murder, if only for the record.

The interview room door opened and Scott appeared, Connor in his wake. The DCs were taking turns in sitting in on interviews to gain experience.

'Thanks for agreeing to come and speak to us,' said Shauna. 'I'm very sorry for your loss.'

'Thanks,' Scott murmured, his head down as he took the seat opposite her.

He looked terrible: his mouse-brown and silver hair a mess, great droopy bags hanging under his eyes, his skin an unhealthy grey. It was only to be expected.

It had clearly begun raining outside. The shoulders of Scott's jacket were darkly wet and so was the cloth hat he was twisting in his hands, apparently oblivious to the edges of the metal badge on the front of it, which had to be cutting into his skin. The badge bore some kind of inscription in copperplate, but she couldn't make it out.

'Would you like tea or coffee?' asked Connor in his high-pitched nasal whine.

As the days of the investigation had passed, Shauna had realised Connor didn't speak like that because he was nervous— it was just how he spoke. She'd caught Alfie imitating him early one morning as she entered the incident room. Before he'd abruptly stopped, Shauna had noticed Jas, to her credit, looking annoyed rather than amused. Connor seemed to have been trying to ignore him. She'd given Alfie a warning frown.

There was gentle ribbing and there was bullying and harass-ment. She didn't want her constables in any doubt which was which.

'Nothing,' Scott answered, adding after a moment's thought, 'thanks.' For the first time, he met Shauna's gaze. 'Can we get this over with?'

His eyes were hazel with black flecks. Red lines staggered haphazardly across the whites like the tracks of drunken spiders.

'I'll be as brief as I can,' she replied. 'When DS Fiske and I visited your home, your mother told us you had been at home with her the night of the third of February. Is that correct?'

'I remember you coming to the door,' said Scott. 'Mum was so pissed off.'

'You were at home then?'

'Yeah, I was there. I would have talked to you. I thought you lot might be around when I heard my shrink's husband got killed. I wanted to get it done, you know. I knew you'd be back if you didn't speak to me. But Mum hates the police. Couldn't stand the sight of two coppers on the doorstep. She just wanted to get rid of you.'

'That was my impression,' Shauna said mildly.

Scott didn't react. His gaze became unfocused. 'I think she took it harder than me. The time I spent inside, I mean. Up until when I was arrested, it was me and her at home, alone. Dad skipped out before I was born. I was all she had. Then I got involved with the wrong people and ended up getting fingered for someone else's crime. After I went away, she had no one. She was never any good at making friends.'

According to the file Shauna had read, the crime he'd been found guilty of was a drug-related revenge killing. The details of exactly why the victim had been murdered hadn't been fully uncovered, but forensic evidence and witness statements pointed to Scott as the perpetrator. It was possible he'd been present but not the actual murderer and gang members had conspired so he took the fall for someone else.

'That must have been difficult for her,' said Shauna, aware they were getting off track. 'So you confirm your mother's state-ment you were at home on the night of the third of February this year?'

The unfocused look in Scott's eyes faded. 'The third? Yeah, I was home.'

'And were you there all evening? Did you go out at all?'

'Nah, I was home all night, playing computer games. I like them. Never guessed how much things changed while I was doing time.'

'Can you remember when your mother went to bed?'

'I don't know. Late. She always goes to bed late. Couldn't sleep well after my conviction. Said she was worried being by herself and worried about what might happen to me while I was inside. It had got a bit better after I came out, but I think her insomnia was a habit by then. The doctor said stress could have contributed to her heart attack,' he added accusingly. 'She wasn't that old. She still had a few years in her.'

'I hope you don't feel we put undue pressure on you or your mother,' said Shauna. 'We're obliged to—'

'Yeah, yeah, I know.' He waved dismissively. 'It wasn't you I was talking about. That shrink was sniffing around though, wasn't she? I don't see why I should have to talk to you *and* her.'

'You shouldn't have to talk to Dr Terrell. She was acting independently and unlawfully. I've spoken to her about her visit to you, and you shouldn't hear from her again. If you do, please let me know.'

'Right. I will. I wondered what that was about. The mental health team at the prison was good. They helped a lot. I was pretty cut up to be locked away for something I didn't do. They helped me get through it.'

'I'm glad to hear it.'

Shauna was ready to wrap up the discussion. She had Scott's confirmation he'd been with someone else at the time of the murder. It was unfortunate that person was now deceased, but both she and Will had witnessed his mother's statement. His alibi wasn't rock solid, but they had nothing to link him to Thomas Edwards except his therapy sessions with Edwards' wife. It felt safe to leave things there unless something else turned up.

'Shame about Dr Edwards' husband,' said Scott.

'Yes.'

'I hope you catch the bugger.'

'We're doing all we can.'

'Just...make sure you get the right person, okay?'

Shauna gave a thin-lipped smile. 'Naturally. Thanks for taking the time to come and talk to us.'

'It's not like I've got much else to do, is it?' Scott said, rising to his feet.

'Could I ask something?' Connor said quietly.

'Go ahead.'

'Mr Scott,' he said. 'One last question. Do you remember what game you played that evening?'

Shauna suppressed a smile of approval. Connor had been to

the Will Fiske Academy of Police Questioning. An analysis of Scott's computer would quickly verify or deny his claim.

'The one where you drive around and shoot stuff.'

'Carjack?' asked Connor.

'Yeah, that's it. Ever played it?' He was standing, looking down at the young constable.

'I have. It's a good one. I'll show you out.'

CHAPTER TWENTY-SEVEN

Her heart sinking to the pit of her stomach, Molly opened the text message.

Stop being a bitch. You know you're just being dramatic, blowing everything out of proportion. And staying with your parents isn't helping. They only hear your side of the story and agree with you because you're their daughter. They don't know the full picture. But we both know the truth. Don't run away from your problems, Molly. Face up to them. Talk to me like an adult. Our marriage is worth saving, but only if you're prepared to fight for it.

She saved the message as her solicitor had advised and then blocked the number. It had to be the tenth time Daniel had used a new number to contact her. She needed to get another sim card. This latest message was mild compared to many he'd sent, but she didn't doubt he would cycle back to calling her horrible names and making outrageous accusations. He'd even accused her of going back to her ex from Sixth Form, saying she must have continued an online affair throughout their marriage and she'd returned to Cambridge in order to be with her lover. Then he'd accused her of being a lesbian. His imagination was leading him down some strange paths. Or maybe he was only making wild accusations to goad her into responding, saying anything that popped into his head, hoping to get a reply.

He seemed so different from the man she'd thought she'd been marrying, but of course the real Daniel had always been there, lurking under the surface.

How had she *ever* fallen in love with him?

The moment when she'd realised *he* was the problem, not her, was like a beacon in her mind. Whenever she wondered if she was doing the right thing, if Daniel might have a point, she returned to it to strengthen her resolve.

The village where they were renting a house had been so small it only had one pub, and every Tuesday night was quiz night. She'd agitated to go for months. The isolated life that suited Daniel so well had become like a prison to her. She yearned for company.

After much prompting and suggesting, he'd finally agreed they could go. She'd been almost gleeful.

Perhaps that was what had set him off. She'd been too happy. He didn't like it when she was happy. Or perhaps he'd only been irritated by the fact she might enjoy being with people other than him.

To simply dress up was another pleasure for her. She usually slopped around in jeans and a jumper, the Scottish climate not allowing anything lighter even in summer. Sometimes, she stayed in her pyjamas all day. To wear a skirt, blouse and cardigan, and to put on tights, heeled shoes and to make her hair look nice had been a rare treat.

Until he saw her.

He'd walked into their bedroom, taken one glance, turned around and stalked out again without a word. She hadn't even had a chance to ask him how she looked.

'Daniel?' she'd called after him. 'Is something the matter?'

When no answer came, she'd gone after him, following him down the narrow stairs, her heels tapping on the bare wood.

She'd found him sitting in an armchair, his phone in his hand, scrolling.

'What's wrong?' she asked again, more softly, and a little afraid. Uncertain, apprehensive, she'd felt as if she'd crossed an unseen, unanticipated line and was about to face the consequences.

'Nothing's wrong,' he'd replied. 'I decided I'm not going. But you go. Go and enjoy yourself.'

The words belied his tone, which was cutting, ironic, bitter. *Go and* enjoy *yourself*, as though 'enjoy' meant something entirely different.

'I won't if you don't want to,' she'd said. 'The idea was we would go together, as a couple. We could meet some of the locals and introduce ourselves at last. Have some fun.'

Daniel gave her a look so sharp it cut her to the core. 'I'm sure you're more than capable of having *fun* without me. You certainly look as though you are.'

She'd looked down at her clothes. They were pretty but conventional, not suggestive at all. Her skirt ended below her knees, and her heels were only a couple of inches high. 'What do you mean?'

'I mean...' he leapt up and threw his phone onto the armchair with such force it bounced onto the floor, '...you're dressed like a *slut!*'

The accusation was so ridiculous and Daniel's reaction was so extreme, she'd giggled out of nervousness.

'Oh, I'm funny am I? My embarrassment at being the husband of a woman who dresses to pick up men is amusing to you?'

He leaned in until his face occupied her vision and she was held by the glare of his eyes.

'Darling, please,' she replied, 'don't be silly. You know I love you. I just thought it would be nice for us to go out for once.'

'If that's how you want to see it, then go.' He picked up his phone from the floor and sank into the armchair once more.

'But we both know that isn't really why you're going. Actually, to be frank, you don't stand a chance of attracting anyone, so I don't have anything to be worried about.'

'I don't...?' She was confused. She felt compelled to defend herself, to say she wasn't unattractive, but if she did she would play right into his accusation that she intended to pick up men.

The idea was ridiculous. The demographic of the small village swayed heavily into retired city escapees and crusty old farmers. The pub couldn't be any further from a nightclub cattle market.

'In fact...' Daniel had turned to face her, '...it's about time I set you right on your appearance and save you from continuing to embarrass yourself. You seem to have got the wrong impression, maybe from some bloke who was flattering you to try to get into your knickers, but...'

He had launched into a lecture about her various physical faults. She was already too aware she was no beauty, but what she hadn't anticipated was the thoroughness and detail of Daniel's list. He even included a few items she hadn't noticed.

Over the course of the next three-quarters of an hour, he'd dismantled her already fragile self-esteem regarding her attractiveness piece by piece.

She'd thought she didn't value physical appearances highly—especially her own—but she'd learned that she had, just a little. He'd stripped her of her illusions.

In the end, he'd paused and watched her face calmly, all his anger gone. 'I'm sorry, Molly, but it had to be said.'

He opened his phone, and looking down at the screen, remarked, 'It's getting late. If you don't go soon you'll miss the start of the quiz.'

'No, it's fine,' she replied, and then swallowed. 'I won't go.'

She'd gone upstairs to get changed.

She'd been young, inexperienced and vulnerable, and, she had to admit, far too naive and trusting. Growing up with Dad as her model of a typical husband hadn't prepared her for Daniel's awful behaviour. It had made her assume their difficulties must be her fault—an illusion Daniel was quick to uphold, until the night he'd lost it because she'd put on a skirt.

Another thing had made her the perfect victim—she'd needed to be loved, to be the most important thing in someone's life. And, for a while, he'd convinced her she was that to him.

In a way, she still was. He'd travelled for hours to follow her, and now he was spending money he didn't have to stay in Cambridge so he could try to persuade her to go back to him.

But he didn't love her.

She picked up her phone and read the message again. She knew she shouldn't reply. It would only exacerbate the situation, but she couldn't resist.

Our marriage is dead. You never loved me. It was obsession, or a lust for control. Me leaving you has devastated your self-esteem and forced you to take a hard look at yourself. I've shown you you aren't perfect, and you can't stand it.

When you lost me you lost the person you could attack in order to feel better about yourself. You needed me, or not me in particular, but someone. Without a woman to find fault with, you have no vent, no relief, nothing to bounce off when self-doubt hits. Feeling low about not having money? Pick on Molly, make her cry, blame her for your problems, make her the scapegoat for being a failure.

We're done.

I'm done.

Piss off and leave me alone, creep.

She pressed Send and then turned off her phone.

At least things were better at home. Mum had agreed to abandon her insane plan to approach the murder suspects. Her mother behaved really oddly sometimes. And Becky was back to normal after her meltdown. Dad had discovered the cause—a toy elephant in her school bag—and removed it. Her sister had an irrational terror of elephants, as they'd discovered on a rare family excursion, when they'd visited Whipsnade Wild Animal Park. The toy had made its way into her bag somehow, and when she'd found it, she started screaming and smashing up her room. Molly had retreated to the living room, unable to help. Only Mum and Dad could get her sister to calm down. She'd always been useless in that regard.

She heaved a sigh and stood up, deciding to go out. If she walked into town she could go to a café and kill some time, though they all would be busy with tourists on a Sunday. Daniel had found her at the Botanic Garden because he knew she had fond memories of the place, but Cambridge had hundreds of cafés. She should be safe enough, and what could he do to her in a public place? Even at the Garden he'd left her alone after she'd pulled her arm from his grip and walked away from him.

She put on her coat and stepped out into the chilly March air. The days were longer but the temperature had only risen a little. Frosty mornings were still the norm, and snow threatened.

At the end of the driveway, she looked up and down the street. It was empty. She walked to the end of the road and out onto Queen Edith's Way, where she waited at the traffic lights to cross.

Daniel's accusation that her parents were siding with her was ironic. They had accepted her back, but they hadn't shown a lot of interest in *why* she was back. It wasn't that they weren't as kind and loving as they'd always been, it was more that, emotionally, they weren't *there*. When Mum had spoken about her regrets in the car, a flash of hope had hit her, a light in the gloom. But then it had all come to nothing.

It was clear she was on her own.

'Molly,' said a voice.

She started.

Daniel had appeared from nowhere.

'Fancy seeing you here.' He had a menacing, leering expression, reminding her of a hunter who had found his quarry. But something simmered under his predatory look: rage. 'I got your message. Think you're quite the psychiatrist, don't you? Planning on following in Mum's footsteps?'

'What are you doing?' she demanded. 'Have you been watching my parents' house?'

'Don't flatter yourself. I happen to be staying at a B and B nearby, and I thought I'd stretch my legs. I saw you waiting here and ran to catch up with you. But let's not look a gift horse in the mouth. What do you say we go for a coffee and hash things out? I forgive you for what you said. I understand you aren't feeling yourself these days.'

'There *are* no B and Bs anywhere around here. You've been hanging around my parents' house, waiting for me to leave.' She looked up and down the street. The only pedestrians she could see were far away at another set of lights.

'That's ridiculous. You've been watching too many police dramas. Where are you going? If you don't want to go for a coffee, we can walk together, and talk.'

'I don't want to talk to you. If you have anything to say to me, go through my solicitor. They're sending the divorce documents to your address in Scotland.'

'But how am I supposed to receive anything? I'm not in Scotland.'

'*Then go back there,*' she hissed, surprising herself with her own viciousness. But she'd endured years of his bullying and abuse and it felt good to vent.

Daniel's eyes narrowed. He glanced about, and then grabbed her upper arm, his gloved hand gripping her bicep like a vice.

'Ow! Let go! You're hurting me.' She began to struggle.

He dragged her close. 'I'm *not* going back to Scotland. I'm not going home without you. Why are you doing this to me? Nothing I did warrants you treating me this way. *Nothing*! You're just a whiny little bitch who can't take a bit of criticism.'

'Let me go!' yelled Molly, trying to yank her arm away from him. He was holding her so tightly he was cutting off her blood supply. She swiped his head with her free hand to try to make him release her.

He did.

Then he slapped her face so hard she fell down.

Tyres screeched and a car stopped. For a moment she thought she must have fallen in the road. She heard a car door open.

Someone shouted, 'Oy, what do you think you're doing? Are you all right, miss?'

Quick footsteps sounded and a figure loomed over her, cutting out the weak light. She looked up, seeing only a blurry silhouette as tears of pain and shame flooded into her eyes.

Daniel took off.

'Yeah, run! Fucking coward, hitting a woman!' the man called out. To her, he said, 'Do you want me to call the police? Here, let me help you up.'

Molly lifted her hand, and the man took it and her elbow and gently pulled her to her feet.

'I take it you know him,' he said. 'I'll call the police for you, shall I?'

'No, it's okay.' She touched her cheek. It was wet from her tears and warm from Daniel's blow.

'You should press charges, love. Don't let him get away with it. I've met a few bastards like that in my time. If you let him get away with it, he's just going to do it again. If not to you, to someone else. They don't change unless someone makes them.'

Molly had wiped her eyes and as her vision cleared she got a better look at her Good Samaritan: A middle-aged man, burly, balding and in need of a shave, wearing a donkey jacket. His car, an old Audi, was parked at the kerb, its hazard lights flashing.

She sniffed back her tears and touched her cheek again, still in shock. Daniel had emotionally and mentally abused her for years, but this was the first time he'd ever raised a hand to her.

'Thanks for stopping and helping,' she said. Greater even than the shock and pain of being hit was her embarrassment it had happened in the middle of the street. She felt like a stereotype of a domestic violence victim, degraded, to be pitied. Her burgeoning self-esteem at taking control of her life was crumbling.

'You don't need to thank me, dear. Only a heartless bastard could see a woman being beaten and not stop to help. Is he your boyfriend or your husband?'

'Husband,' she replied meekly, feeling stupid. 'That's the first time he's hit me,' she tried to explain. 'Or—'

'It won't be the last,' the stranger warned.

'It will. I'm divorcing him.'

'Ah, I see. Good for you. So he's losing it. Getting pushed over the edge.'

'Yes. You know what? I *am* going to call the police.' The man who had helped her was right—Daniel was becoming deranged. He could be turning dangerous. She wouldn't have believed he was capable of violence, despite his warning at the Botanic Garden, but she'd been proven wrong. And he'd been stalking her. Who knew what else he might do? She needed to document his assault. It might be useful for the divorce, too, when they went to court.

'Smart move,' said the man, pulling a mobile from his jacket pocket. 'I'll call, and you can speak to them yourself.'

CHAPTER TWENTY-EIGHT

Grief was odd. Some days, if Shauna kept herself busy, pushing through the hours on a wave of activity and distraction, she was sometimes able to avoid remembering what had happened. Other days, from the moment she opened her eyes, no matter what she did she had to drag herself through it. Showering, eating, driving, working, talking, even watching TV were all torture until finally exhaustion and then sleep overtook her. Existence was pain, and she foresaw no end to it, not until she died.

Until death do us part.

That was what she'd sworn, twice, but both times she hadn't the slightest inkling of how the promises would play out.

Today was going to be one of the hard days.

She knew the signs. She'd woken with a heaviness in the pit of her stomach like she'd swallowed a bowling ball. The slightest physical movement would feel as though she was immersed in treacle; every word she spoke would sound hollow and meaning-less; everything she saw would appear dull, lifeless and unreal. It was like she didn't belong in the world. She was only a kind of zombie, inexplicably living on after everyone who had ever meant anything to her had died.

Though it was a Sunday, she could still have gone into the station. She could have worked on the Edwards case. She probably should have gone in. There was plenty for her to do, but she hadn't had the stomach for it. So much for Bryant's hopes she would make his life easier.

Her only relief on one of these particularly bad days was to go birding. Something about being in a natural environment, in stillness and quiet, eased her soul.

She lifted her binoculars and scanned the landscape. She hadn't been out to Wicken Fen since Thomas Edwards' body had been discovered and her phone had spooked a short-eared owl. Rumour said a glossy ibis had been spotted here not long ago. She'd never seen one in real life, only pictures. Sighting the bird would be a high point in what promised to be an otherwise low day. If she could get a photograph of it, all the better. But her careful examination of the lake drew a blank ibis-wise.

While she was waiting for the bird to show, she pulled a dog-eared notebook from her inside jacket pocket and thumbed through it. The earliest pages contained the names of species she'd spotted when she'd first taken up birdwatching. She smiled at her beginner birds—wren, nightingale, mistle thrush—but each sighting had brought her a brief burst of happiness during a terrible time, when she hadn't known if she would be able to endure living.

As she turned the pages, the birds grew rarer. By the middle of the slim book, the ticks for each sighting of a species no longer appeared, only the names alone. Having exhausted the range of local avian wildlife, she'd begun to travel farther afield, visiting places for the express purpose of seeing birds that only lived in or visited the area. Her pastime had become more challenging but that had been good. The more difficult her task, the more it distracted her from painful thoughts and memories, and the rewards of achieving her goal brought a bigger spike of happiness.

She turned to the latest, half-filled page. Her most recent

entry was the short-eared owl. Now she wanted to fill in the line beneath it.

Lifting her binoculars again, she adjusted the focus, and then slowly swept from left to right, seeking a sleek chestnut brown head and tell-tale long, downwards curved beak. It was a flocking bird, so she might expect to see a few grouped together, and in the poor light from the overcast sky, the plumage might appear black.

Plenty of birds were out there on the flat, marshy land, but she couldn't see any glossy ibis. To while away the time until her target species might arrive or appear from a hidden spot, she watched the other birds.

One of the reasons she'd chosen to come to Cambridge was close access to prime birding sites. The wide expanses, watery landscapes and vast skies were ideal for many species. With luck, she could spend years there and always find something interesting to see.

And when she ran out of new birds to spot? She didn't know and tried not to think about it. Getting through days like this were enough and perhaps all she could ever expect.

Her phone vibrated in her back trouser pocket. After her experience with the short-eared owl, she'd made sure it was on vibrate only this time. She ignored it. Whoever it was, the person could leave a message. She didn't want anyone dragging her back to reality right then. And if the matter was urgent, the person would phone again.

After a minute or so, her phone became still.

Relieved, she focused on a group of Canada geese, all paddling along in one direction. They weren't British natives and, in fact, damaged other species' habitats, but she had a soft spot for them. She liked their cheeky behaviour and honking cry.

Then, briefly, a smooth, dark, chestnut brown head bobbed into view in the unfocused background beyond the geese. Excitement sparked inside her. Could it be what she thought it was? She gently eased the wheel on her binoculars a few degrees around. As the geese blurred, the bird behind them sharpened.

There it was!

A distinctive beak curved out and down. The colour was spot on. It *had* to be a glossy ibis.

If she could get a photo, she could study it later to confirm the sighting. Not moving her head lest she lose sight of the bird, she put down her binoculars and picked up her camera.

Her phone vibrated again.

Dammit.

Trying to ignore the incoming call, she raised her camera and looked through the lens, trying to find the ibis. It didn't take long before she spotted the bird again. She could only see the head and part of the neck poking above a stand of reeds, but it was unmistakeable.

Her phone continued to vibrate.

The ibis wasn't in focus. The reeds were in the centre of the lens view, and so her camera was automatically using the distance as the focal point. She switched to manual and lifted the camera again. Gently, she adjusted the lens the tiniest bit, sharpening the image. But then the bird moved. Its lines softened and blurred.

And still her phone buzzed.

She put down her camera and irritably snatched it from her pocket. The screen stated Will was calling. He knew it was her day off. Was it something urgent?

'Someone better have died,' she muttered before accepting the call. 'Yes?'

'Shauna, it's Will.'

'I know,' she snapped. 'What is it?'

'Sorry, is this a bad time?'

She paused before replying, 'Kinda. Has something happened?'

'What do you mean?'

'With the case, Will. The case we're working on, remember? Mr Edwards, murdered in cold blood. That one.'

'Um, it *is* a bad time. It's okay. I'll let you go.'

'No, wait.' She closed her eyes in a long blink and breathed slowly in and out. 'I thought you were phoning me on a Sunday because there was a crisis.'

'No... I'm not working today either.'

'Oh, yeah.' She winced. 'I forgot. Is everything okay?'

'Yeah, everything's fine. It's just...I was looking at the free paper, and I noticed there's a photography exhibition on, about birds. I wondered if you wanted to go.'

'Right. I hadn't heard about it. Thanks for letting me know. I might pop along later.'

'No, I meant...'

He paused, and what he was *actually* asking her dawned on her. She winced some more.

He went on, 'I meant, do you want to go together? I thought it would be good to talk about something other than murder for a change.'

'That's...nice of you to ask.'

'Shauna, I only mean as friends,' he said gently. 'It isn't a big deal. If you don't want to go, it's fine. I can understand if you can't move past my stupidity at the pub the other night.'

'No, that's forgiven and forgotten.' He had seemed genuinely remorseful, and everyone made mistakes. God knew, she'd made plenty herself.

'Great,' he said. 'Then you don't fancy it?'

'I'm just not sure if it's a good idea for us to see each other outside of work.'

'Really? Maybe socialising is frowned upon in the Met, but we're a bit friendlier in Cambridge. I don't want to make things awkward though. Forget I asked. I'll see you tomorrow.'

'Wait. I'm sorry. I'm being an idiot. You did catch me at a bad time.' It was touching he'd remembered her interest in birds and had thought of her when he read about the exhibition. The idea of rejecting him felt churlish, and spending time with someone *might* help banish her terrible state of mind. 'I would like to go to the exhibition with you.'

'Great. I'll text you the details. We can meet there this afternoon.'

As Ruth waited for Phillipa to gather her things from the back seat of the car, she looked over at Ronnie, the security guard. The man wasn't making any secret about staring at them. She wondered how much he and the rest of the prison staff had been gossiping about her friend.

Poor Phillipa. She had so much to contend with: her husband's murder, police scrutiny, her home holding dreadful memories, and the investigation dragging on, delaying the funeral. How could she even attempt to come to terms with it all?

'You can lock it,' Phillipa said. She'd retrieved her briefcase and shoulder bag.

Ruth pressed the button on her key fob and they set off towards the prison. The car park was emptier than usual.

'It was a good idea to suggest I ease back into work on a Sunday,' said Phillipa. 'But you needn't have come in with me.'

'I thought a quiet office would be less stressful,' Ruth replied. 'It's no trouble to be here with you. I want to make sure you're okay. I still think you're going back too soon.'

'It's better for me this way. Takes my mind off things.'

Ronnie watched them walk the entire distance, his gaze intent under the brim of his tightly pulled down hat.

'Morning ladies,' he said as they passed him.

'Good morning,' they chorused in reply.

Once they were safely out of earshot, Ruth hissed, 'I should ask him if he doesn't have anything better to look at.'

'You could,' replied Phillipa, 'but he hasn't, has he? He gets paid to watch us, check no one's up to anything nefarious.'

'You're too kind. He might have to watch us, but he doesn't have to stare.' Ruth was tempted to tell her friend how Ronnie had behaved the day after Thomas's murder, gloating over his tidbit of scandalous news, but she held back. There was no point in adding to Phillipa's woes.

They passed through the two sets of security doors and entered the main office. Only Stella was in.

'Welcome back, Dr Edwards. It's nice to see you again.'

After saying hello, Ruth asked Phillipa to come to her room. Looking somewhat surprised, she followed her. When they were inside, Ruth closed the door.

In answer to Phillipa's puzzled look, she said, 'Sorry, I don't mean to be mysterious. It's nothing to worry about.'

'This is about Thomas,' said Phillipa resignedly.

'Yes. Would you like some coffee?'

'No thanks.'

'Sit down,' said Ruth as she went to the coffee machine. 'I'll have to get some water. I'll only be a minute.'

'Are you sure this can't wait until lunch? I have a lot to catch up on.'

'I know, but I'd rather talk now. I won't be long.'

Phillipa looked uncomfortable as Ruth left the office. On her return, she hadn't sat down. She was looking out of the window.

'Another dreary day,' said Ruth. 'I wish it would warm up. We could do with some cheeriness around here.'

Phillipa turned around, and for a second Ruth saw the same blank expression she'd observed when her friend was unaware she was being watched at the hospital. She was still somewhat in shock, Ruth supposed.

At the house, Phillipa had spent most of her time in Molly's room, and at meals she was polite but quiet and distant. The murder had been a taboo subject, out of fear of upsetting her. Ruth hoped what she was about to suggest wouldn't exacerbate her grief.

She made herself some coffee. 'I understand this might be difficult for you, but I want to talk to you about the murder suspects.'

'Apart from me, I assume?' replied Phillipa dryly as she sat down.

So far, so good.

One thing Ruth liked about her friend was her understated wit. She'd also appreciated her intelligence and, if she was honest, she'd been a little envious of her sophistication. Up until the murder, Phillipa had always seemed to have it all together, which was a marked contrast to Ruth's chaotic life. If she was honest, she'd always envied her friend a little. She had a feeling Phillipa wouldn't have missed the signs of autism in her own child, or had her other child cut contact and disappear, or live in a dirty, messy house.

She gave a snort of derision. 'Not in my wildest dreams could I imagine you would hurt Thomas.' She sat opposite her friend and took a sip of her hot beverage.

'I'm glad someone thinks so. The police certainly don't.'

'I know. They seem determined to prove it was you.'

'Well, they'll never prove it.'

'Exactly. So—'

'Ruth,' Phillipa interrupted, 'you've been incredibly kind and helpful since this whole terrible debacle began, and your family has, too. I can't thank you all enough. But the last thing I want to do is sit around talking about my husband's murder. I'm not sure how discussing the suspects is going to be helpful.'

'I understand, and I don't want to cause you any further pain, but have you considered what might happen if the detectives don't find the murderer? Murders are rare in Cambridge, and the police have received a lot of media attention. People are worried and looking for answers. They want to know who did it and they want the person behind bars so they can relax and go on with their lives.'

'You think the police might *frame* me for the murder? That's a little far-fetched.'

'Not frame you as such, but point the finger. All they have to do is to convince the CPS they have a case and you could end up in court. Then, who knows what might happen? Miscarriages of justice aren't unheard of, even these days.'

Phillipa frowned and looked over Ruth's shoulder to the view out of the window. 'I know the police don't like me, for some reason, but I strongly doubt it'll come to that. And, in any case, what has this got to do with the other suspects? Unless... don't tell me you still want to figure out who the murderer is. I remember you mentioning it when you came to see me in hospital.'

'Would that be so strange? If it is one of your former patients, you know we're both in a better position than the police to make an educated guess. We have the suspects' histories and diagnoses, and a good understanding of human psychology. I thought if we went over what they'd told you during their therapy sessions...'

'But we're hardly impartial either, and even if we look at my session notes and form an idea, are the police going to take any notice? If I give them a name, they're only going to think I'm trying to divert their attention away from me. I'm not comfortable with this, Ruth.'

'*I* would tell them, not you, though...' she continued ruefully '...I'm not exactly in their good books at the moment either.'

'Why's that?'

'It isn't important. Look, if you feel this isn't something you want to do—which is entirely understandable in the circumstances—I'm happy to do it by myself.'

Phillipa didn't answer for a moment as she appeared to consider the request. 'Ruth, I...' Her words petered out. 'I really wish you wouldn't do this. Some of the suspects are dangerous men. What if the murderer finds out you implicated him? He already killed Thomas. What's to stop him coming after you or Dom or Molly? Or not even the actual murderer, but the ex-inmate you implicate, who might want to take revenge if he finds out. What you're doing is foolish and dangerous.'

'Don't you want to see your husband's killer brought to justice?' Before she could answer, Ruth continued, 'When I thought I'd lost Molly forever, you were there for me. Now I want to help you in return.

Phillipa sighed. 'I see that, but please let this go, Ruth. *Please.*'

She got up and walked out.

Ruth slumped in her seat. She understood her friend's point of view, but she didn't see how it would hurt to go over the suspects' case notes.

The door opened, and her heart rose as she thought Phillipa had changed her mind. But it wasn't Phillipa, it was Anders.

Apparently reacting to her disappointed expression, he said, 'Am I intruding? I can come back later.'

Gathering up her emotions, she assumed what she hoped was a professional demeanour. 'No, please come in. You're in today too? This is starting to feel like a normal workday.'

'Just catching up on some paperwork. I'm glad you're here. I'd been hoping for an opportunity to discuss something...delicate.'

'Of course. Close the door and sit down, Anders. You know I'm always ready to listen to staff concerns.'

He drew up a chair, his expression pensive. 'Firstly, I was wondering if everything's okay.'

'Yes,' Ruth replied, confused. 'I mean, considering everything that's happened recently. Why do you ask?'

'The meeting on Friday?'

As soon as the word 'meeting' left his lips it hit her. 'Oh, I'm so sorry!'

She'd called a team meeting and then completely forgotten about it. 'What happened? I hope you didn't wait for me for long.'

'No, not long. And it was fine. Everyone knows you've been under a lot of stress lately. We discussed the usual topics. Stella may have already sent you the minutes.'

She shook her head. She really needed to get a grip. 'I'll have to apologise to everyone.'

'I'm sure there's no need.' He paused. He had the look of holding something back.

'Is that all you wanted to talk to me about?'

'No.' He paused again. 'Ruth, you know I'm not a gossip, right? I don't think anyone could accuse me of that.'

'No, not at all. I would never say that of you.'

'Good. I want you to understand I'm saying this with good intentions, not because I mean anyone any harm.' His features twisted with discomfort.

Ruth said, 'I think it's best you tell me what's on your mind.'

'Okay, I'm just going to spit it out. I have concerns about Dr Edwards.'

'Oh, is that all?' she replied, relieved. 'I happen to agree with you. I didn't want her to come back so soon, but she insisted it's better to have something to do to take her mind off the investigation. The poor woman's been through so much...' Her words petered out as she registered Anders' continued look of discomfort. 'Is something wrong?'

He fingered the neck of his shirt. 'That isn't exactly what I meant. The other members of the mental health team and I have found Dr Edwards very difficult to work with. She's abrasive, cold and antagonistic and has been so ever since I met her when

I came here three and a half years ago. I didn't say anything for a while—as I said, I'm not a gossip—but when I did, I found everyone agreed with me. Her attitude has only become worse over time. No one wanted to say anything to you because you two appeared to be such good friends. The others thought you must condone her behaviour, but as I've come to know you better, I don't think that's the case. Now she's back, I felt compelled to mention it.'

'You're absolutely right,' Ruth spluttered. 'I would never condone poor behaviour from anyone in our section.' She was amazed—so amazed, she didn't quite believe him. She would have to speak to the others one-to-one before she did anything.

There didn't seem to be much more to say. 'You've given me a lot to think about. Thank you for bringing this to my attention.'

He stood up. 'I'll leave the matter in your hands. I feel guilty for mentioning this right now, after Dr Edwards has suffered a terrible loss, but I thought I'd better say something.'

'I'm glad you did, Anders. Thank you again.'

CHAPTER THIRTY

Will had changed from his usual pea jacket and was wearing a longer coat and a hat, something like a fedora but with a wider brim. The change in clothing meant Shauna didn't spot him immediately as he waited for her outside the Kettle's Yard gallery in central Cambridge. Her gaze passed over him, dismissing him as one of the trendy professionals who thronged the city.

A spark of familiarity drew her attention back, and at the same time, he spotted her and waved. Surprised, she recognised him and her mind re-jigged, slotting this new impression of her DS into place. She crossed the space separating them, dodging shoppers.

Ever since she'd first met him, she'd had the impression Will fancied himself, and his behaviour at the pub had confirmed her suspicion, but she had to admit he did look good in his non-work gear.

'Sorry I'm late,' she said as she reached him. 'Had a hell of a time finding somewhere to park.'

'No problem. Cambridge is a nightmare for drivers, in case you hadn't noticed yet. I usually don't bother driving if I'm not working. I cycle or get an Uber.'

'That would have been a better idea, but I was coming in from out of town. If I'd gone home to drop off my car before coming here, I would have been even later.'

'Been busy?'

'Just birdwatching.'

'You really love it, don't you?'

'Yeah, I do. Shall we go in?'

Will pulled open the door to the gallery, and they stepped from the noise and bustle of the street into the hush and stillness inside. Visiting the gallery was free, so they walked directly into the first section. This part of the exhibition focused on birds of prey. Shauna hadn't heard of the photographer, but as she looked at the pictures she was immediately blown away by their quality.

She stopped in front of a photograph in order to study it closely. Somehow, the photographer had managed to capture a close-up of a peregrine falcon mid-dive. How had he done it? Behind it was a grainy, out-of-focus image of a block of flats. She guessed the photo must have been taken from the window of an adjacent block. The sign next to the picture only stated the species, not the location or technical details of the shot.

'Cool,' Will commented, peering over her shoulder. 'A wild creature within the urban environment. I like it.'

Shauna shot him a sidelong glance. Was he being sarcastic? He seemed serious.

'This bird's on my wish list,' she said.

He laughed. 'What do you mean? I take it you don't want to own one. You want to see it?'

'I've already seen it, but I'd like to get a picture. Never got a good shot of it, though, not even perching. They nest high up. It's the fastest animal on the planet and can dive at over two hundred miles an hour. Getting it in focus while it's in a stoop like this is nearly impossible.'

'You're kidding.' Will looked at the photo again with new

respect in his features. 'Two hundred miles an hour? It's lucky we don't have speed cameras for birds. What does it eat?'

'Other birds.'

'Yeah, stupid question.' He straightened up and wandered off to look at the other photographs.

Shauna continued to examine the image of the falcon, wishing the gallery had included more information. She opened her bag and fished for a pen and an old receipt, and then copied down the photographer's name. Maybe she'd be able to find contact details and ask him directly. He probably wouldn't mind answering an email.

When she'd finished jotting down the information, she slid the receipt into her purse and moved onto the next picture. This one showed a golden eagle feeding its chicks. Again, she was impressed by the photographer's ability to get the shot. He must have taken it from above the eagle's nest, almost certainly on a mountain somewhere in the Scottish Highlands, although the birds also lived in Northern Ireland. From the colour and angle of the light, it seemed to have been taken in the early morning, too, which meant the photographer must have hiked up the mountain in the dark.

'That's a good one,' said Will looking over her shoulder again.

'Yeah, it's stunning,' she replied. 'Golden eagles are amazing. For their courtship ritual they take a stick or a rock, fly to a great height, drop it, and then dive down to catch it mid-air. The male and female birds both do it.'

'Kind of showing off to each other?'

'More like demonstrating their hunting prowess, I think. They mate for life, so they don't want to be tied to a partner who can't help them feed the chicks.'

'How romantic.' He squinted at the photograph. 'That's a bit grim. Can you see it?'

'What?'

Without touching the surface, he pointed at a section within the nest. Camouflaged by its baby feathers, the shrunken remains of a second chick could just be seen behind the first. 'One didn't make it.'

'Ugh, I didn't notice,' said Shauna, 'but you're right. They usually lay two eggs, but only one chick survives to adulthood—the strongest or most demanding. Survival of the fittest, from one generation to the next.'

'You really do know a lot about birds, don't you?'

She shrugged. 'It's my hobby. How about you? What do you do in your spare time?'

'Nothing much. Play a bit of five-a-side. Watch horror films.'

'Horror? You don't get enough of it day to day?'

'Funnily enough, it seems to help me forget. When the films are hammed up and ridiculous, it makes everyday nastiness seem unreal.'

'Hmm, I can see that.'

They both fell into silence. But it wasn't uncomfortable, it was familiar. When your job involved you in tragedy and violence as a matter of course, an unspoken understanding developed, a shared suffering that didn't require stating; that was better left unstated.

Will wandered away again to look at some more photographs, and then disappeared into the next gallery. Shauna studied the next photograph, a goshawk.

She could easily spend all day here and still not be fully satisfied. She felt awed, jealous and inspired to improve her skills. She would need to buy more equipment to achieve anything approaching the standard in the exhibition. On the other hand, she didn't have anything else to spend her money on, so why not?

As she was looking at the photograph of the goshawk, however, she began to feel uneasy. Coming to the exhibition had been a good idea, helping her to banish the ghosts fogging her brain, but now her troubling emotions had subsided the Edwards case had reared up in her mind once more.

She was frustrated by the slow progress. Though most of the evidence was in, it had yielded no promising leads. They were at a dead end, except possibly for Scott, who had the weakest alibi of all the ex-prisoners. The problem was the motive. He'd said his therapy sessions had been helpful. He didn't bear Edwards any animosity, and even if he was lying, disliking the psychologist enough to kill her husband was a stretch. There had to be a better reason. And if hate *was* the motivation, why kill the husband and not Edwards herself?

'You really like this one?' Will asked, making her jump.

She hadn't noticed he'd returned to her side. She must have been staring at the photo of the goshawk for several minutes, lost in her thoughts.

'Uh, no. I mean, I like it, but, actually, I was thinking about something. Will, what do you say we go to the station and look over the evidence for the Edwards case? Go back to the beginning and start again. We aren't getting anywhere. Maybe we'll spot something we missed.'

'If you like. It'll be quiet in there today.'

———

Night had fallen by the time they reached the station, and wispy flakes of snow were swirling through the darkness.

'You wouldn't believe it was March already, would you?' Will asked unwinding his scarf as they walked in.

'DS Fiske!' exclaimed Beth, on duty as desk sergeant. 'I almost didn't recognise you. Don't you look nice. What's the occasion? Evening, DI Holt.' Her gaze flicked to Shauna and then back to Will. The woman she'd been dealing with waited patiently.

'No occasion,' Will replied. 'Just doing a little overtime.'

'Right. I thought you two weren't working today.'

Shauna was about to open the security door leading to the offices, when she caught sight of the face of the person the sergeant was helping.

'Excuse me,' she said, 'aren't you Dr Terrell's daughter?'

A crimson flush spread over the woman's features as she replied, 'Yes. You're the detectives working on Thomas Edwards' murder, aren't you? I'm sorry about my mum. She was only trying to help.'

'We know that,' said Shauna, 'but she really shouldn't interfere. That isn't your fault, though. Why are you here? Is it something to do with the case?'

'No, no. It isn't anything to do with that.'

'Right, I see. What a coincidence we should see you again.' Shauna hesitated, noticing a red mark on her cheek, darker than her blush. 'Can I ask why you've come into the station?'

The woman turned a deeper crimson and she appeared about to cry. 'Oh God, this is so embarrassing.'

The desk sergeant mouthed *domestic violence*.

A horrible sense of dread filled Shauna's stomach. 'Look, why don't you come in? You can sit down and have a cuppa while you make your report.'

Shauna checked the woman's name with the desk sergeant: Molly Markson. Yes, that was it. She would talk to her about her mother's behaviour after she'd made her report about her assault.

If there was a chance to avoid the situation with Dr Terrell escalating, Shauna wanted to take it. She didn't want to have to charge the doctor with anything. It would only complicate matters and create more paperwork. And she didn't believe the psychiatrist's interference was malicious. Emotions ran high for all concerned after a murder, and people behaved out of character for what were often the best intentions. In any other circumstances Terrell would be a law-abiding citizen. It was clear she was only concerned for the well-being of her friend and frustrated that the case seemed to be going nowhere.

Shauna could understand. She was frustrated too.

She'd told the officer taking Markson's statement to ask her if she would mind discussing another matter after she was finished. While she was waiting, she had a call to make.

The person at the other end answered after three rings.

The voice was female and sounded young. According to the information Connor had passed on, she was thirty-one.

'Hello,' said Shauna. 'Am I speaking to Phoebe Matthews?'

'Uh...who is this?'

'I'm Detective Inspector Holt. I'm sorry to disturb you. I'm investigating a case and I was wondering if you could help with our enquiries.'

Shauna heard quiet whispering. *'Not now. Go and play. Mummy's on the phone.'*

A child whined in the background.

'Is this a bad time?' asked Shauna. 'I can call back later.'

'No, no, it's fine,' the woman replied, adding quietly but urgently, *'Go and play! I'll be there in a minute.'*

'You *are* Phoebe Matthews?' Shauna asked.

'Yes. Is this about Pip?' There was a note of quiet sadness in the woman's voice.

Slightly taken aback, Shauna replied, 'Do you mean your sister, Phillipa?'

'Yeah, I used to call her Pip. I couldn't pronounce her name when I was little, and Pip stuck.'

'Right. I take it you heard about the murder?'

'Murder! God, no. What murder?'

'You didn't know your sister's husband had been killed?'

'Her husband? I didn't even know she was married. He was murdered? How awful.'

'Mummy!' the child complained.

'Shhh!'

A high-pitched cry of outrage and frustration was followed by the sound of small feet stamping away from the phone.

'It sounds like you aren't in regular contact with Phillipa.'

'No.' Phoebe sighed. 'I haven't seen her since I was a little girl.'

'And yet, when you received a call from the police, you automatically assumed it was something to do with her.'

'Yes, I expected I would hear some bad news about her one day. I thought she would probably get herself into trouble again.'

'Again? We don't have any record of your sister.'

'I think she had a few run-ins with the police, but she was young at the time. Maybe they've been wiped from the system.'

It was certainly a possibility, especially if Edwards hadn't been charged with any other crimes.

'If it's her past you want to ask me about,' said Matthews, 'I'm afraid I can't help you. I'm much younger than her and I don't remember. I'm just going by what my mum and dad said.'

Connor had also given Shauna information on Edwards' parents. Her father was dead and her mother had Alzheimer's.

'They didn't talk about her much after they kicked her out,' the sister went on, 'so I could have it wrong.'

'She was made to leave home?'

A heavy sigh came down the line.

'It was probably wrong of them, but I think they must have reached the end of their tether. Pip was always difficult, Mum told me once, right from the minute she was born. Always crying, never sleeping. And as soon as she was mobile she was into everything. They couldn't leave her alone for a second. She would be climbing the curtains or trying to open the windows.'

Shauna was about to remark that some children were hyper-active—thinking hyperactivity hardly warranted being chucked out onto the street—when Matthews continued,

'She was always getting into trouble at school for one thing or another, and when she wasn't at school they never knew where she was. She got caught shoplifting lots of times and she took drugs from an early age. I think she was in a gang that harassed homeless people too? I'm not sure. When she did come home, she would bully me mercilessly. I *do* remember that, but it was the second pregnancy that was the final straw for my parents.'

'The *second* pregnancy?'

'Yes, she got pregnant for the first time at thirteen. Mum and Dad were horrified. They were devout Christians, so they forced her to have the baby and give it up for adoption. Six months later, she was pregnant again.'

Another heavy sigh.

'What happened then?' asked Shauna.

'They gave her up to Social Services when she was nearly due. Said they couldn't cope anymore. I think they were trying to protect me from her too. She went into a children's home but, within a few months, she'd run away. That was the last we knew. All these years, I've been expecting to hear she'd died of a drug overdose or something. I'm sorry about her husband. What was it you wanted to talk to me about?'

'Just background info. You've been very helpful. Thank you.'

Shauna hung up.

The phone call had been quite the eye-opener. Phillipa Edwards clearly had big issues as a child, though Shauna wasn't sure what to make of the news. Had she been abused by her parents and that was the reason for her anti-social behaviour? Phoebe must have been only three or four when her sister was forced out of the family home, so her recollections couldn't be relied upon.

Whatever the truth was, Edwards had certainly turned her life around since she was a teenager.

———

When Shauna opened the door to the interview room, Molly Markson was obviously still deeply upset. Her cheeks were flushed and she didn't make eye contact.

The officer left, and Shauna took her seat. 'Thanks for coming in to make a report. So many domestic violence victims don't, and if they manage to get out of the relationship, their abusers go on to hurt others.'

Markson seemed to relax a little. 'That was the first time he's actually been violent. He never hit me before, or I would have left right away. Maybe he knew I would and that's why he held back. Now I'm divorcing him, he doesn't have a reason to control himself. He doesn't have anything to lose.'

'Oh, we'll give him a reason to leave you alone. Don't worry about that.'

The young woman shook her head. 'I don't think you'll find him. I don't know where he's staying, so I couldn't give an address. I came here because I wanted it on record for the judge to see.' She touched her cheek self-consciously. 'You can't have a no-fault divorce. I didn't know until I talked to a solicitor. You either have to live apart for a couple of years, or you need to justify to the court why the marriage is over.' She smiled, and for the first time met Shauna's gaze. 'Daniel just made it easy for me.'

The path of the conversation was making Shauna uncomfortable. She wasn't there to discuss marital violence. 'I hope it goes smoothly for you. We have other means of locating your husband than his address. I don't know the ins and outs of your case, but it sounds like he'll end up with an assault charge. That should definitely help to persuade the judge.'

Suddenly, Markson hunched over, buried her face in her hands and began to cry. Shauna snatched tissues from a box and offered them to her before moving around the table and patting her on her back.

'I'm sorry,' Markson said between sobs. 'It's just…it's just it's all been so much. Leaving Scotland and coming home. I hadn't spoken to my parents for years, and then I turned up on their doorstep with a suitcase. But the next day the murder was reported, and Phillipa came to stay, and no one, no one…' She began bawling again.

The door opened. Will peered around the edge. His eyes widened, and Shauna gave him an *I didn't expect this either* look. He quickly withdrew and softly closed the door.

Markson looked up at the sound anyway, her face wet with tears.

'It's okay,' said Shauna. 'It was just my sergeant checking up on me.'

The interruption appeared to bring her somewhat back to

normality. She began to wipe her eyes. 'Oh my God. I'm so sorry.' She blew her nose. 'I don't know what came over me.'

'It's fine. It's the shock just beginning to hit. It's a perfectly normal reaction to being assaulted.' Shauna was repeating something she often said to victims to reassure them, but she did feel for the woman. She'd clearly been through a lot, and then when she'd finally broken out of her abusive marriage, it seemed her mother was preoccupied with someone else's problems. That had to hurt. Markson was already weak and vulnerable. Domestic abusers wore their victims down psychologically over the years.

'You're doing the right thing, you know,' said Shauna. 'Leaving your husband, I mean. His behaviour would only have become worse over time. You're very brave. Things will get better.' She bit her lip and hesitated before adding, 'I know how hard it is.'

'Do you?' The young woman looked at her curiously.

Should she backtrack and give a professional response, telling her she knew from her experience as a police officer? Or should she be genuine? The latter would be better. Hearing others have been through the same as you made you feel less alone and powerless. Not that she'd ever met anyone whose story matched her own.

'I do,' she replied eventually. 'You'd be surprised how many women have been in your situation, and men too. People don't like to talk about it, and abusers are very clever at persuading their victims to not tell anyone what's happening.'

'I would never have imagined a police detective could—'

'It was a long time ago, before I joined the service.'

Markson appeared to mull this fact over. She wiped her eyes again. 'The worst thing about it is I feel like such an idiot. I was so stupid, so easily taken in. I don't know how I let it happen.'

'You need to stop blaming yourself. The first step to moving on is to forgive yourself. You were the victim. If you want someone to blame, make it your soon-to-be ex, okay?'

She nodded and then straightened up. 'I should go. My dad texted me just before you came in. He's on his way to pick me up. He'll be here soon.'

'Right, well, before you leave, I want a quick word about your mother.'

Markson groaned and covered her eyes with one hand. 'I'd forgotten about that. I tried my best to persuade her not to go to that man's house. I'm so sorry.'

'I'm glad we're on the same page about it, and you weren't involved except for happening to be there too. Molly, what your mother did was very serious. When I said she could jeopardise the murder investigation, I wasn't exaggerating, and when I said she could be arrested, it wasn't an idle threat.'

'I understand. I'm so sorry,' she repeated.

'Can I ask you what Dr Terrell's attitude was after you left Baram Scott's house? Does she intend to continue approaching the people of interest in our enquiry?'

'No,' Markson replied emphatically. 'She was quite shaken up by what happened. She said she wouldn't do it again. I'm sure she won't.'

'Good,' said Shauna. She was watching the woman carefully. Though she was verbally in agreement, she seemed to be holding something back. 'So she's going to stay out of the case from now on?'

'I-I think so. She definitely isn't going to talk to any more ex-inmates.'

Shauna didn't reply immediately, hoping Markson would fill the pause, but she didn't. Terrell was her mother, after all. Shauna couldn't expect her daughter to side with the police against her.

'Just so long as she understands she could be doing more harm than good by her actions. If she really wants to help us catch Thomas Edwards' murderer, the best thing she can do is not interfere.'

'I'll tell her.' Markson's phone pinged, and she checked a text. 'I really should be going. Dad's waiting for me.'

'All right, I won't keep you any longer,' said Shauna. But as the woman stood up, she asked, 'By the way, is Phillipa Edwards still staying with you?'

'She's going home today.'

'I see. Your mother must be sorry to see her go. They seem to be close friends.'

'Yeah, though...'

Shauna waited, interested to hear what reservation Markson seemed to harbour.

But her phone pinged again. 'I really must go.'

Maybe she was only resentful of Edwards taking her mother's attention.

'I'll show you out.'

'Thanks.'

Shauna led her through the station.

When they reached the security door, Markson said, 'Thanks for what you told me. About it happening to you too, I mean. It makes me feel less stupid.'

'You aren't stupid,' said Shauna, holding the door open, 'And it isn't your fault.'

If only she could convince herself of the same, but she'd given up on that long ago.

CHAPTER THIRTY-TWO

As Shauna began to walk back to her office, a sudden emotional reaction to her conversation with Molly Markson began to well up. She had to get out of sight fast, so she took a detour to the toilets.

She opened the door and saw with relief the room was empty. Quickly locking herself into a stall, she only just had time to lower the seat lid and sit down before anguish and despair hit her. Hunched over, she wept, tears dripping freely from her eyes. Despite her best efforts, sobs escaped her lips.

Long experience had taught her the spasm would pass in a few minutes. But until it did, her feelings were beyond her control. Over the years, she'd tried counselling, medication, mindfulness techniques...anything and everything that might help. Some things *had* helped, but nothing had completely put to an end these moments of total loss of self-control.

She was beyond fixing. All she could do was try her best to hide her flaw. So far, she seemed to have succeeded. No one in the police service, as far as she was aware, knew about her past. If her weakness were revealed, it would compromise her professional reputation. Her superiors might doubt her abilities, or, at the very least, she would draw her colleagues' excruciating pity. She needed to appear confident and in control.

Gradually, her crying eased and her breathing evened out. Within another couple of minutes, her composure returned. She tore off some toilet paper, dried her eyes and blew her nose. She listened.

Nothing.

Opening the stall door, she peeked out. The room remained empty.

At the wash basin, she discovered her face was a predictably blotchy mess. Her eyes were swollen and red, and irregular patches of colour patterned her cheeks. She'd never been one of those graceful weepers whose attractiveness increased as they sobbed their hearts out.

She splashed her face with cold water and patted it dry with a paper towel. She'd left her handbag in the office, so she couldn't put on eye make-up, brush her hair or do anything else to disguise the evidence of her anguish.

The door banged open. Shauna started.

It was Beth.

'What a day!' she exclaimed to Shauna's back. 'As well as that assault, I've had three brawling drunks, a mugging report, and a homeless woman having a psychotic break. Glad it's finally over.'

She disappeared into a stall.

Shauna quickly left. What she most wanted and needed was to go home, drink some wine, and lose herself in trashy television. Her episode had exhausted her. But it had been her idea to do some more work on the Edwards' case. If she left now, Will would find it weird.

She turned a corner—and almost walked directly into Bryant. The man was in full uniform. The shiny buttons of his jacket seemed to rush at her face and she jumped backwards in shock.

'DI Holt,' he said, oblivious to her surprise and alarm. 'I didn't expect to see you here, but I'm impressed by your commitment. Have you had a breakthrough on the case?'

'Not yet, sir,' she replied, her head down. 'Still working on it.'

'Hm, that's not the news I wanted to hear. The press conference the other night didn't go well. People need to feel safe in their homes, they need reassurance, and they look to us for that.'

It was an old spiel she'd heard many times in her career. What he really meant was, *I need something to get the press and higher-ups off my back.*

'We are making progress,' she said. 'As soon as we have something concrete I'll inform you immediately.'

'Good.' He hesitated. 'Is everything all right?'

He leaned closer, as if trying to get a closer look at her face.

'Yes, everything's fine. I have to get back to work. As I said, as soon as I have something concrete, I'll inform you.'

She skirted around Bryant and continued on her way.

It had been exactly the wrong time for her to see him. She already felt like shit. Having pressure applied only made her feel worse. Did he think she didn't want to solve the case? And she hadn't forgotten the chilling phone call. She'd played it off as probably a nutcase trying to scare her, but she was only human. She *had* been frightened, just a bit. She had as much reason as anyone to find the murderer.

Hoping her face had calmed down a bit, she went into the incident room. Will was at his desk watching CCTV footage on his monitor.

'Bryant's here,' she said. 'Did you know?'

'No. He mustn't have a social life either.'

CCTV footage of the supermarket car park where Phillipa Edwards had been discovered was playing on Will's screen. She'd watched the same recording herself several times and not seen anything useful. All it showed was Edwards wandering among the parked cars, looking confused. But something about the scene Will was watching looked different.

'What's that?' she asked. 'Something new?'

He looked up and took a double take at her face, but didn't comment on it. 'The security supervisor forgot they had another camera covering the same area. This recording arrived a few hours ago.'

She pulled a spare chair over and sat down. 'Anything interesting?'

'Not yet.'

A line of trolleys appeared on the screen. Then a young employee came into view, pushing the end of it. Edwards was in his way. She moved to one side and rested her hand on a car bonnet, looking around confusedly. The young man pushed the trolleys into a bay and began to walk back to the store. As he passed Edwards, he stopped and spoke to her.

Shauna had seen the interaction many times before from a different angle. After a short dialogue, the shop worker left Edwards, but he soon returned with the store manager. Another conversation ensued, during which shoppers passed by, giving the group curious looks. Eventually, the manager, employee and Edwards walked off screen as they went into the supermarket. An ambulance had been called not long after.

Shauna focused on Edwards. Though the video quality was poor, she did *appear* confused.

'I hope that kid got mentioned in dispatches,' Will remarked. 'He spotted something wasn't right with her immediately.'

'Or he fell for her play acting. Go back to the start.'

He clicked on the beginning of the clip, which started before Edwards entered the car park. Shoppers were arriving and leaving on foot and in their cars. Everything looked normal. Shauna watched the spot where Edwards had walked in. The psychologist had stepped through a gap in a tall hedge, a short cut from the public footpath.

The area was closer and better defined in the new recording.

Edwards came into view, stepping through the open space. Her expensive, professional woman's attire seemed at odds with her behaviour. Her type would have usually arrived by car, not on foot, and not via a gap in a hedge.

'Pause it,' said Shauna.

Will tapped the relevant key.

'Go back to the beginning again.'

As the video began to play once more, she leaned in, peering closely—not at the place of Phillipa Edwards' entrance to the car park, but a different portion of the hedge.

'Look.' She pointed, her finger nearly touching the screen.

'What?'

The recording played on.

Edwards stepped through the gap.

'Go back again,' said Shauna, 'and watch this spot.'

Patiently, Will restarted the footage.

She didn't want to tell him *what* to look for, only where to look. She needed him to see it too without her prompting. She wasn't entirely convinced her imagination wasn't playing tricks on her.

'There's someone else there!' he exclaimed.

He hit pause again and edged the recording back a couple of seconds.

Though the bushes had lost their leaves for the winter, they were thick. The recording was also grainy and the daylight was weak. The figure of Edwards approaching behind the vegetation was barely visible. Yet the indistinct shadow was obviously too large to be only one person.

'Let it play,' said Shauna. 'I want to see what the other person does.'

A second or two passed. Edwards stepped into the car park and began to wander among the cars. Shauna kept her gaze glued to the remaining dark spot in the hedge. It didn't move for twelve seconds. What was the man or woman doing? Watching Edwards? Waiting for something?

Then the figure walked slowly away until disappearing from the screen.

As the person turned, Shauna also thought she'd seen a tiny flash of light in the region of their head, though she wasn't sure.

'We've got more footage than this,' said Will. 'I originally cut it to just before Edwards arrives. Give me a minute, and we can see what happens earlier.'

After Will found the original recording, they watched again. What looked like two people walking together moved along the other side of the hedge and then stopped. The pair parted company. Moments later, Edwards stepped into the car park. The stranger turned, and then he or she was gone.

There could be no doubt about it. Phillipa Edwards had arrived at the car park with a companion.

'Well,' Shauna said, 'I'd call that a significant development.'

'So has she been faking her amnesia all along?' Will asked.

'I suppose not necessarily. The annoying thing is, we can't see how she looks before she steps into the car park. If she was putting it on, we might see a change in her behaviour.'

'She didn't have any drugs in her system. We know she wasn't doped up. She either knows who she was with that morning or she's forgotten, the same as everything else.'

'Who could it be, I wonder,' Shauna mused. 'She's lived here five years, but, according to the address book in her phone, she doesn't have any friends in Cambridge except the Terrells.'

'She can't have been with Dr Terrell. We were interviewing her when Edwards turned up.'

'What about her husband?'

'Didn't Dr Terrell phone him at home while we were with her?'

'No,' Shauna replied, the light dawning. 'She spoke to her daughter, Molly Markson. Don't you remember? Terrell was worried about her daughter and her husband due to the murder. She said something like, *Tell your dad. He must have left with*…I can't remember the name. It must be another child of theirs. But he wasn't there when she called.'

They paused. What did it mean? Shauna felt the puzzle pieces were slotting together, but she still didn't know what she was looking at.

'Just because Mr Terrell wasn't home at the time,' she said, 'that doesn't mean it's him behind the hedge.'

'No. It's quite a leap. On the other hand, who else does she know? According to what we've found on her phone and laptop, the only people she sees socially are the Terrells.'

Another pause.

'Should we bring him in?' Will asked.

Shauna chewed her lip. 'Yeah, let's do it. Tomorrow.'

CHAPTER THIRTY-THREE

Dad had made spaghetti bolognese for dinner. As always, his version of the humble dish was delicious. Dad wasn't great with housework, but he could certainly cook.

Only no one seemed to feel like eating.

Mum was quietly glum, slowly moving forkfuls of spaghetti to her mouth and taking forever to chew and swallow while staring vacantly at the table. Molly was still feeling shaken up by the incident with Daniel. Even Becky was getting more food on the floor and herself than in her mouth.

Dad said, 'She hasn't been right since the elephant incident.'

'What?' asked Molly.

'Becky hasn't got over the toy elephant turning up in her school bag. Don't you remember?'

'Oh, that. Really? It's been days.'

Her father shrugged. 'It takes her longer than most children to recover from an upset. It's part of her condition.'

'Did you ever find out who put it there?'

'No. I told the teacher about what happened and she said she'd look into it, but I haven't heard anything. It must have been one of the other kids. Some of them are little devils. They know exactly what sets another child off and they do it for fun.'

'That's a little harsh, dear,' said Mum, suddenly breaking out of her musings. 'All the children have special needs. That's why they're at a special school. I'm sure it wasn't malicious. It was probably an accident, someone trying to be nice by giving her a toy to take home.'

Dad raised his eyebrows but appeared to decide it wasn't worth arguing about. He looked at his plate and was silent.

'Poor Becky,' Molly murmured.

Mum's hand rose to her mouth, and she shook her head. A stifled sob escaped her lips. 'I can't believe...'

'It's all right,' said Dad, patting her other hand. 'She'll be fine in a day or two.'

'No, I'm not upset about that nonsense.'

She put her fork in her bowl and then sank her head into her hands.

'What's wrong, love?' asked Dad.

Her voice muffled, Mum replied, 'Here's Molly feeling sorry for her sister when *she's* the one who deserves pity. That awful, awful man. Hitting my...' Her words trailed off.

Molly reached out to touch her mother's shoulder. 'It's all right. I'm okay now. It was a shock when...but he didn't really hurt me. And the police said they would probably be able to find him and charge him, even though I couldn't give them an address. I suppose they'll ask at all the local hotels and B&Bs. He's probably registered under his real name. He didn't have a reason not to, until he hit me.'

But Mum gave a strangled sob and her shoulders shook. She mumbled something, but Molly couldn't make it out.

'Ruth, love!' said Dad. 'Let me find some tissues.' He pushed back his chair and left the table, returning moments later with the tissue box. He put it down in front of Mum and drew his chair closer before patting her back. 'Don't worry. It's all over now. Molly's here, safe and sound. And Daniel won't be coming within two feet of her ever again. I can guarantee it.'

'Oh, Dad, you don't have to be my white knight,' said Molly.

'I'm not afraid of him. He's got his anger out now. He took me by surprise, that's all.'

'That *isn't* all,' her father retorted. 'These things don't happen out of nowhere. It's clear he's been treating you terribly. You're well rid of him.'

Molly couldn't deny Daniel had behaved like an absolute arsehole, but she hated the idea of her parents worrying about her. 'You're right, but it's over now. And things could have been worse for me. I could have had nowhere to go. But you took me in, even though I hadn't contacted you for years. You accepted me back without question.' Perhaps it was because her mother was already crying, but Molly found herself tearing up too.

'Goodness,' said Dad. 'Did you imagine we would turn you away?' He shook his head. 'You should know you're always welcome here, love. *Always*. When did we ever give you any other impression? I only wish I'd known how bad things were. When we didn't hear from you for a while, I just thought you were busy and in love. That's how things are when you're newly married. Wrapped in your own little bubble. And then the time passed so quickly. It came as quite a shock when I realised we hadn't seen you for five years, or heard from you for almost as long. We did think about paying you a visit, but travelling with Becky is so hard and Scotland is so far. We kept putting it off.'

Molly wasn't sure how she felt about her father's take on the years of no contact. She'd felt guilty about not answering her parents' emails and changing her phone number. But it appeared that Dad, at least, had barely noticed. Had Mum been the same? She wasn't saying anything, just quietly weeping.

In one way her father's obliviousness was a relief, but it also hurt she hadn't been missed. It was another example of the same inattention she'd experienced for the majority of her life. Then she chided herself. Her parents' lives weren't easy.

'I don't think it would have made any difference if you had visited,' she said. 'Daniel probably would have persuaded me to not let you in. He'd already persuaded me to stop communicating with you. It took me a while to see what he was doing, that he'd been manipulating me right from the beginning. It was years before I understood *he* had the problem, not me, and nothing I did would ever be good enough, that *I* would never be good enough.

'The divorce petition has gone in now, and the solicitor said it should be straightforward as neither of us has much in the way of assets. Now I have the assault charge too, it should go through even more easily. Hopefully, in another few months I'll be free and able to start again.'

'That's the best way to look at it,' said Dad. 'You're still a young woman with your whole life ahead of you. There's plenty of time for you to meet someone else, someone who'll be good to you. It's not the end of the world. You can put it all behind you and move on.'

'Yes, I can, and I will.'

Her father reached over the table to squeeze her arm.

Mum continued to cry. Occasionally, she wiped her eyes with a tissue, but she didn't seem able to snap out of it.

'Ruth,' said Dad, 'Don't take on so. Everything's okay now.'

But her mother only shook her head. A moment later, she stood up and tottered mechanically out of the kitchen. Then came the sound of her footsteps going upstairs.

'I'd better see she's all right,' said Dad, getting up.

Becky hadn't seemed to notice all these goings on. She continued to play with her food.

Molly fetched a cloth to clean her sister's face. She had a sudden impulse to hug her sister, but Becky couldn't bear that kind of contact.

CHAPTER THIRTY-FOUR

There had been a time when Shauna thought she might finally be able to move on from her past, but now she knew it was not to be.

In the beginning, pain had overwhelmed her. Her memory of the time was hazy. Weeks and months had passed, but she had little recollection. Then, somehow, reality had broken into her nightmare. She'd come to understand that, while life had stopped for her, for everyone else it had carried on as normal. Relief from her agony had arrived in brief patches, when she could step back into her old life as if the unspeakable hadn't happened.

The periods of respite grew longer, and she'd joined the police service. Due to having, as Will had put it, no social life, she'd been able to devote herself utterly to her work. Her superiors interpreted this as an exceptional level of commitment and rewarded her with promotions. For a time, things had seemed to go well. Somehow, she'd even got married again, deluded she wasn't irrevocably broken.

But her bouts of despair resumed and increased. Each time she sunk deeper into the well, and it grew harder to climb the mossy, slimy walls of her prison and drag herself out. She'd divorced her kind, patient husband, knowing she couldn't be the partner he deserved, and applied for a transfer to a quieter area of the country, hoping reduced work pressure might help her return to her state of just-about-coping. What a joke. It hadn't worked, and there was nothing she could do about it.

'It slots together, doesn't it?' said Will. 'Dominic Terrell was having an affair with his wife's colleague, and in a fit of jealousy he kills her husband. Then Edwards covers up for him because she's still in love with him and doesn't want him to go to prison.'

'Yeah,' Shauna said, dragging her mind back to the task at hand. They were walking up the Terrells' garden path. 'It would explain why there were no signs of a fight at the murder scene.'

'Thomas Edwards would have known Dominic Terrell because their wives were friends,' said Will. 'He wouldn't have been alarmed to see him in his house. Maybe Dominic and Phillipa even planned the whole thing. If Phillipa Edwards divorced her husband she would only get half of his inheritance, maybe not any of it. I'm not sure if inheritances are shared in a divorce. But with her husband dead and no kids in the picture, she stands to get it all. Maybe Mr Terrell's planning to divorce his wife after the kerfuffle with the murder investigation dies down, and he and Phillipa will ride off into the sunset, set up for life.'

'Makes sense.' Shauna rang the doorbell. 'Let's see how he reacts when he finds out he's a suspect.'

The door opened. Molly Markson stood in the entrance. 'Oh, hello. Is this about Daniel? Did you find him?'

'Er, no, sorry,' Shauna replied. 'Other police officers are dealing with your case. Is your father home?'

'Yes, I'll...' she paused, mid-turn, and faced them again. 'Why do you want to see him?'

'If you would please ask him to come to the door?' asked Will.

Looking troubled, Molly said grudgingly, 'All right.'

She closed the door until it was only just ajar and called

'Dad!' from the hall, followed by, 'It's the detectives from the murder case.'

A moment later, Dominic Terrell arrived wearing a pinny. 'What can I do for you?'

'We'd like you to come to the station to answer some questions.'

'You...what? Why?'

Molly appeared at his side. 'Why do you want to talk to my father?'

'This is police business, Mrs Markson,' said Shauna. 'I'm not at liberty to discuss the matter. Mr Terrell, would you come with us?'

'Wait...I...Are you arresting me?'

'You aren't under arrest,' Will replied, 'but it would help with our inquiries if you would submit to an interview.'

'But why?' Terrell asked. 'How on Earth could I—'

'Are you refusing?' asked Shauna.

'I don't know,' he said. 'I'm wondering if I need a solicitor. Please wait a moment.' He closed the door.

'He isn't going to do a runner, is he?' Will asked.

'He'd better take his apron off.'

A discussion could faintly be heard going on in the hall. About a minute later, Mr Terrell reappeared wearing a winter coat. 'I'll attend an interview, but I have to leave by two to pick up my daughter.'

'As you wish,' said Shauna. 'It shouldn't take long.'

———

'Thank you for consenting to a DNA swab, Mr Terrell,' said Shauna.

'It's not a problem. I don't have anything to hide.'

'Can I ask how long you've known Phillipa Edwards?'

Terrell knit his fingers before replying, 'My wife invited Phillipa to a gathering at our house when she was new at the prison, about five years ago. I met her then. Ruth often does that when someone joins the team, to help ease them in.'

'So you've known her about as long as your wife has.'

'Yes.'

'Do you see her often?'

'I see my wife every day.'

'Don't play games, Mr Terrell.'

He rolled his eyes. 'After the welcoming party, I began to see her occasionally when she and Ruth were doing something together. They're friends. And of course she came to stay with us following the murder.'

'So you're saying you've only seen Dr Edwards while your wife was present too?'

'Yes.' He frowned.

'Have you ever been to her house?'

'No.'

'How would you describe your relationship with Dr Edwards?'

'Acquaintances.'

'Nothing more?'

After a pause, Terrell replied, 'I see what you're implying, but I love my wife very much. I've never had an affair and never will, and certainly never with someone like her. And if you think I'm a murderer, well...' he shook his head '...anyone who knows me would tell you how ridiculous that sounds.'

'Someone like her?' asked Shauna. 'What do you mean?'

He shrugged.

'I can't say I'm much of a judge,' said Shauna, 'but I'd say Phillipa Edwards is an attractive woman, especially for someone her age. Would you say so, DS Fiske?'

Will's eyebrows shot up. 'Er, yes, ma'am.'

Shauna turned back to Terrell. 'It seems she isn't unattractive, so I'm guessing you must have meant something else when you said *someone like her.*'

'I didn't realise you wanted to discuss the relative beauty of my wife's co-workers,' said Terrell acidly. 'Had I known, I would have brought along my score sheet.'

'I get the impression you don't like Dr Edwards,' said Shauna. 'Is that correct?'

'Does it really matter?' he asked. 'She's my wife's friend and she needed a place to stay after her husband was murdered, so we put her up for a few weeks. Whether I like or dislike her doesn't come into it.'

'Really? I prefer to like the people who stay in my house.'

'I'm happy to admit my lovely wife rules the roost in our home. If she wants to open our house to a friend, then that's what we do. I didn't have a serious objection. The woman needed somewhere to go, so she came to us. Now she's gone back to her own place. End of story.'

Shauna rested her elbows on the table. 'So you're denying you've ever had a romantic or intimate relationship with Phillipa Edwards?'

'I am. Categorically.'

With the sense of a conjurer performing a trick, Shauna took the evidence bag containing the handkerchief from the box at her feet and placed it on the table.

'Does this look familiar to you, Mr Terrell?'

His mouth hanging slightly ajar, he looked from the handkerchief to her and back again before bursting into laughter. 'Are you saying that's mine?!'

'You tell me.'

He wiped a tear from his eye. 'I mean, I suppose...' His voice trailed off and his expression suddenly turned serious. 'I don't think it can be, unless the police have been secretly raiding my washing line. Where did you get it?'

'Please answer the question, Mr Terrell.'

'No, it isn't mine.'

'You're positive?'

'Yes, I'm positive.'

Shauna leaned back in her seat, cueing Will to take over while she watched Terrell.

He took out his notebook and flicked through it. 'Mr Terrell, can you tell us what you were doing the night of the third of February this year?'

'The third? That's when the murder took place, isn't it?'

Neither Will nor Shauna answered.

Terrell sighed. 'Molly, my daughter arrived that night from Scotland, for a visit, about eight o'clock. We spent the evening together.'

'You, your wife, and your daughter?' asked Will.

'Correct.'

'Did you leave the house at all that evening?'

'No...oh...yes, I did. Molly was hungry, and we'd already eaten. I went out about ten o'clock to get a takeaway.'

'How long were you gone?'

'Probably about three-quarters of an hour.'

'How did you pay for the food?' asked Will. 'Do you have a receipt?'

'I always pay for that kind of thing with cash. I don't want to risk them swiping my card details.' A sudden realisation seemed to hit him. His face fell and he began to look worried. 'Look, I can see what you're thinking. But that's just silly.'

'Do you remember where you bought the takeaway?' Shauna asked.

'Uhhh...' Terrell coloured. 'It was weeks ago. If you give me a minute, I'm sure I can think of it. Not many places are open that time of night.'

'Your house is...what would you say?' said Shauna, '...about half a mile from the Edwards'?'

'That's enough!' Terrell exclaimed. 'I refuse to answer any more questions.'

'Can you tell us your whereabouts on the morning of the fourth of February?' Will asked.

'I said, I'm not answering any more questions. I want to speak to a solicitor.'

'On the night of the third and the morning of the fourth of February,' said Shauna, 'were you at any time in the company of Phillipa Edwards?'

'I *said*...I want to leave. You haven't arrested me, so I'm free to go.' He got up.

Shauna also stood. 'Thank you for your time, Mr Terrell. We'll be in touch.'

CHAPTER THIRTY-FIVE

Dom had briefly mentioned something about a police interview, adding dismissively that it was 'a load of stuff and nonsense', but Ruth was worried nonetheless.

Yet she couldn't seem to say or do anything about it.

Here, under her bedclothes, she felt safe and secure, as if nothing in the world could harm her or her family ever again. It wasn't true, of course. Molly had been hurt by her husband and, before that, by herself and Dom, though they hadn't realised it at the time. She wanted to say or do something about her mistake, but somehow she couldn't. She could only lie here.

What are you doing, Ruth? What's wrong with you?

She could see herself from above, a bird's eye view of her body under wrinkled covers, messy greying hair peeking out.

At the same time, she could feel the warmth and soft darkness of her safe place.

Voices outside the bedroom door.

Molly and Dom, speaking quietly, but she could still make out the words.

'It's been three days, Dad!' Molly admonished. 'We need to do something. Call a doctor, or at least tell her co-workers what's really going on. Maybe they can help.'

'We can't, not without her permission. We don't know how it will affect her standing and reputation. She might even be forced to resign.'

'Maybe that wouldn't be such a bad thing. Maybe she can't handle work anymore and needs to do something else.'

'I'm sure it's just a phase. We mustn't over-react, and we definitely mustn't do anything without your mother's say so. She probably just needs a break, some time to rest and recuperate. She was dreadfully upset by Daniel's assault on you and she's been under a lot of stress from the murder investigation. She'll snap out of it soon, I'm sure.'

'And what if she doesn't? What if this is it?' A thread of fear ran through Molly's angry tone.

'Then we'll do something, but not now. Not yet.'

'Then when? How long do we let this go on?'

'Let's see how she feels tomorrow and take it from there, okay? I have to go and pick Becky up now.'

The landing floorboards creaked as Dom walked away.

Seconds later, the sound of the front door opening and closing floated in.

Ruth hadn't heard Molly move.

Tap, tap, tap.

'Mum?'

She wanted to answer but her tongue and throat felt swollen and numb.

The doorknob rattled and light from the hallway spilled into the room.

'I brought you some tea.'

Ruth sensed her daughter's form moving through the bedroom. The mattress sank to one side as she sat down.

'I put a couple of sugars in it,' she said. 'I know you don't normally take sugar, but you've hardly eaten anything recently so I thought...' She sighed.

Ruth felt the touch of Molly's hand on her shoulder.

'Is there anything else I can get you?'

'No, dear,' Ruth managed to whisper. 'I'm fine, just very tired.'

'You can't still be tired, not after three days in bed!' Molly inhaled sharply. 'Sorry, I didn't mean it. I'm just worried about you.'

Ruth couldn't muster an answer.

———

When Molly had gently tapped her parents' bedroom door with her knuckles, she'd been holding onto a fragile hope her mother might be feeling better, that Dad's prediction she would 'snap out of it soon' had come true.

Nothing had changed.

Her mother lay on her side under the bed covers, a hump graced by the minimal light from the window. The air leaking out of the room was stale and held the trace of morning breath. The curtains were closed. Daylight spilled from their edges and settled on surfaces: the covers on the double bed, the old-fashioned, free-standing wardrobe with one door ajar, the bowed front of the chest of drawers and items cluttering its top.

Molly had a feeling her dad never hoovered or dusted in here. He probably didn't see the point as guests would never enter it. The room wasn't quite at hoarder level, but it wasn't far off. She itched to go through the place and throw out all the useless junk that had built up over the years before cleaning it top to bottom. But Dad would think up some excuse to stop her.

He would say he was getting around to having a clear out and she shouldn't bother herself. Like this problem with Mum, he would put off acting on it indefinitely, refusing to face painful facts.

Molly put down the mug of tea on the night-stand and sat on the bed.

After a brief conversation, during which Molly nearly lost it, she lapsed into silence.

At school and university, when her friends had bitched and vented about run-ins with their parents, she'd heard plenty of stories of screaming matches, slammed doors and thrown crockery. Her own store of tales of family life had been feeble in comparison. Voices were rarely raised in her home while she was growing up. Dad was usually cheery and Mum calm, though somewhat vague and distracted.

This new version of her mother filled her with alarm.

Biting her lip, Molly wondered if she should call an ambulance. Mum wasn't physically sick, as far as she could tell, but something had gone wrong with her mentally.

'How are you feeling? Are you up to eating anything? I could make you some soup.'

A small sigh escaped her mother's lips but no words followed.

She noticed a silvery track leading from the corners of her eyes to the pillow, where a wet patch darkened the white cotton.

In an effort to lighten Mum's mood, she said, 'Becky's okay. I know all her routines now. I took her to school this morning and explained you aren't well. The teacher said they'll keep an eye on her. She said people often think autistic children aren't aware of what's happening around them, but they often understand more than we give them credit for, so she was grateful I told her.'

Her words provoked no response.

Mum's open, unfocussed eyes seemed to mock her.

It was as if she were in a play, pretending to be dead. She was present but also absent.

Just like she'd been for most of Molly's adolescence.

Memories of the time flooded in. The years Molly had spent in the shadows, hoping one day her parents might notice her, yet feeling guilty for desiring attention. She recalled the missed celebrations: her eighteenth birthday, A level results day, getting into university. All she'd ever received was her parents' quiet congratulations. Organising a party or going out to dinner would have been too disruptive and too much effort in their already busy lives.

Had it been a relief to them when she'd gone away to university? Had they been grateful for one less burden, or perhaps they'd been relieved they no longer had to even pretend to care about her? How had they really felt about her coming home?

The hurt reached a crescendo. She had a sensation of being at the top of a roller-coaster, about to tip over the edge.

Sobs wrenched their way out of her throat, and she thrust her face into her hands. 'Mum, for god's sake! First Daniel, and now you. I can't take any more! Why are you doing this?'

Her mother's weight slowly shifted on the bed. She sat up and Molly felt her arm slide around her shoulders. She pulled her close and whispered, 'I'm sorry, love. I'm so very sorry.'

But Molly couldn't stop crying. Her chest heaving hard, she wept on. The dam had burst and years of resentment and bitterness gushed forth.

'Don't touch me!'

She threw off her mother's arm and leapt to her feet. 'Stop pretending! You don't give a shit about me and you never have! Is it any wonder I ended up married to an abuser? It's *your* fault I was so easy to manipulate. Your and Dad's fault I was in such desperate need of attention. Your fault I craved acceptance so badly I was willing to overlook anything, just so long as I felt like *someone* loved me. Anyone! All this time I've blamed myself, but it wasn't me, it was you. How could you do it, Mum? How could you?'

Throughout her tirade, her mother had wordlessly watched, her eyes wet and wide.

Molly finally ran out of words. Unable to bear the sight of her mother's blank expression, she turned away.

'You're right,' Mum whispered. 'It's all true. Everything you said. We did neglect you. I see that now. I think I've known it for a while, but I didn't want to admit it to myself. Of all people, I should have seen what I was doing, but I was blind. I've been blind about so many things.'

Molly heard her mother climb out of bed.

In her crumpled nightgown, her hair a bird's nest speckled with grey, her face wrinkled and pale, she looked older—frail, old, and tired.

'I'm sorry, I didn't mean...' said Molly. But she had meant it. Only she didn't want to hurt this woman she loved.

Mum moved closer. 'I can't take back the past, but if there's any way I can make this up to you, I will.'

'Oh, Mum.' Molly's tears broke out afresh.

Her mother hugged her. 'Let's try to start again, shall we? I want to do what I can to fix our family.'

The doorbell rang.

CHAPTER THIRTY-SIX

'I'd like to speak to your father,' said Shauna. 'Is he home?

'No,' Molly Markson replied, 'he's gone to pick up my sister from school. Why do you want to see him? Does he have to come into the station for another interview?'

'When will he be back?' Shauna asked.

'Not long. Five or ten minutes.'

'Right. We'll wait for him.'

Will returned with Shauna to their unmarked car. After shutting the door, she relaxed in her seat and exhaled.

'Something's up with her,' Will commented.

Dominic Terrell's daughter had been crying. The same as Shauna, it didn't do her looks any favours.

'Do you think she knows?' he asked.

Two marked police vehicles sat behind them on the road, the uniforms inside them awaiting Shauna's nod.

'She could have a good guess,' she replied. 'But whatever's bothering her, it isn't to do with us turning up. She couldn't have known we were coming.'

'What if she phones him and tips him off?'

'It's a possibility, but I don't think he's stupid enough to abscond, especially not with his young daughter in tow.'

The DNA test result had been clear: the handkerchief found at the crime scene belonged to Dominic Terrell. The DNA link, plus the man's inability to account for his whereabouts at the time of the murder were sufficient to take him into custody, according to DCI Bryant. He had insisted on making an arrest.

'You have a clear association and no alibi,' he'd said in reaction to Shauna's look of doubt. 'What else do you want?'

'More concrete evidence would be nice,' she'd replied.

'That's what your search warrant is for. Look, it's a story old as time. The jealous lover killed the husband. Go and find your evidence, DI Holt.'

A car appeared at the end of the road, slowing as it approached. Terrell sat in the driver's seat and the figure of a girl could be seen in the back.

Even at the distance, Shauna saw Terrell take in the three vehicles parked on the road in front of his house. When he was a few metres away, he made eye contact with her. A stony expression settled on his face. He indicated and pulled into the driveway.

At the sound of tyres crunching on gravel, the front door opened. Molly Markson stood in the doorway.

Terrell got out.

Shauna and Will did the same, and she beckoned to the uniforms. The noise of car doors opening and slamming resounded in the quiet street.

Terrell was helping his child out of his car, which was odd because she looked about twelve or thirteen. He turned to Shauna as she reached the bottom of the driveway. 'Please allow me to take my daughter into my house, then I'll do whatever you want.'

'I'm afraid—'

'Molly! Take Becky inside.'

The younger woman ran to him in her slippers.

'Mr Terrell,' said Will, 'we have a warrant to search your house. I'd like to ask you to—'

The young girl collapsed.

Without any warning she'd suddenly dropped to the ground, as if her muscles had lost all their strength. Then she began to shriek. The sound she made was incoherent, wordless. Her hands clasping each side of her head, she writhed on the gravel.

Surprise made Shauna hesitate. She'd had no idea the Terrells' other daughter had a learning disability.

'Damn you!' Terrell thundered, his face pale and eyes staring. 'How dare you come here and upset my family!'

'It's all right, Dad,' said his older daughter, raising her voice over her sister's cries. 'Come on, Becky. Come on, let's go in.'

Though she tugged at the girl's arms her efforts were futile. Her sister continued to move from side to side and kick her legs.

'Ma'am?' one of the uniforms asked.

'Yes,' Shauna replied. 'Go ahead.'

The four police officers walked briskly past the scene on the drive and stepped into the house, putting on their gloves and carrying evidence bags.

'Dominic Terrell,' said Shauna, 'I am arresting you on the suspicion of...'

As she gave the caution, she had misgivings.

Bryant had been pushing for a quick resolution to the investigation from the beginning. He seemed to care more about results than getting things right. And the handkerchief thing seemed wrong to her. It was too obvious. Too neat.

Molly Markson was standing behind her father, her mouth agape as Shauna cuffed him. Her sister continued to writhe and scream at her feet. Leading Terrell away, Shauna couldn't meet the young woman's gaze.

CHAPTER THIRTY-SEVEN

Her legs a little shaky after spending so long lying in bed, Ruth walked carefully down the stairs, gripping the bannister rail.

There was a commotion going on outside. Dom was back and Becky was having a meltdown from the sound of it, though she couldn't think what might have triggered it. Another elephant in her school bag? Dom was too hard on the other children at the school, but he was right that one of them might easily do such a thing to another pupil.

The front door stood ajar. Molly had gone out, presumably to help with Becky.

Ruth shivered in her nightie. She should probably put her dressing gown on and go out to see if she could help. She'd been utterly useless the last few days as she'd been coming to terms with her terrible mistakes. She could see that now. But she was feeling better. It wasn't too late to put things right.

Voices came from outside, faint over the sound of Betty's screaming.

It was probably the neighbours.

She turned to go upstairs to fetch her dressing gown, but a figure in black appeared at the front door, pushed it open and stepped inside.

She gasped and clutched the bannister.

The figure was quickly followed by another.

Police officers!

The first spotted her standing on the stairs. 'We're conducting a search, ma'am.'

———

Dom was under arrest. She could hardly believe it. She had to do something quickly, before things got out of hand.

It was well after five o'clock and the officers searching the house had finally left, taking her husband's mobile and all the laptops in the house with them. Ruth hadn't been allowed to leave while they were there, presumably to prevent her from removing evidence. But she hadn't wanted to at the time. It wouldn't have been fair to leave Molly alone to care for Becky while they were being 'raided by the police'.

How often had she heard patients refer to the experience in passing? Though they usually used a different word for the constabulary. Never had she ever imagined her family might be subjected to the same invasion of privacy and humiliation.

They had lived in the same house for over twenty-five years and were on first-name terms with the neighbours. She would have to explain to them what had happened. No doubt they would all be polite and sympathetic to her face, but her family would be the subject of gossip for weeks to come. And, for the foreseeable future, that's what they would be known for. Every new arrival to the street would be informed of their history.

Number 17 was searched by the police once, looking for evidence of a murder! And the husband was arrested. Can you believe it? Most exciting thing to happen around here in a long while. But you don't have anything to worry about. It's generally very quiet and friendly.

Wincing at the sting of the imagined gossip, Ruth looked out the living room window. All *was* quiet, as though the police cars and the constables with their latex gloves had never been here; as if Dom hadn't been taken away in handcuffs like a criminal.

Becky was finally settled in her room watching television. She'd taken ages to calm down. Molly was in the kitchen.

She went to speak to her older daughter.

'Molly, I'm sorry, I know this is completely the wrong time, but I have to go out.'

Molly put down the knife she'd been using to chop vegetables.

'What? Why?'

'I have to go into work.'

'Can't it wait until tomorrow? I'm making dinner. Why do you have to go now? We should talk about what's happened to Dad and figure out what we're going to do.'

'I agree,' Ruth replied, 'and we will. But I need to go in. I'll be as quick as I can and we can talk when I get back.' If she told her why she had to visit the office now, Molly would be angry at the very least. She might even try to stop her.

Before her daughter could voice more protests or ask more difficult questions, she left.

At the prison, most of the Mental Health Unit team had gone home for the day. Only Stella remained at work in the main area and the light was on in Anders' office. The glass window above Phillipa's office door was dark.

Relieved to see the admin team leader still at her desk, Ruth approached her.

'Dr Terrell! What are you doing here? Are you over the flu already?'

'I'm feeling better, thank you. Stella, you have a master key to all the desks, haven't you?'

'Yes.' She opened a drawer and began riffling inside it. 'Did you lose yours? Not surprising if you haven't been well. Are you sure you should be back so soon? Wouldn't it be better to wait until tomorrow and get a good night's rest?'

'Actually, I...'

There was no point in lying. Stella would see her go into Phillipa's room with the key.

'I need to check something in Dr Edwards' notes.'

Stella had found the key. Her eyebrows rose sceptically as she sat poised with it in her hand.

What Ruth was doing was out of the ordinary. She would never normally look at another professional's files, certainly not while they were out of the office.

'You need to...?'

Ruth held out her hand for the key. After Stella passed it over, she felt the administrator's gaze on her back as she walked to Phillipa's room.

She turned on the light and closed the door.

———

Three thick, A4 notebooks sat in a pile in the large drawer of Phillipa's desk. Ruth lifted them out and sat down.

She used similar books herself for jotting down notes during sessions with patients, notes that would inform formal reports detailing the subject's state of mind, any progress or regression in their mental state, and medications prescribed.

Why had Phillipa been reluctant for Ruth to read hers?

Having a colleague read your notes *did* feel intrusive. The jottings were made in the moment without expectation of later scrutiny. No matter how confident you were in your practice, no one enjoyed opening themselves up to judgement. She'd tried to make it clear to Phillipa she wasn't evaluating her work, that she only wanted to help find Thomas's killer, that a second set of eyes on what the suspects had said during their sessions might shed some light.

Nothing she'd said had made any difference. Phillipa had refused. Why?

The dates the books covered were written on their fronts. She put two of the books on the desk and opened the remaining one. Phillipa's handwriting covered the first page, long, slim, slanting words running from side to side.

She began leafing through, looking for the names Ableton, Drake and Scott.

She recalled from her previous look at the suspects' official files that Phillipa had begun treating Ableton a year ago, and Drake had seen her a year before that, but not since. Scott had been assigned to Phillipa when he arrived at Shelby four and a half years ago and had attended assessments regularly.

The date was written at the top of each page along with the inmate's name and other relevant details. She scanned the notes her friend had made. At first, she didn't see anything remarkable. The usual histories of traumatic childhoods, highly charged emotions, delusions and twisted thought processes. Then something caught her eye. She re-read the sentence, a simple comment made at the end of a session, as if an afterthought.

This particular inmate hadn't been seen by Phillipa for another three months. Ruth flipped the pages, moving forwards in time. When she read the text relating to the next session closely, alarm grew within her.

The inmate's answers to Phillipa's questions were innocuous enough on the surface. They were replies Ruth might expect to read anywhere in her friend's notebooks, and Phillipa's comments were similarly workaday, but certain things were beginning to add up. She read to the bottom of the page and went straight back to the top to read again. Then, she jumped ahead three months.

The notes from the next session, coupled with the fact of Thomas Edwards' murder, painted a picture far darker than anything she could have imagined.

It was too much.

She slammed the book closed and threw it on the desk as if it burned her fingers. She stared at it, afraid to believe the conclusion her mind had jumped to. Was she over-thinking it? Or could she possibly be right?

CHAPTER THIRTY-EIGHT

The apparent progression in the Edwards case warranted a small celebration, according to Will. He'd persuaded Shauna to go to the pub with the other police officers again and, though she harboured reservations, she'd agreed.

The atmosphere did seem more comfortable than last time, she had to admit. No one had given her more than a second glance or a quick greeting when she'd arrived. She saw Will at the bar, chatting to Beth. He hadn't noticed her. He was wearing the same cocky look he'd worn when he'd made his faux pas with her.

Some people never learned.

But he appeared to be having some success with Beth. Her face was a little flushed and she was smiling.

He spotted her.

When he waved her over, Beth took her drink and left.

'Don't let me spoil your fun,' said Shauna.

'What?' Will looked confused.

'Beth seems nice.'

'Yeah, she's great,' he replied. Then understanding dawned on his face. He gave an embarrassed chuckle. 'Am I that obvious?'

Shauna shrugged. 'You aren't doing anything to be ashamed of. There's no law against workplace relationships.'

'Yeah, but I don't want to get a reputation as a womaniser.'

She guessed it was probably too late for that, but she didn't mention it. Will's pint glass was nearly empty, so she offered to buy him another, and then they found an empty bench seat at a four-seater table. The opposite seats were occupied by a couple of constables Shauna didn't know very well. Both looked quite drunk, from the sloppy smiles they gave Will and Shauna as they sat down.

The constables ignored them after that, continuing a whispered conversation, their heads close together.

'Are they a couple?' Shauna asked Will quietly.

'They're married,' he replied, before taking a sip of his pint and then adding, equally quietly, 'but not to each other.' He laughed softly and went on, 'You must think the Cambridge office is a hive of sexual indiscretion.'

'No, I really don't. Romantic relationships are inevitable when people spend a lot of time together, especially when they're working a stressful job. Things weren't any different at the Met.'

'Well, the pressure will be off us soon,' said Will. 'We picked up plenty of stuff at the Terrells' house. Dominic Terrell's laptop might reveal something, or Forensics might find traces of the victim's blood on his clothes. Or his phone records could show he was in the Edwards' home when the murder took place.'

'He's too smart to have had his phone on him, and there aren't any laws against having an affair.' Shauna glanced at the couple on the other side of the table. 'The best the prosecution could make of that is it gives him a motive. Even if he can't prove his whereabouts that evening or when Phillipa Edwards arrived at the supermarket the following day, it won't be enough for the CPS to go ahead with a prosecution, no matter what Bryant says. We need something that clearly and firmly puts him at the crime scene.'

'Maybe he'll tell us something tomorrow,' said Will. 'A night in the cells might loosen him up a bit. A confession would be great.'

Terrell hadn't given them anything at his interview, sticking to his story that he'd gone out to get a takeaway the night of the murder and the morning after he'd been shopping after dropping his daughter at school. Connor had requested the CCTV footage from the relevant shop.

'He's too clued up to confess,' said Shauna.

She took a sip of wine, closed her eyes, and rested her head against the tall seat back.

'Ironic, isn't it?' said Will.

'What?'

'Ruth Terrell was so set on finding the murderer,' he went on, 'and it was her husband all along.'

She opened her eyes.

'Yeah,' she agreed, though without conviction.

'What do you think about Phillipa Edwards going missing?'

Another team had been sent to her house at the same time she and Will had attended the Edwards', but the psychologist hadn't been home and all efforts to trace her had been fruitless so far.

'It's a little early,' Shauna replied, 'but unless she turns up soon, when we catch her she's going to find it hard to argue she wasn't an accomplice.'

She wondered what the atmosphere in the Terrell household was like. Not good, that was certain. Molly Markson had enough problems without her father being arrested for murder. And that poor kid with a disability. She would be missing her dad. The unease she'd been feeling since Bryant had insisted on arresting Dominic Terrell rose up again. She felt deathly tired as well. 'I think I might go home.'

'Me too. It's been a long day.'

Shauna drained her glass.

'Where are you parked?' Will asked.

'Just a couple of streets away.'

'I'll walk you to your car.'

'No, it's fine. It isn't far, and the roads are well lit.'

'If you're sure…'

He was already scanning the pub. Shauna saw his gaze alight on Beth on her way to the loo.

'I'm sure,' she replied. 'Could you…?'

'Sorry.' He stood up and she slid out of the bench seat.

'See you tomorrow,' she said.

Outside, frost after rain had turned the streets into an ice rink. Shauna wished she'd thought to bring her soft-soled boots to change into, but her car was only a short distance away. As long as she trod carefully, she should stay upright.

Her tiredness was due to the breakthrough in the Edwards' case. It was always the same. When things seemed to be drawing to a close, her adrenaline levels would drop and weeks of poor sleep would catch up with her.

She turned the corner into the street where she'd parked. In contrast to the main road, here the streetlights were few and far between. Pools of darkness spread out between the soft circles of light.

Quick footsteps sounded from behind and someone barged into her. She was flung forwards. Her face smacked into the pavement, and air erupted from her lungs. The person was on top of her, pressing a knee into her back.

She couldn't breathe, and her face was a mass of agony. Was her nose broken? The icy surface was slick with her blood.

'Bitch!' a voice hissed in her ear. 'Think you're so smart, don't you? So did Thomas Edwards.'

A hand grabbed her hair and jerked her head backwards, straining the ligaments of her neck.

She could barely move. She writhed feebly.

A knife blade touched her throat, its edge cut into her skin.

With the remaining air in her lungs, despite the pressure on her chest, she managed a small squeak.

'Hey!' a voice shouted. 'What are you doing?'

The pressure on her suddenly disappeared. Running feet pounded the pavement. She lifted her head and caught a glimpse of a figure in a heavy coat speeding into the darkness. Then her assailant was gone.

CHAPTER THIRTY-NINE

'I'm fine,' said Shauna, the dressing on her nose muffling her voice. She hadn't dared to even glance in a mirror yet, but she guessed she must look a sight. Her face felt puffy and bruised, and though the doctor had said he didn't think her nose was actually broken, it would be a close thing, judging from the damage. She was waiting for the x-rays to arrive.

Will peered at her sympathetically. 'You don't *look* fine.'

'Thanks.'

'What do you want me to say? You can't expect to walk away from someone smashing your face into the pavement looking like a beauty queen. That must hurt. Have they given you painkillers?'

'Paracetamol.'

'The strong stuff. Better watch you don't get addicted.'

Will was trying to keep things light, but Shauna heard something else underlying his tone.

'This isn't your fault, you know,' she said. 'Whoever did this must have been stalking me. If they hadn't jumped me tonight, it would have been another time.'

He grimaced, looked down and shook his head. 'I should have walked you to your car. If I hadn't been chasing tail...'

'It's not your fault.' She shifted painfully as she reached for the cup of water the nurse had brought her.

'What's that?!' Will exclaimed, staring at her neck.

He'd seen the cut. It was too shallow for stitches and it had been cleaned up, but it was still visible.

'He had a knife,' she explained.

'He was going to slit your throat?! Jesus. I thought he'd only roughed you up a bit, to give you a warning. I didn't realise he was trying to kill you.'

'I don't know that he wanted me dead. All I know is—'

'Come on, Shauna!'

She didn't know what to say. She was trying not to think about it. In the end, all she found to comment was, 'Someone certainly feels strongly about the Edwards case.'

'And it isn't Dominic Terrell,' said Will. 'Unless he magicked himself out of custody. Was it definitely a man?'

She thought back. The force with which she was pushed to the ground, the weight on her chest, the voice in her ear... 'I'm pretty sure it was.'

'Because if it wasn't Dominic...'

'I know.' The implication was clear. If Dom Terrell *was* the killer, the only other person who might want to scare her would be Phillipa Edwards. If Shauna's attacker wasn't a woman, that meant the real murderer was still on the loose.

'Did the voice sound the same as the one on the threatening phone call?' asked Will.

'That was so distorted, it's impossible to say. It's a shame we didn't announce we'd taken Dominic Terrell into custody today. Then the real murderer would have left me alone and let Terrell take the blame. You'd think Bryant would have been shouting it from the rooftops.'

'You underestimate our DCI,' said Will. 'He was waiting for the *morning's* news, the one most people read. He's received a lot of flak from the press. He wanted to make a big splash.'

'Shit. That makes sense.'

Even worse than the pain of her injuries was the knowledge they were back to square one, and they'd arrested an innocent man. She knew she should have gone with her gut and stood up to Bryant.

'Where are you going after you're discharged?' asked Will.

'Home, of course. The doctor said to rest for at least 24 hours, so I won't be at work tomorrow.'

'Today, you mean. It's gone two.'

Two o' clock in the morning? She hadn't realised she'd been at the hospital so long. The ambulance had arrived quickly. Unfortunately, the person who'd called it had disappeared as soon as it was clear she was safe. It was a sad fact that the public often didn't want to get involved.

'You live alone, right?' Will asked.

'Is it that obvious?'

'I don't think it's safe for you to be by yourself right now. We know what the killer is capable of. He followed you from the pub, and he might know where you live. What's to stop him breaking in and trying to kill you?'

'I have to go home, Will. But don't worry. I have good locks.'

He looked sceptical. 'So did Thomas Edwards.'

'What can I do? I can't afford to live in a hotel until the investigation's over, and that might not be any safer anyway.'

'You *could* stay with me,' said Will, 'but I share with another bloke, and, you know, bachelors' flat and all that.'

She could imagine. 'I'm sure I'll be fine.'

'What about... Do you have a spare room?'

'You want to come and live with me?!'

'You don't need to pull that face. I'll have you know I *am* house trained.'

'I don't think that would be a very good idea.'

'Why not? It would be better than living on your own. Seeing another man around the place would definitely put the murderer off trying anything again.'

'Just...no. I'm sorry. I appreciate the thought. It's nothing personal. But, no.' Over the weeks they'd worked together she'd grown to like Will, despite his flaws, but she couldn't stand the idea of another police officer in her home. She would never feel she was off duty. Even another person in her private space was too much. She couldn't bear him to witness her darkest moments.

Yet a gaping hollow opened up inside her at the thought of returning alone to her cold, empty rental. She generally relished solitude, but now was not one of those times. She attempted a confident smile. Her entire face protested.

'Don't decide right now,' said Will. 'Promise me you'll think about it. If you're worried I'm going to be in your face all the time, don't be. I'll stay out of your way if you like, but it would make me feel a lot better knowing you aren't on your own.'

Tears pricked her eyes. 'I promise I'll think about it.'

CHAPTER FORTY

It was four am, and Shauna could finally leave. The x-ray showed her nose wasn't broken. A nurse had removed the wadding and applied a lighter dressing, and the doctor had sent her on her way with a prescription for more paracetamol. She loved the NHS, but it couldn't be accused of coddling patients.

'Come on,' said Will. 'Let's get you home.'

He'd waited with her the entire night. She'd tried to get him to go but he'd refused, insisting on staying until she was discharged.

'Will, really, there's no need. You've done more than enough. You've been here hours. You need to get some sleep before you have to go to work.'

Ignoring her, he said, 'I was just thinking, your car must still be parked near the pub.'

She sighed, defeated. 'Ugh, yeah. I'd forgotten. It doesn't matter. I'll pick it up later.'

'How about we both go to your car now, and I drive it to your place? If you feel up to it.'

'No, I can't impose on you anymore. Please, just go home.'

'You aren't imposing. If we get your car now, it would stop me from worrying about you dragging yourself out of bed today to collect it.'

'Then I'll get it tomorrow. It won't be going anywhere.'

'Yeah, but you probably left it somewhere with restricted parking. You'll get a fine.'

Shauna tried to remember, but casting her mind back to yesterday evening only conjured the sensation of an unbearable weight pressing her into an icy pavement, hot breath on her neck, and a sharp blade at her throat. She shivered. 'It's okay. I'll just pay it.'

'Oooh, bold words from Lady Moneybags.' Will grinned, but then his expression turned sombre. 'Seriously, I'd feel better if I could help you with something.'

Was he *still* blaming himself for not walking her to her car?

'You've already helped me far more than necessary,' she said. Realising he wasn't going to take no for an answer, she added resignedly, 'If you insist.'

'Great.' He pulled his phone from his coat pocket. 'At this time in the morning we'll get an Uber in a few minutes.'

Shauna put on her coat, noticing for the first time her pocket was torn. She guessed she must have had her hand in it when she was jumped. Her bag also bore the scars of her attack—it had been scraped down to raw leather on one side.

'Two minutes,' said Will, pocketing his phone. 'Must be a record. On the road out front. I said it wouldn't take long, didn't I?'

They walked to the pick-up point near the hospital's public car park. Though it was March and four fifteen AM, a warm breeze was blowing, carrying a green scent. Spring had finally arrived.

———

Will pulled up a few doors down from Shauna's tiny, terraced house, in one of the few available spaces.

'I'll come with you to your door,' he said, setting the hand-brake and turning off the engine. 'It'll only take a minute. I can walk home from here.'

She lacked the willpower to protest, even though it was a bit silly to walk her literally three houses. All the adrenaline in her system from being attacked had dissipated, and she was ready to collapse. Her nose throbbed badly, the painkillers she'd been given already wearing off. All she wanted to do was pop two more and go to bed. She expected she would sleep into the afternoon.

Will handed her the keys. After they got out, she locked her car and they walked to her house. Distant sounds of ever-present traffic filtered through the early morning quiet, but her street was peaceful. Her front door stood only a step from the pavement, across a space so narrow it didn't deserve the term front garden.

She slipped her house key into the old Yale lock and turned to Will. 'I'll be okay now, thanks.'

'Sure you don't want me to come in?'

'I'm sure. Thanks for everything. You've been great. I appreciate it.'

He frowned. 'I haven't done anything out of the ordinary. We look out for each other, right?'

'Yes,' she said. 'Yes, we do.' She didn't realise until the words were out of her mouth, but she really meant it. Something had changed. She no longer felt like an outsider.

'Okay, I'll head home,' Will said. 'I hope you get a good sleep. I'll give you a ring this afternoon, or maybe tomorrow.'

'All right, but if anything happens with the Edwards' case, or if you need me for anything, let me know.'

'I will. Good night.'

She turned the key and pushed at her door. As always, it stuck against the jamb. She gave it another push and it swung open. Before going inside, she turned to watch Will walking away. His hands were stuffed in his pockets and his head was down. She hoped he didn't have far to go. She hesitated for a second, tempted to call him back and invite him in for a cup of tea or coffee, to stay with her until she felt comfortable being left alone. But the moment passed.

Her dark, poky hall confronted her. She stepped inside and closed the door, shoving it until the lock clicked shut. The light switch was inconveniently far from the entrance, halfway between the front of the house and the living room. When she'd moved in, she'd concluded early twentieth century electricians hadn't had much of a clue, and later electricians hadn't bothered to rectify the mistake.

She slid her hand along the wall, feeling for the switch.

Thinking about the light reminded her of another one—the little flash on the CCTV footage of the supermarket car park when Phillipa Edwards' unknown companion had turned to leave. Something around the area of his head had caught the sunlight and reflected it. Something glass or metallic.

An image flashed into her mind: two large male hands twisting a rain-sodden hat, and between them on the hat's front, a metallic badge.

Baram Scott's hat.

The man accompanying Edwards the morning after the murder had been Baram Scott.

She heard a faint swoosh of wood moving over carpet and a tiny squeak. In her months in the house, she'd heard the same sounds every time she'd opened her living room door.

She froze.

A figure stepped into the hall, darker than the surrounding darkness.

Her lungs found sudden life, sucking in a great gasp.

Then Scott was on her.

A hand clamped over her mouth and another grabbed her waist, dragging her forwards. She fought, but she was like a doll in the strength of his grip. He jerked her towards the living room. Her feet went from under her and her knees hit the polished floorboards of her hall. Slipping and fighting, she was hauled the rest of the way into the room. He threw her onto the carpet.

His hand left her mouth, but as she opened it to shout, he forced a ball of material in, right to the back of her throat. Another strip of material went around her face, preventing her from spitting the ball out. She couldn't breathe. There was too much stuff in her mouth. It was cutting off her air supply. She heaved and writhed as her body instinctively struggled for oxygen. Dimly, she became aware he was binding her wrists and ankles.

By shaking her head vigorously and working the muscles of her mouth, she managed to ease the substance in her mouth forwards a little. Finally, she breathed through her nose.

She was lying face downwards and rough carpet fibres were pressing into her cheek. Pain emanated from her back, as if Scott had been pressing his knee into it, but she wasn't sure if that was from the original attack. For several seconds, every-thing had been a blur of terror.

It must have been Scott who had attacked her earlier.

She was so tightly bound she could only wriggle a little. Scott's footsteps sounded around her head as he seemed to search for something, but only soft scrapes and creaks reached her ears, as if he was trying to avoid disturbing her things too much.

'Forget it,' said a female voice. 'Let's go.'

Shock stilled Shauna's movements. Someone else was there too. She recognised the voice instantly. After all, who else could it be? Phillipa Edwards was here too. She must have conspired with Scott to murder her husband. The 'missing hours', the amnesia, she'd been faking all along.

'She must have stuff hidden in here,' Scott replied. 'Everyone does. Jewellery, cash. I still think we should take her purse.'

'No,' Edwards insisted. 'We agreed.' She added, her voice heavy with exasperation and irritation, 'We can't leave any DNA behind. It's risky enough coming here. If I hadn't been able to pick the lock—'

'But we're wearing gloves,' protested Scott.

'It's still possible to leave a trace,' said Edwards. 'It doesn't matter how careful you are. How would we explain that in court? And we don't have time for searching. It's nearly morning. If we don't leave soon, someone's bound to see us.'

Scott grunted, as if in frustration.

What were they planning? They didn't want to leave any sign they'd been in her house. They were going to abduct her, take her somewhere, but make it look like she'd disappeared. Should she try to disturb or break something to leave signs of a struggle? If she could just bang on a wall it would wake her neighbour. The walls in these terraces were like paper. But if she did that, Scott might just decide to kill her here and now.

There was a knock at the door.

Silence clamped down as Scott and Edwards froze.

Shauna struggled and tried to cry out, but she could barely breathe, let alone shout.

Something descended on her neck, crushing it. The sole of Scott's boot.

'Fuck,' he whispered.

'Just ignore it,' murmured Edwards. 'Whoever it is, they'll go away in a minute.'

Shauna whimpered.

No air was entering her lungs. Darkness was closing in.

All she could hear was Scott's ragged breathing.

A movement. Was Edwards moving over to him? The pressure on Shauna's neck suddenly increased. She thought her spine was about to break.

'This is your fault,' Scott quietly hissed. 'I should have cut her throat when she walked in. We'd be long gone by now.'

'No,' Edwards replied softly, barely audible, 'this way's better. They won't come after us immediately. We'll be out of the country before they put two and two together, if they ever do.'

A second knock at the door.

'*Fuck* this,' whispered Scott. 'I'm going to kill her now. Get away out the back. You can do what you like, but if you—'

The letterbox rattled. 'Shauna!'

Will.

'It's only me,' he went on. 'Just checking you're all right. I noticed...' His voice trailed off.

Silence.

A third knock.

Shauna clung onto consciousness like a rope flung to someone drowning. With the little strength she had left, she tried to yell, to warn him, to tell him to leave and call for back up.

The letterbox opened again. 'Shauna!'

He sounded panicked.

'Get him in before he wakes someone up,' Edwards ordered. 'Remember, we don't want any blood.'

No!

Shauna couldn't hold out any longer. She slid into oblivion.

CHAPTER FORTY-ONE

She'd been a fool, Ruth told herself as she buttoned her coat in the hallway. A self-centred, unseeing fool, professionally and in her personal life.

If it was the last thing she did, she would put right all her wrongdoings. At least she still had time and things were not irretrievable. She *hoped* they were not irretrievable. She would try again to tell the police what she'd discovered in Phillipa's notebooks. Last night, at the station, they'd said no one was available to speak to her, but this morning the detectives should be at work. Or, failing that, someone else could take her statement.

If only she'd realised her mistake in time to save Thomas Edwards' life. She couldn't bring him back, but she could make sure his killer was caught and brought to justice.

'Where are you going?' Molly asked, emerging from the kitchen.

'To the police station.'

'You're going to try to see Dad?'

'No, they won't let me. I'm going to talk to the officers in charge of the case.'

'Will they speak to you?'

'I don't know. I'm going to try.'

'I want to come with you.'

'No, there's no need.' Ruth attempted a smile, though she guessed it probably came across as a ghastly grimace.

Molly's gaze was unblinking and doubtful.

'This isn't like last time,' said Ruth. 'I know what I'm doing now. Finally.'

The crease between her daughter's eyebrows only deepened.

Ruth sighed. 'Molly, no one knows better than me how stupid I've been. But...' She sought the right words. How to explain what she'd discovered to a non-mental health professional? She gave up. 'You'll just have to trust me. Though, Lord knows, I haven't done much to earn it.'

'Oh, Mum, don't say that. It isn't true.'

'You're just being kind.' She checked her car keys were in her pocket, musing, 'That was part of the problem, I think. You're so sweet and kind and forgiving. If you'd acted out like most teenagers would have in the same circumstances—going off the rails, getting into drugs, self-harming—I might have taken notice. But you were always a quiet, good girl.' Her chin trembled before she mastered herself enough to continue, 'You were languishing from neglect right in front of my eyes, and I didn't see it.'

'We can talk about that another time,' said Molly quickly. 'But if you're going to speak to those detectives, I have to come with you.'

There was something she wasn't saying.

'Why?' Ruth asked. 'I'm more than capable of talking to them myself. You know that.'

Her daughter cast a glance upwards before explaining, 'When I was at the police station reporting Daniel's assault, the lead detective spoke to me about you. She warned me about how much trouble you could get into if you didn't stop what you were doing. I reassured her you wouldn't be involving yourself in the

case anymore. Now here you are interfering again. I feel like…'
She paused. 'I feel like, if I don't go with you, something bad
might happen. You might end up in the cells like Dad. For my
own peace of mind, I have to come too.'

'I see,' said Ruth. She exhaled heavily. 'If it will make you feel
better…'

———

After they dropped Becky off at school, the route to the police
station was unusually clear of traffic. After weeks of regular
sleety showers, the blanket of cloud that had been ever-present
was breaking up. A warm spring sun peeked through the gaps,
and clumps of wild snowdrops were flowering on the grass
verges.

She managed to find parking in a side street. After pumping
the meter with as much change as it would take, not knowing
how long she might be at the station, she set off to walk the
short distance with Molly.

'Mum,' her daughter said, 'are you absolutely *sure* about this
thing you have to tell the detectives? They aren't going to be
very receptive after what you did.'

'I'm certain. This is different from before. I'm not trying to
do their job for them. This is my professional opinion based on
evidence. I think they'll listen if I tell them that. I've been an
expert witness in Crown Court trials. If they don't listen and it
comes out later they ignored key information, it'll look bad on
them. The police care a lot about their public image.'

The police station doors registered their arrival with a jerk
before drawing apart, rumbling along their tracks. Ruth strode
through the doorway. The lobby was empty except for some
scruffy plastic chairs backed up against one wall and a uniformed
officer behind a glass screen.

Ruth approached the policewoman.

'Good morning,' she said briskly. 'I'd like to speak to Detectives Holt and Fiske, please.'

The officer glanced at Molly before replying, 'What is it in relation to?'

'I have information about a case they're working on at the moment. And I want to know if there's any news on my husband. He was arrested yesterday. His name's Dominic Terrell.'

'Right.' The officer picked up a phone. 'If you wouldn't mind taking a seat?'

'No, thank you,' Ruth replied, resting a hand on the counter. 'I'll wait here.'

'*Mum*,' whispered Molly.

The policewoman gave a small cough before jabbing the phone keypad with one finger.

After a sotto voce conversation, she said, 'I'm afraid the detectives aren't able to speak to you at the moment. If you give me your details—'

'Are they out interviewing suspects?' Ruth blurted, alarmed.

'I really can't say, but if you give me your contact details, I'll pass—'

'I have to speak to them now. I have to warn them. If they aren't here, someone needs to take my statement.'

What if they were alone with the murderer?

'That isn't going to be possible,' replied the policewoman firmly.

'It's okay, Mum,' Molly said. 'You can talk to them later. Give her your phone number.'

'No, this is urgent,' Ruth said.

'It's Dr Terrell, isn't it?' said the officer.

Molly gave a soft groan.

'It isn't going to be possible for you to speak to Detectives Holt or Fiske right now, and no one is available to take your statement. You can either leave a message or your contact details. Take your pick.'

It was clear the woman thought she was talking to a crackpot.

'I have information vital to solving Thomas Edwards' murder,' said Ruth forcefully. 'In my professional capacity as a forensic psychiatrist, I demand to be listened to.'

Molly tugged on her arm. 'Come on, Mum. The detectives aren't here. We can come back another time. I'm very sorry,' she added to the officer.

'No,' said Ruth. 'I know how it looks, but...'

The policewoman was watching her with pity. 'Go home with your daughter, Dr Terrell. Someone will be in touch about your husband.'

'I'm not leaving until I speak to someone.'

'Mum!' Molly exclaimed. 'You're in a bloody police station, for God's sake, not a department store. Come on. Let's *go*.'

Her daughter had turned crimson. Ruth took a deep breath and paused. The last thing she wanted to do was cause Molly more distress. 'You're right,' she said to her. 'I'm sorry.'

Turning to the officer, she went on, 'Please tell the detectives to call me as soon as they can. They have my phone number. I know how this looks, but I do have some important information for them.'

'All right, Dr Terrell. I'll pass the message on. You take care.'

The officer's phone rang. Lifting the receiver, she listened, and then held up a hand, indicating they should wait. The call over, she smiled and said, 'Your husband is being released, all charges dropped. He'll be out in a few minutes. You can wait over there.' She nodded at the chairs.

'Thank God,' said Molly.

Ruth didn't resist as her daughter pulled her over to the seats.

Perched tensely on the hard plastic, Ruth waited.

How could she look Dom in the face knowing she was indirectly responsible for his arrest? When she explained how stupid she'd been, he would forgive her. Of course he would. He was that kind of person, and he loved her. But would she ever forgive herself?

A soft touch on her arm dragged her from her contemplations.

'It's going to be all right, Mum,' said Molly.

The security door opened and Dom emerged. His clothes a mess of creases, his grey hair an unkempt halo, deep wrinkles etched into his face and dusky pouches under his eyes, he looked awful, but Ruth didn't think she'd ever been happier to see him.

'You two were quick,' he said as the three of them hugged tightly. 'They only told me I was being released ten minutes ago.'

'We were here for something else,' said Molly.

'Oh?'

'I'll tell you later,' said Ruth. 'Let's go home. You must be exhausted.'

However, as they were walking to the car, she gasped and stopped in her tracks.

'What is it now?' Molly asked irritably. 'Please don't tell me you're going back to the police station.'

'What an idiot I've been,' said Ruth, opening her handbag. 'I've been trying to speak to those two detectives face to face, when all along I had the woman's phone number!' She took out her purse and fished in it for the card Holt had given her when she'd come to the prison.

Molly rolled her eyes as she waited, her arm entwined with her father's.

Ruth tapped the number into her phone.

It rang four times, then she heard, 'Hello, you've come through to the voice mail of Detective Inspector Shauna Holt...'

'Hmpf,' said Ruth. 'She isn't answering.' After waiting for the beep, she left a short message, simply asking for a return call on an urgent matter. That was better than trying to condense what she had to tell them into a few sentences.

They went home, and Dom went straight to bed. When he surfaced in the early afternoon he looked much better. In the intervening hours, there had been no call back from the detective. Ruth had spent the time tidying up and making a pile of things to take down the dump. Molly left to collect Becky from school, and the daily routine continued in the Terrell household.

Still no response arrived from Detective Inspector Holt.

CHAPTER FORTY-TWO

Vibration and the hum of a car engine were the first things to edge into Shauna's awareness. The side of her face was pressed into soft plastic. A car seat? She was upright, propped up by her left shoulder. Wetness lay under her cheek. Her saliva? Or blood? Her jaw ached unbearably around the wad of sopping material in her mouth. She remembered the gag and experimentally tried to move her wrists and ankles. She was still tied up. Her muscles complained with cramps and spasms.

She opened her eyes.

No.

Will.

They'd got Will too.

He was unconscious, facing her, slumped halfway down the seat. A gag bit into his face and his arms were behind his back.

Behind him, beyond the car window, a scene flowed past. Flat, brown fields speckled with green shoots ran all the way to the horizon. A patch of rose in the clear sky signalled the coming dawn. She was facing east, which meant they were travelling south. There was no hard shoulder, so they weren't on the M11. Balsham Road? Babraham? She wasn't sure.

She recognised the interior of the car. It was hers! Scott or Edwards must have taken her keys out of her bag.

She slid her eyes sideways, not wanting to move and alert her captors to the fact she'd woken. Edwards was driving. Scott was looking out the side window.

Where were they taking her and Will?

She recalled snippets of their conversation in her house.

We can't leave any DNA behind, Edwards had said, and *This way's better. We'll be long gone before they put two and two together.*

She'd been trying to avoid drawing the obvious conclusion from Scott and Edwards' actions, but she couldn't avoid it any longer.

They—or, rather, Edwards—had a plan intended to confuse the police somehow. Were they taking them somewhere remote where their bodies wouldn't be found for ages? Her absence from work would be expected, and while Will's would be unusual, it still might take a day or two before anyone did any digging. The medical staff at the hospital would report he had stayed with her after the attack and they'd left together. She guessed Edwards was using her car to make it look like she'd driven away of her own volition. With her house empty, no signs of a struggle and her car gone, no one would suspect foul play until it was too late.

They were on their own. If they didn't get themselves out of the situation, they were going to die.

Will's eyelids fluttered and he gave a soft groan. Then his eyes snapped open. His body jerked, and he whipped his head around wildly.

Scott looked over his shoulder and laughed. 'Pretty boy just woke up. She's awake too. Kept quiet about it.'

Edwards spared them a dismissive glance before returning her attention to the road.

Will's gaze met Shauna's. He blinked twice before understanding seemed to calm him.

Then sudden fury twisted his features. He brought his knees up and drove his feet into the back of Edwards' seat. She was jolted forwards. The car swerved violently, throwing Shauna into the passenger door and cracking the back of her head against the window.

'Hey!' Scott yelled.

The car continued to swerve as Edwards fought to bring the vehicle back under her control, swearing loudly. Shauna slid across the back seat into Will, her body rigid as she anticipated a crash.

But Edwards began driving straight again.

Scott pulled out a knife and leaned over the back of his seat, saying to Will, 'Do that again and I will *cut* you.'

Will glared out his hatred at the man, but he didn't move. A tense silence passed before Scott turned to face forward. Addressing Edwards, he said, 'Stop the car. We do it now and dump them. Then get the fuck away.'

'No.'

'Stop the car!'

'We either do it my way or you're on your own,' said Edwards tersely. 'We had a plan before and you changed it, and look what happened. I had to make up all that nonsense about losing my memory. You messed things up once, I'm not going to let you do it again.'

Scott chuckled, his mood abruptly changing. 'Ha! I got you good though, didn't I? You should have seen the look on your face.'

'You're a bastard,' said Edwards. 'You know that? Making me watch my own husband being murdered.'

'Oh, don't give me that crap. If you gave a shit about him why did you get me to kill him?'

'Just because we had an arrangement, that doesn't mean I want to see the dirty work.'

'Why should you get away with not seeing it? It's like everyone these days, happy to buy meat from the supermarket but would never set foot in a slaughterhouse. You want someone dead, you should know what you're asking for.

Anyway...' he shrugged '...I thought you might like it. Turn you on.'

Edwards made a noise of disgust.

Scott slid a hand down her thigh. 'That's not how I remember it.'

She smacked it away.

'Fear makes people hot for it,' he remarked. 'After, I mean, when they know they're not gonna die.'

Shauna gave a shudder.

When Edwards didn't reply, Scott muttered, 'I was the one taking all the risks. If I'd got caught, who would have believed me if I'd said you put me up to it?'

'There's the real reason,' Edwards declared. 'You wanted me implicated too. You wanted me present at the crime scene, not away on a trip, in case the police figured out it was you. Then it would be easy to convince them I was involved. What you forgot is, I'm the one paying. *I* provide the money, *you* take the risk. That's how these things work. We aren't Bonnie and Clyde.'

'Who the fuck are they?'

'Never mind.'

Will's gaze was on Shauna's as they listened. Too late, they were finally understanding what had happened. Who could have guessed a forensic psychologist would be in cahoots with a convict, scheming to have her husband murdered?

'I still say this is too complicated,' Scott grumbled. 'We should keep things simple. If I'd only been able to slit her throat last night—'

'You would be facing another twenty years for murder. It's lucky you didn't manage it. I don't know what you were thinking.'

'It was too tempting. I couldn't resist. It was a nosy little bitch like her who got me put away last time. But anyway, I had to clobber the bloke when he came to the door, and they must have marks on them from the gags and ties. It'll be obvious they were murdered. Why go to all this trouble?'

'You're over-estimating the intelligence and determination of the police. Besides,' Edwards added with a note of amusement in her tone, 'this is fun. Don't you think they deserve some payback for all the trouble they've put me to? Hounding a grieving widow?'

As she spoke, she half-turned towards Scott. Her expression was like nothing Shauna had ever seen in her before. Her eyes were shining with exhilaration. She looked truly *alive*.

'Stop worrying,' she told Scott. 'We'll do things properly this time. My way. It's the next turning, isn't it?'

The car slowed and turned, sending Shauna sliding into Will. The tyres crunched on dirt or gravel, and the vehicle juddered as the road surface became bumpy. Then they hit a patch of exceptionally rough ground, bouncing her in her seat.

Her feelings about her impending death had cloaked her aches and pains, but this latest assault brought everything flaring up again. Her jaw felt like it was about to part company with her skull, the bindings around her wrists and ankles were instruments of torture and her back was so knotted, she didn't think she would ever stand straight again—assuming she got the opportunity.

An angry cry of pain burst from her throat. As well as raging against these evil lowlifes who were planning to murder her, she was furious with herself. She hated that she hadn't seen through Edwards, and that she was showing weakness.

Scott and Edwards laughed.

The car stopped. Edwards swivelled in her seat to fully face Shauna for the first time.

'Self-righteous bitch,' she spat. 'Thought you were so clever, didn't you? *I intend to catch your husband's murderer, Dr Edwards.* Instead, you and PC Plod ended up getting caught yourselves. What a pair of clowns.'

Will brought his feet up again and tried to kick Edwards in the face. She moved out of the way just in time.

Scott roared, 'That's it!' He lifted the knife to stab Will in the leg, but Edwards seized his wrist.

'Calm down. If they catch us before we leave the country, you don't want his blood on you. We're nearly finished. We only have one last step to go, then we're done.'

'All right, all right, keep your hair on.' He kissed her, hard.

This time, she didn't reject him.

He pulled away. 'Yeah, I'll make a nice little murderess of you yet.'

She gazed at him inscrutably. For all Shauna could tell she could have been planning to sleep with him or kill him. The mask had risen again.

They got out without another word, slamming the car doors heavily. The car rolled a little. Edwards had forgotten to set the handbrake. The locks clicked shut. Shauna struggled to look out the back window, craning her neck to see what Scott and Edwards were doing.

They were kissing again, clutched in an animalistic embrace, his hands roving her body, groping, squeezing.

The car was parked in a hollow with rough scrub growing up the sides. It wasn't possible to see what lay beyond the vegetation. Another car was parked a short distance away.

Edwards thrust Scott forcefully away and pointed at the car. Together, they moved to the rear of the vehicle and placed their hands on the boot. They began to push.

Shauna swung around to look out the front.

Before them stretched a wide lake.

It had been no mistake that Edwards hadn't set the handbrake.

Shauna began to shake.

No! Not like this. Anything but this.

From somewhere distant, she heard muffled screaming.

The person screaming was herself.

CHAPTER FORTY-THREE

Ruth sipped coffee, indecision plaguing her. She checked her phone in case she'd missed a message from DI Holt, but there was nothing. How many times had she looked at it in the last hour? She'd lost count.

Should she try calling her again? The woman clearly wasn't taking her seriously. It was only to be expected. She'd muddied her reputation with the police through her own stupidity. But that didn't make what she had to tell her now any less important.

'Everything all right, dear?' asked Dom. He was helping Becky play a game on her tablet.

'Yes. I was just thinking about the murder case.'

'It's best to put all that behind us.'

Molly glanced up from a magazine, giving her a dark look.

That was the problem. If she insisted on returning to the police station and forcing the detectives to listen to her, Molly would be angry, and she might spill the beans to Dom about her prior interference. Her husband was an angel, but even he had his limit. If he discovered the idiotic things she'd done, he might reach it.

On the other hand, she had a public duty to give the police

the information. More than that, she felt responsible for what had happened. She of all people should have spotted the signs.

'Mum, let's do something,' said Molly, closing her magazine. 'We have a couple of hours to kill before dinner. You don't mind if we pop out for a while, do you Dad?'

'Not at all. I think that's a lovely idea. You two have hardly spent any time together since Molly got back.'

'Okay, Ruth replied hesitantly.

What was Molly up to? Was she helping her return to the police station without Dom knowing?

'Good,' he said. 'Have some mum and daughter time and take as long as you like. I'll hold the fort while you're gone.'

'You're always holding the fort,' said Ruth.

'That's my job. Chief Fort Holder.'

'I just need five minutes to do something,' Ruth said, 'then we'll go.'

Molly's disapproving gaze followed her out of the living room.

———

She'd been right to send an email before they left. As soon as Molly closed the front door she said, 'Don't get the wrong idea. I only want to go for a walk with you, nothing else. I know what's on your mind and I don't want you getting into trouble again.'

'Oh, very well. I suppose you're right. I've left Detective Holt a message and I sent her an email just now too. I think I've done as much as I can. It's time I concentrated on other responsibilities I've been neglecting, like you.'

'I'm a grown-up, Mum. You shouldn't feel responsible for me.'

'But I do, and I should have been more—'

'You don't need to say it.' Molly smiled. 'Dad's back home, Becky's fine and I'll be rid of Daniel soon. Let's have a nice walk and talk about happy things.'

She put her arm through Ruth's and they set off.

'You haven't told me anything about your time in Scotland,' said Ruth.

'Ugh, I'm not sure I want to talk about what it was like living with Daniel yet. Too many bad memories. But Scotland itself was lovely.'

'Then tell me about that.'

Molly began to describe the village in the Highlands where she'd lived: the little cottages, the gruff farmers and the old, retired farm labourers; the rain and the heather; deer stepping out of the dawn mist.

Ruth clasped her daughter's arm tighter as she listened.

Their route took them past an area of parkland bordering a narrow stream. The brook gushed over a stony bed, swollen with spring rain, and the line of trees and shrubs bordering the road were edged with green.

The beauty of the scene struck her as if she were seeing it for the first time. She felt as though, for years, she'd been seeing everything through a grey gauze, and now it had been lifted.

She sensed a good future ahead. Come the summer, the sad events of the bleak winter would be behind them. Molly would be free of her nasty husband and beginning a new, happier life, and the murder would have retreated in their minds to a story to be retold at dinner parties.

Molly's stories had lapsed to silence.

'Scotland sounds beautiful,' Ruth said, 'but I'm so glad you're home again.'

'Me too.'

'Do you remember going to the Botanic Garden when you were little?'

'Yes, I do. I loved it.'

'So did I. We used to have so much fun. We should go there again, soon.' Ruth sighed. 'Where did the time go? Never mind. Now you're home again, we can make up for all the lost opportunities.'

'I'd like that,' said Molly. 'Mum, I can't see how I'll be able to afford to move out for a while. You can't rent a place around here on entry level wages.'

'Don't worry about it,' said Ruth, squeezing her daughter's arm. 'You'll always have—'

She was yanked from her feet. Someone had grabbed her from behind, pulling her arm out of Molly's. The person was dragging her into the trees bordering the road.

Overcoming her shock, she struggled and opened her mouth to shout or scream.

The sharp edge of a knife pressed into her throat.

'One word, and I'll kill her,' said a man's voice. He was talking to Molly.

She remained on the pavement, her body rigid, her face chalk white and her hands at her mouth.

'Get in here,' barked the man.

At the same time, he continued to haul Ruth backwards, his arm an iron band around her chest. Her heels cut channels in the leaf mould as she was dragged, too scared to resist.

'Please,' Molly begged. 'Don't hurt her. Don't hurt my mum.' She looked from side to side, up and down the road.

'In here!' the man commanded.

Her expression etched with fear, she stepped under the overhanging branches.

When the man reached a patch of dry, bare soil, he stopped. They were in heavy shade. The road was only a few metres away and open parkland stood in the other direction, yet it was unlikely anyone would see them unless they looked closely.

Ruth prayed for a dog walker to happen by and raise the alarm, but all she could hear was the road and Molly's soft whimpers.

The man was panting. Her back pressing into him, she moved with his breaths. He had to be Thomas Edwards' murderer. Somehow, he'd found out what she'd told the police.

But how was that possible? She'd only sent the email a few minutes ago.

'Let her go,' Molly sobbed. 'Please! I'll do anything. I'll come back to you. I promise I will. Just, please, please don't hurt her.'

I'll come back to you?

It wasn't the murderer after all. The man was Molly's husband!

'Too late,' Daniel hissed. 'Much too late. You made sure of that, didn't you, Molly? Setting the police on me even though all I did was grab your wrist. You burned your bridges. Our marriage is over. But the police won't catch me for this. They'll never catch me.'

'Is that what this is about?' Molly asked. 'I'll withdraw the charges if that's what you want. And I won't mention any of this to anyone. That's right, isn't it, Mum? We won't say a word. I understand you're upset and hurt, but this is insane. You're making a huge mistake. Please.' Molly dropped to her knees. 'Please let her go. I'll come back to Scotland with you if that's what you want.'

'No, you're lying. You don't mean any of it. You never did. It's all been lies. You never loved me.'

He was shaking violently. Ruth's body shook with his. She wanted to say something to calm him down, but fear was freezing her mind as well as her tongue. The knife blade had already sliced into her skin, and blood was dribbling down her neck.

All she'd wanted to do with the rest of her life might never happen. Dom would be a widower, Molly and Becky would be motherless. She would never have the chance to make up for her mistakes.

'I *did*,' Molly protested. 'I did love you. I mean, I do love you. I love you, Daniel. P-please put the knife down so we can talk. You wanted us to talk, didn't you?'

'Huh, you can't even lie convincingly to save your own mother's life. You were always useless. I don't know what I ever saw in you. What's the saying? Swear on your mother's life. Do you swear on your mother's life, Molly? Do you swear?'

'I do. I do swear. God, please.'

Cars passed on the road, their drivers oblivious to the drama taking place under the trees. Ruth could see the headlines in tomorrow's papers: Woman slain in broad daylight. Would Detective Holt be assigned to her case too?

She managed to squeeze out a whisper: 'Molly, run. Call the police.'

The knife bit deeper.

She squealed in pain.

'Shut up,' Daniel breathed in her ear. 'If you make another sound, it's over. Here and now.'

Where was everyone? If only someone would walk past and happen to look into the trees in just the right place. That would be all it would take. The police would be here in minutes.

Molly raised a hand, entreating him. 'Let her go. Take me.'

'It hurts, doesn't it?' said Daniel. 'It hurts to see your mother like this. But what about *me*? You saw I was in pain but you didn't give a shit! And you caused it. You hurt me, and you didn't care, you bitch.'

Molly hugged herself and rocked. 'I do care. I care...'

'Like I said, it's too late.'

His tremors had begun to ease, and he sounded calmer. His grip was slackening.

'We can't go back now,' he went on. 'We'll never get back what we had. Like you said, we're done.'

Closing her eyes, Ruth hoped his crisis was coming to an end. He'd wanted to scare her daughter and have the final say. Now he'd made his point, he would probably let them go.

'But you have to be punished,' said Daniel. 'You do understand that, right? I have to teach you a lesson so you don't do this to some other poor sap.'

'All right,' said Molly. 'I understand. I've learned my lesson. I really have. Put the knife down, Daniel.'

'No, that isn't what I meant. Frightening you isn't your punishment. I have to hurt you like you hurt me. You have to suffer.'

She looked up at him, her eyes wide. 'I-I don't understand.'

'It's simple,' Daniel replied maliciously.

What did he mean?

A possible answer crept into Ruth's mind, filling her with dread.

He shifted position, adjusting his hold on her.

'You'll never forget this moment,' he said. 'For the rest of your life, this will be the first thing you think of when you wake up in the morning, and the last thing on your mind before you sleep.'

His grip around Ruth's chest tightened unbearably. She couldn't breathe. She jerked and writhed, trying to break free, but he was too strong.

'Goodbye, Molly. Sweet dreams.'

The blade plunged into her neck.

Agony seized her.

Molly shrieked.

Dimly, she felt the knife jolt out again. The arm that had held her for so long abruptly released its hold. The ground rushed up at her. As her face hit the dirt, her hands were already clasping the cut on her neck. Hot liquid gushed between her fingers.

There was the sound of another body falling.

Daniel faced her, mouth agape and eyes staring. He had sliced his own throat. She watched his life spurting away before darkness descended.

CHAPTER FORTY-FOUR

Shauna's car hit the water nose-downwards but quickly righted itself, bobbing on the surface before slowly beginning to sink. She stopped screaming, absolute dread silencing her. If she could have chosen the worst possible way to die, it would have been this, the death that had haunted her for years. When she'd managed to block the horrifying scene from her waking imagination, it had returned—continued to return—as a recurring nightmare, the herald of what she'd come to call one of her 'bad days'.

Water was already pouring in, soaking her feet. Soon, it would rise to the roof and the car would sink to the bottom of the lake. She guessed Edwards and Scott had chosen this place because the water was deep. It would cover the car, and her and Will's bodies wouldn't be found for a long time, if ever.

She became aware of a thumping sound, dragging her from her frozen shock and terror.

It was Will. He was kicking his door and window, his body buffeting hers as he tried to escape.

But that wouldn't work. Their murderers had locked the car before pushing it into the lake. Only something hard and sharp would shatter the glass.

Her chest heaved as she panted, blood rushing in her ears,

clammy sweat coating her skin. She had to stop panicking. She had to control her fear. If she could think straight, there might be a way they could survive.

The water was up to her knees.

She twisted around to look out the back window. No one stood among the trees and grass at the edge of the lake. Edwards and Scott hadn't hung around to watch them die.

She shouldered Will, yelling at him to stop. Her gag had narrowed, wet with her saliva, and though it still muffled and distorted her words, he understood. His eyes were frantic with fear as he looked at her for an explanation.

Turning to face him, she lifted her feet onto the seat and then pushed against his thigh until her back was pressed against the door. Though her wrists remained tied, she managed to reach into the door pocket.

After her first husband had driven into a river with their children strapped into the back seat, her world had imploded. Their deaths had been something she'd thought she would never recover from, and in fact she never had. She hadn't wanted to. It felt wrong to move on from something like that, as if it were an insult to their memories and all they'd ever meant to her.

Another effect of the dreadful event was that, for years, she couldn't get in a car without being reminded of what had happened. Each time she'd driven anywhere, she'd had to take a minute to calm herself and push away the memories. One thing that had helped had been equipping her vehicle with multiple safety devices to use in case of a crash. Not that she'd ever thought for a moment she would ever be in the same position as her poor kids.

Her fingers brushed a plastic and metal surface.

She'd found it!

Gripping the seat belt cutter tightly, she quickly swivelled to let Will see what she had.

'Turn around,' she said, though it sounded more like *Ur a'ou*.

The water was already rising over her thighs, brown and icy, but after facing her window again and moving closer to him, she managed to locate the bonds around his wrists. Scott had used zip ties, no doubt specially bought for the purpose. She pushed the cutter between Will's hands, fearing she would cut him too, but she guessed he would forgive her in the circumstances.

Working by touch alone, it was hard to figure out if she had caught the zip tie on the cutter. She could feel resistance, and as Will wasn't yelling in pain, she inferred it wasn't him she was slicing. Straining with effort, she pushed upwards, trying to ignore the water closing over her hands.

The resistance broke.

Will's hands moved apart!

At the same time, the cutter slipped from her grasp.

There was a flurry of movement as Will spun around and pulled down his gag.

He was saying something. He touched her hands and must have realised they were empty.

'Fuck! Where's it gone?!'

She heard splashing behind her as he searched for the cutter.

The water was up to her chest. She was lifting off her seat, becoming buoyant.

'The window!' she yelled. *Er 'in oh!*

But he didn't understand. He'd begun bashing it again.

She swung to and fro, trying to find the cutter. Her hands only met cold, liquid emptiness.

'Hammer, Will. There's a hammer.' That was what she'd tried to say, but all that came out was garbled nonsense.

The deeper the car sank, the faster the water rose, greater pressure forcing it in and the air out. As the level reached her shoulders, her earlier, brief hope they might survive started to fade.

Will had given up trying to break the window and was searching for the cutter again. Why did he think freeing her hands would help if they couldn't get out? Maybe he was just panicking.

Water rose up her neck.

'Hammer!' she screamed. 'There's a hammer in your door!'

Only maybe there wasn't now. Maybe it had washed out of the pocket and it was floating somewhere under the opaque surface.

CHAPTER FORTY-FIVE

'Mum,' said a voice.

Molly.

'Mum, can you hear me?'

Fingers touched Ruth's cheek, and she opened her eyes.

She was alive!

Thank God, she was alive.

Molly's face hung over her, concern written in every feature. 'Mum, the doctor said you mustn't try to speak, okay? The knife...' her eyes filled with tears and she swallowed before continuing '...your voice box has been damaged. It has to heal. You mustn't speak, or you could make it worse.'

Ruth nodded.

Her daughter's expression relaxed.

Relief that she was still in the world, that Molly's husband hadn't killed her, suffused her body and mind. She'd thought she'd lived the final scene of her life, and it was far more grisly and tragic than she'd ever imagined. No last goodbyes, no telling her family how much she loved them or apologising for the things she'd done wrong. Her chance to make amends snatched from her; an ending come too soon.

She lifted her hand from the hospital bed, anxious to communicate.

'Do you want a pen and some paper?' Molly asked.

Ruth nodded again, and then pushed herself to a more upright position as she waited. Jagged pain dug into her neck, and she felt stiff bandages swathing her throat. Grimacing, she thought of the scar she would carry for the rest of her life.

But, *she was alive.*

Molly handed her a biro and opened a notebook before placing it under her hand.

Daniel? Ruth wrote.

Her daughter bit her lip and looked down. 'He died before the ambulance arrived,' she said softly. 'The crew focused on you because you still had a pulse.'

By the time Molly reached the end of her reply, tears were dripping from her eyes and her voice had grown high and breathy.

Ruth took her hand and squeezed it.

Molly grabbed a tissue from the box next to the bed and pressed it into her eyes before blowing her nose. 'I don't know why I'm crying about him. Not after everything he did to me.'

There was so much Ruth could say to her, so much professional advice to give. How many sessions had she spent with prisoners who had received news of the death of a loved one? Too many to count. Each patient's reaction to grief was different, yet the help she offered was often the same.

But, for her daughter, she thought of a better response.

She picked up the pen again.

I love you.

Molly read, and then she sobbed.

When she regained some control, she said, 'I love you too, Mum.'

Everything's going to be all right.

'I know. I just...I'm so sorry for what Daniel did to you. If I'd known he could hurt you or Dad, I never would have come home, knowing he might follow me. He could have killed you. If he'd succeeded, I don't know how I would have lived with myself.'

Don't blame yourself. You couldn't have guessed this would happen.

'He said, once, that I didn't know what he was capable of. He was right. I'd come to understand he was narcissistic and jealous and abusive, but I had no idea he was capable of murder.'

He's gone now. You don't need to worry about him anymore.

Molly sighed. 'The police are going to tell his parents. I'm so glad. I don't think I could do it myself.'

Where are your dad and Becky?

'Oh, sorry. I forgot to say. Becky's at the neighbour's. They said they would be happy to take her for a few hours and she seemed okay about it. And Dad's gone to get some tea. We've both been here waiting for you to wake up. He should be back soon.'

Ruth put down her pen and rested her head on her pillow, closing her eyes. She must have been given painkillers, but her neck still hurt. And she felt exhausted. It was the shock, no doubt.

A new concern popped into her mind, and she took up the pen again.

Where's my phone?

'If you put it in your bag, it's here. I brought your bag with me in the ambulance.' Molly lifted the handbag onto her lap and looked inside. 'Here it is.'

Ruth checked it, but there were no messages or missed calls.

'Don't tell me you're thinking about work at a time like this.'

I was wondering if the detectives had got back to me.

'Mum!'

I couldn't say anything this morning because your dad was there, but I uncovered some information relating to the case. I think I know who the murderers are.

'This is ridiculous! You're obsessed.'

Ruth had continued writing. *I read Phillipa's case notes – the notes she takes during sessions to write her reports from. But the notes on one of the inmates were very different from the reports she wrote.*

Molly read and frowned.

At last, her daughter seemed to be taking the matter seriously. Ruth was relieved. She was personally in no condition to go chasing up the detectives and persuading them to act on her information. Perhaps Molly would do it instead.

'How were they different?'

I won't go into the details, but it was clear she thought this prisoner had psychopathic traits.

'That isn't so strange, is it? There must be a lot of psychopaths in the prison system.'

There are. So it makes no sense that she covered up the fact.

'I suppose not. Why do you think she did it?'

Before Ruth could write an answer, Molly's mouth fell open. 'Do you think they were having an affair?'

They would never get away with a physical affair, but an emotional one, maybe.

'And you think, when this man was released, he killed Phillipa's husband out of jealousy?'

Not exactly. I don't think it was jealousy as such. I think Phillipa put him up to it.

Molly gasped, and her eyes as she lifted them to meet Ruth's were wide. 'You think the two of them planned it? That's what you've been trying to tell the detectives for the last two days? No wonder you were agitated. But...' she bit her lip '...it's a bit far-fetched, isn't it? How can you be sure? Phillipa couldn't have mentioned *that* in her notes.'

You're right. She didn't. But I think she may be psychopathic too. Tears started into Ruth's eyes, and she had to squeeze them shut and take a couple of deep breaths to get her emotions under control. When she'd achieved a measure of calm, she wrote on.

I've been so blind. Not only about you, my dear, as you were growing up, but at work too. Phillipa had me twisted around her finger. I thought she was lovely, which was exactly what she wanted. Her colleagues didn't like her. To them, she was mean and rude, but she manipulated me into being her friend. She probably lied about enjoying similar pastimes and so on. It was classic psychopathic behaviour, and I missed it. Just as I missed how much pain you were in.

'I don't understand. How could a psychopath become a psychologist?'

They probably exist in most professions, dear. Do you see now why it's so important the detectives receive this information?

'I suppose so. But you already sent it to them, right? I don't see what else we can do.'

They might not have taken any notice due to my past involvement. I've created a bad impression so they might not trust anything else I say. But if you talk to them, maybe they'll listen to you.

Molly's shoulders slumped. 'You just nearly died, Mum, and I had to watch Daniel stab you and then kill himself. I don't think I'm up to it.'

I know it will be hard. But there's a murderer and his accomplice running around loose. Can you please try? I feel responsible for Thomas Edwards' death. I want to try to see justice done on his behalf.

'I understand. All right. I'll call them from my phone. Maybe they'll pick up if they don't recognise the number.'

Ruth explained the female detective's number was the last one contacted on her mobile.

Molly stepped away from the bed and made the call but after a moment she said, 'It's gone to voicemail. I'll leave a message.'

As she was speaking, Dom returned bearing two plastic cups, tea bag strings hanging over their edges.

'You're awake, love! Wonderful. Has Molly explained you mustn't speak?'

When Ruth nodded, he grabbed her hand and held it, continuing, 'What a terrible fright you've had. Thank God you're okay. How are you feeling?'

Ruth gave a small nod and smiled. Just seeing her husband made her feel better. She picked up the pen to tell him.

He read her note. 'I feel the same, darling. I always have.'

Molly rejoined them at the bed.

'Who were you phoning?' Dom asked.

'The detectives handling the murder case. Mum had some information for them.'

'Oh! I bet you didn't get through.'

'No, I didn't. How do you know?'

'There was a news report on the television in the waiting room. They're missing.'

CHAPTER FORTY-SIX

Primal fear clamped down on Shauna, freezing her heart.

Was this how it had been for Liam, Charlotte and Naomi?

Perhaps.

But she would not die like this. She would not follow her children.

Not yet.

She would not give into the darkness that had swallowed their lives and threatened to swallow her for so many years. She would not let *him* win.

Frigid wetness slapped against her chin and her head bumped the ceiling. She would have to try to find the hammer herself. She tried to climb over Will, but he shoved her back. They struggled. What was he doing? Why was he fighting her? Did he think she was panicking?

He turned her around and there was movement at her hands, a tugging at the tie securing her wrists. He'd found the cutter!

She was free.

He took a breath and dipped below the water. She felt his fingers searching for her ankles, and in another second they were unbound too.

Meanwhile, she'd ripped the gag down, yanking it over her

lower lip. Her head was tilted back, forehead pressed up to the ceiling, yet water spilled into her mouth, muddy and cold. She spat out the material in her mouth, choked and coughed.

Will resurfaced.

'There's a window hammer in your door,' she gasped.

His face was half-submerged, but his eyes registered understanding.

He disappeared under the surface again.

Only an inch of space remained between the water and the ceiling. She pushed her nose and mouth into the gap, breathing in a last lungful of air.

A dull *thunk* echoed in her ears.

He'd found the hammer and hit the window. Had it broken? She hadn't heard the glass shattering but then maybe she wouldn't under water.

A hand grabbed her arm. He was pulling her. It must have worked! He was telling her they could get out.

She clamped her lips shut and sank down. Her eyes were open but she could see nothing except murkiness.

Will's shoes flashed into view. He was pulling himself out of the window.

She had to do the same.

Blindly, she groped for the exit. Her hands met hard, sodden surfaces, a metal edge and rough shards, and then nothing.

This was it.

Clutching the bumpy edges, heedless of broken glass, she heaved herself through. Her lungs were already protesting the lack of air. By chance, her foot hit the outside of the door. She kicked at it, launching upwards. Her head broke the surface.

She was looking at the centre of the lake.

She twisted around, her waterlogged clothes threatening to drag her under. She trod water, propelling her arms and legs backwards and forwards to stay afloat, and tore off her coat and shoes.

Where was Will?

The car had floated metres from the shore.

Her foot bumped something.

She dove down and groped in the murk. Her hands met wet textile. Will was moving, still alive, probably disoriented, trying to figure out which way was up. Holding onto him, she dragged him upwards with all her might.

His head burst from the water and he gave a great whoop as he sucked in air.

'Take off your coat,' Shauna shouted, pulling on the collar.

The coat came free and, together, they swam in the direction of the shore.

It had been a close thing, but they'd survived. Now all they had to do was get out, flag down a passing motorist and call Cambridge Central.

Baram Scott and Phillipa Edwards stepped from between the trees.

They *had* stuck around to make sure she and Will had drowned after all.

Scott was holding his knife.

'Swim out to the middle,' he said. 'Set foot on this bank and I'll kill you.'

'Not happening,' said Shauna, gasping. 'You'll never kill us both. Give yourself up. It's over.'

She sounded more confident than she felt. She didn't fancy her and Will's chances of tackling an armed man while soaking wet and exhausted, in the water or out of it.

'It isn't over until you two are dead,' Scott retorted. 'Swim out and die easy or I'll slit both your throats.'

Edwards leaned closer to him and whispered something. He shook his head and pushed her away, making her stumble in the long grass.

Taking advantage of Scott's momentary distraction, Will asked softly, 'What's the plan?'

As if she had one.

She replied, 'Overpower Scott and get the knife off him.'

It was either that or succumb to the chilly water and 'die easy'. Her arms and legs were already aching with the effort of staying afloat, and her teeth chattered with cold.

If they were going to play a waiting game, it was clear who would win. The murderers had picked the area because it was deserted. No one would see what was happening and call 999. She and Will were on their own.

Edwards had got to her feet. She clenched her fists and screamed, 'Have it your way then, moron!'

She stomped out of sight.

Scott ran after her.

'Swim in, Will!' Shauna hissed. 'This is our chance.'

She hastily front-crawled to the shore and climbed onto the bank, slipping and sliding in the mud and slimy green vegetation. Water ran from her clothes. Will made it out a few metres away.

She squatted down. Where had Scott and Edwards gone? A narrow slice of their car was visible between the bushes.

'We've had it!' a voice yelled. It was Edwards. 'Don't you get it?'

'And whose fault's that?' Scott asked angrily. 'I told you—'

'We don't have time for this! Get in.'

'I'm not leaving until—'

'Fine! Have it your way.'

A car door opened.

'Oy, get out of my car! You're not going *anywhere* without —*Ooof!*'

There was a thump of something hitting the ground.

Shauna sprang up and ran into the hollow where the car was parked. Edwards was in the driver's seat and two figures struggled on the ground.

Will and Scott.

Will had jumped him while he was distracted by his argument with Edwards. Will was on top and holding onto the wrist of Scott's knife-bearing hand.

The car door slammed shut and the engine started. Edwards

was going to get away, but if Shauna didn't do something to help Will he could be killed.

She cast around and instantly saw what she needed. At the same time, the car pulled forwards and then hard right, peeling out onto the road.

Scott kicked Will off him, sending the young DS sprawling. Shauna raced over.

Will was on his back. As Scott lifted the knife, Shauna hoisted the rock and smashed it onto his head. The rock hit the ground and Scott dropped onto Will, blood oozing into his hair.

Shauna stood still, panting, her hands loose at her sides.

Will was staring up at her, white-faced and frozen under the unconscious man. 'Is he dead? Did you kill him?'

'I don't know.' She kicked the fallen knife out of Scott's reach, just in case. 'Let's get him off you.'

With effort, she rolled the heavy man onto his back.

'If you get into trouble,' Will said, sitting up, 'I'll say it was him or us. You didn't have a choice.'

'Will, it *was* him or us, and I *didn't* have a choice. And when I said we have to overpower him, I meant we should do it together. Anyway...' she bent closer to Scott '...he's still breathing.'

She began to search him.

'Shouldn't you leave him alone?' asked Will.

'I'm looking for a mobile. Unless you know of a telephone box around here.'

Being sarcastic helped with the shock of what she'd done, but her hands were shaking as she rifled through Scott's pockets.

CHAPTER FORTY-SEVEN

Shauna had barely had time to shower and change before she received the call from Bryant. Baram Scott wanted to talk, but he would only speak to her and Will. It was late in the day and she wanted to do nothing more than open a bottle of wine and try to forget what had happened. But Scott's full recovery wasn't guaranteed. They might not get another opportunity to hear what he had to say and possibly use the information to catch Edwards.

A uniform was standing guard outside Scott's room at Addenbrooke's. The officer nodded politely at Shauna but didn't speak. She was in no mood for chit-chat either. She'd been blocking her ordeal from her mind ever since the police cars and ambulances had arrived at that lonely spot by the lake.

Will arrived a few minutes later with the recording equipment. He appeared surprisingly unscathed by his brush with death. She was sure the same couldn't be said for herself.

No, something *had* changed in the young detective sergeant. He looked a tad older and the jauntiness had gone from his step.

'How are you?' she asked as he reached her.

'All right. You?'

'I'll live. So Bryant's given our suspect a guard. Wonders will never cease.'

The uniform stared ahead.

'Are you okay with doing this?' Shauna asked Will.

'Yeah. It might be the only time the bastard talks.'

She pushed the door open.

Scott lay half-reclined in bed, bandages swathing his head. Blood had seeped through the dressings and leaked across the skin of his face, pooling around his eyes. She comforted herself that while she might not look great, her would-be murderer looked like absolute shit. A nasal cannula was supplementing his airflow. Handcuffs secured his wrists to the bed rails.

His lips curved into a sneering smile. 'Nice to see you, detectives.'

Shauna carried two plastic chairs to Scott's bedside and Will plugged the recorder into a power outlet.

'What's that?' Scott asked.

'It's for recording the interview,' Shauna replied.

'No, I don't want to be recorded. If you turn that thing on I'm not saying anything.'

'Mr Scott,' she said tersely, 'you consented to a formal interview and waived your right to legal representation.'

'I changed my mind.'

'Right, in that case...' She lifted the chairs to return them to their previous spot next to the wall.

'Wait. I'll talk. Don't you want to hear what I have to say?'

'Not really.'

She did. She wanted to find Edwards, though now they couldn't use his statement against him in his trial, and she wanted him to receive a very long sentence. But she wasn't going to stick around if he was going to waste their time.

'Could you unplug the recorder please, DS Fiske?'

'I'll tell you what Phillipa did,' Scott blurted, 'right from the start. If I'm going down for a murder she planned, I don't want her getting away with it. I'm gonna take her with me.'

Shauna asked, 'You'll tell us where to find Phillipa Edwards?'

'Yeah.'

She put down the chairs and sat on one. 'I'm all ears.'

'It was her idea,' said Scott, 'right from the start. She put me up to it, knowing I was going to get out soon. Said she was sick of her boring marriage, boring husband, boring respectable lifestyle. She wanted to cut free, live again, she said. Only she wanted all the money, not have to divvy everything up in a divorce.'

'So you're saying it was Phillipa Edwards' fault you murdered Thomas Edwards,' said Will, sitting down, 'an innocent man who had done you no harm, in cold blood in his own home.'

'Yeah, it was her fault,' replied Scott, though uncertainly, as if even he recognised the ridiculousness of what he was saying.

'Right,' said Shauna. 'Do you know where she is?'

'I'm not sure. I'm thinking about it. I'll get to it in a minute. I have to tell you the rest first.'

Shauna folded her arms.

'We planned it so she wouldn't be there. She would be away at a conference or something like that. She said her husband was a stuffy old fart who always kept to the same routine. She knew exactly what room he would be in at what time of day, and I could use the information to find him and kill him fast, then get out quick. After things had cooled down and she had the inheritance, she was going to sell the house, cash everything in, and me and her would go live somewhere hot and sunny. She reckoned we'd never have to work again.'

'Very romantic,' said Will.

'Where is Phillipa Edwards now, Mr Scott?' Shauna asked.

He wasn't telling them anything they didn't already know or could have guessed. Was he stringing them along, playing for time to allow Edwards to escape? Probably not. He had to know he was heading for a long custodial sentence and he would never see his girlfriend again. Shauna concluded he just wanted attention. That was why he'd come to the station to be interviewed after his mother died. It had been nothing but attention-seeking. And now he was taking the opportunity to state his version of events, too, mitigating his role in the crime in order to boost his self-esteem.

'I'm still thinking,' said Scott.

'Well, let us know when you come up with something,' said Shauna, rising to her feet.

'Do you realise another man could have gone to prison for what you did?' asked Will angrily.

Should she tell him there was no point in appealing to the moral integrity of someone like Scott? Perhaps it was better to allow him to hold onto his faith in humanity while he still could.

'Oh yeah,' Scott chuckled. 'The handkerchief. I was forgetting. That was her idea too. Her shrink friend's husband's wasn't it?' His eyes widened. 'Was that the same cow who came to my house the day my mum died?'

'Tell us about the handkerchief,' said Shauna, sitting down.

Though whatever Scott said was inadmissible in court, they might be able to use the information to question Edwards, assuming they caught her.

'It's pretty simple,' he replied. 'She wanted to throw you pigs off the trail. So she took it out of her friend's washing basket one time when she was visiting her. She was going to plant it before she left for her conference, but after I threw a spanner in the works she shoved it under a chair, quick, before we left. She told you they never had visitors, didn't she? She knew you'd have to ask how it got there.'

Shauna was sick of this evil, disgusting man, sick to the pit of her stomach, but curiosity overcame her desire to get out of his presence.

'Why *did* you 'throw a spanner in the works'? Why didn't you follow the plan and wait until Edwards left before murdering her husband?'

A sly smile crept over his face.

'She's a weird one. Had a thing for me like I've never seen.

Loved me and hated me at the same time. Said we had a *connection*.' He chuckled. 'It's funny. Shrinks think they're so clever but half of them are barmy.' He paused and his expression became serious. 'She was scared of me, I think. She acted like she wanted to control me. So I had to show her who was boss.'

'Oh, you certainly did that, didn't you?' said Will. 'Here you are in a comfortable bed with pretty bracelets on your wrists while your girlfriend is all alone without you for company.'

Scott's lips twisted and he spat, 'Catch the bitch!'

'I'd love to,' said Shauna. 'Tell us how.'

He grumbled, 'I don't fucking know, do I? I don't know where she's gone. I'd tell you if I could.'

'That's exactly what I thought,' said Shauna. 'DS Fiske, I think we've wasted enough time here.'

'One last question,' said Will. 'We know it was you who attacked DI Holt the other night. Did you make the threatening phone call too, or was that Edwards?'

'Phone call? I didn't make any phone call, and neither did Phillipa. Why would we take the risk of you recognising our voices?'

As they left Scott's room, Shauna's mobile rang.

It was Beth at Cambridge Central. 'DI Holt, I was wondering if you heard what happened to Ruth Terrell? It's related to the attack on her daughter the other day.'

She closed her eyes. 'Do I want to know?' The name Terrell conjured up more negative associations than she felt capable of dealing with right now.

'I think you probably do. And I was thinking, as you're at the hospital anyway...'

Shauna listened, and her mouth fell open. She locked gazes with Will. 'And she's here?'

'Yes,' said Beth. 'She was admitted earlier today.'

CHAPTER FORTY-EIGHT

Ruth Terrell looked almost unrecognisable in her hospital bed. Her throat was entirely encased in bandages and a purple-black bruise covered one side of her face. She looked up as Shauna and Will entered her room and her daughter turned around in her chair.

Molly Markson stood up. 'What are you doing here? My mother's been through a terrible ordeal. She can't speak, and she won't be able to answer your questions. She's already sent you the information you need in her email.'

Terrell reached out and touched her hand before writing something on a notepad. Her daughter read the words and said, 'I don't think it's a good idea, Mum. For lots of reasons. You've told the police what you know. It's time to step away now.'

Her mother gave her a pleading look.

'Oh, all right,' Molly said with exasperation. 'But I'm staying here.'

'That's fine,' said Shauna, moving to the other side of the bed. 'We won't be long. I understand this is a difficult time for you all. Dr Terrell, I was very sorry to hear what happened to you.'

She wrote her reply: *Thank you. You seem to have been hurt too.*

Shauna touched her nose self-consciously. 'We had some problems with an arrest.'

'You've arrested someone for the murder?' asked Molly. 'Great!'

'I read your email,' Shauna said to Terrell. 'We have Scott in custody and we're looking for Phillipa Edwards.'

'Phillipa?' exclaimed Molly. 'Mum, you were right.'

'That's why we're here.' Shauna addressed Terrell. 'The information you gave us explains a lot, but I'm puzzled about why you didn't tell us earlier. You were very protective of your friend when we first interviewed you.'

'She didn't know!' blurted Molly. 'She didn't figure it out until later. She wasn't withholding evidence.'

'I'm glad to hear it,' said Shauna.

Terrell was writing again.

My daughter's telling you the truth. It wasn't until I read Phillipa's case notes and heard some reports from her colleagues that I put two and two together. She misled me. I thought she was a good, kind person and my friend. I apologise for my earlier interference. I hope you weren't injured due to something I did.

'No, I wasn't. And, to be fair, even if you had told us your suspicions at the beginning of the investigation, it might not have made any difference. Without any evidence to back it up, your opinion would have been pure speculation. Fortunately for us, Scott and Edwards incriminated themselves. I'd like to know if you have any ideas about where Phillipa Edwards might have gone.'

As Shauna spoke, however, an idea of her own formed in her mind.

Terrell replied, *To be honest, I hesitate to suggest anything. I have no idea how much of what Phillipa told me about her life was lies.*

'I understand,' said Shauna. 'If you do think of something that might be useful, would you let me know?'

'We still have your card,' Molly said. 'If Mum thinks of anything, I'll phone you.'

'Thank you. We'll leave you alone now.'

As she turned to leave, Molly said, 'Thanks for what you said to me at the police station. It's made me feel better and see things in a different light, especially now, after what Daniel did.'

'There's no need to thank me,' replied Shauna. 'It's easy to lose perspective when you're in an abusive relationship. I'm glad what I said helped. I hope you make a speedy recovery, Dr Terrell.'

They left.

Once they were out of the room, Will asked, 'What did you say to the daughter?'

'I just told her the way her husband was behaving wasn't her fault. Sometimes, people need to hear that. They need someone to tell them they aren't to blame.'

They stopped at the lift.

Will said softly, 'You sound like you know what you're talking about.'

'You don't ever give up, do you?' she replied, more sharply than she intended.

He bowed his head. 'Sorry.'

She sighed. 'No, *I'm* sorry. That was rude of me.'

The incident at the lake had set her on edge. Neither of them had mentioned it. There might be a time when they could discuss what they'd gone through, and maybe even a later time when they could joke about it, but not yet.

They awkwardly stared at the lift doors.

'What made you come back to my house after you dropped me off?' she asked. 'If Scott and Edwards hadn't abducted you too...' She swallowed. She wouldn't have been able to cut her ties by herself.

Will replied, 'I noticed Phillipa Edwards' car parked a couple of streets away as I was walking home. It seemed an odd coincidence she would be near your place so early in the morning, so I went back to check you were okay.'

She nodded. 'You're a good detective, DS Fiske.'

'Thank you, DI Holt. You too.' He rocked on his heels. 'We were lucky you had emergency equipment in your car. Most people don't bother, but I'm going to be ordering some online as soon as I can.'

She didn't reply.

After a pause, Will said, 'Shauna, you're right. Your private life is none of my business. I'll stop pushing. But...well, if you ever need someone, I'm here.'

'I appreciate it,' she said as the lift arrived. 'Can *you* drive us to the station? I have a phone call to make.'

———

Road works delayed their return. Stuck in a long queue, they crawled forwards to the temporary lights, only to find themselves in another queue as soon as they were past them. The twenty-minute journey took them over an hour.

In the meantime, Shauna's hunch paid off. She'd made her phone call as soon as they left the hospital, and the Northumberland police immediately went to Phoebe Matthews' house. According to Alfie, who had phoned her with the good news, Phoebe gave up her sister right away, no doubt to Phillipa's chagrin. She'd probably imagined she could bully her sibling into hiding her, as she'd bullied her when she was a little girl.

It was late in the day when they arrived at the station. Alfie, Jasmine, and Connor were still in the incident room, completing paperwork. Shauna had plenty of her own paperwork to do, but with her and Will's testimony and the physical evidence, the case against Scott and Edwards seemed airtight. And even if the Prosecution Service couldn't pin Thomas Edwards' murder on them, assaulting a police officer, kidnapping and attempted murder carried long sentences.

DCI Bryant arrived.

'You heard Northumberland caught Edwards?' he asked.

'Yes, Shauna replied. 'DC Hepplethwaite phoned with the good news while we were on our way back.'

'Excellent work, DI Holt. I knew I was making the right call when I put you in charge.'

'Thank you, sir, but it was a team effort. I had the support of Will and the DCs. Everyone did a fantastic job, especially DC Connor. It was only because he'd managed to track down Phillipa Edwards' family earlier that we were able to apprehend her.'

'Really?' asked Bryant. 'That's good to know. Well done, Connor.'

'Thank you, sir.'

'Yeah, well done,' Jasmine echoed.

Connor flushed and returned his gaze to his computer screen.

'Well done, mate,' said Alfie, somewhat grudgingly.

'We have some sterling officers here at Cambridge Central,' said Bryant. 'I've scheduled a press conference in fifteen minutes to announce the arrests. This case has dragged on too long, setting the whole town on edge. I'd like to calm the public's fears. Only...um...this is rather awkward. Would you mind if DS Fiske sits on the panel?'

'Of course not. Why would I mind?'

'I, er, I think the DCI means instead of you,' said Will, looking embarrassed.

'Oh, you mean because I look like I walked in front of a lorry?' asked Shauna, chuckling.

'I don't want to give the wrong impression,' said Bryant. 'Beaten up officers aren't a good image for us. This isn't downtown Chicago. It's important that the people living in Cambridge have confidence in their police service.'

'Go ahead, Will,' said Shauna. He could take her place at every press conference for all she cared.

When Will and Bryant had gone, she sat in front of her computer.

'We're going down the pub in a few minutes,' said Connor. 'I know it's been a long day and everything, but do you want to come, ma'am? Might be good to unwind.'

'I'm not sure,' she replied, then added, 'Maybe another time.'

'Yeah, leave her alone,' said Jasmine. 'The poor woman wants to rest.'

'I was only asking,' Connor muttered.

It *was* tiredness that was putting Shauna off socialising with her detective constables, not her usual reclusiveness—tiredness, but mostly the need to process the horrible ordeal she and Will had endured. She'd grown to like her little team and feel at home at Cambridge Central.

But she also wanted to think.

It seemed it hadn't been Scott who had phoned her as she'd left the pub weeks ago, and he appeared confident Edwards hadn't either. So who had it been?

Who had threatened her?

She shivered and turned on her computer.

HOLT & FISKE'S STORY CONTINUES IN...

WHEN BLOOD BURNS

For advanced notification of the latest Regan Barry releases,
updates on works in progress and tastes of life in Cambridge,
join the reader group:
https://www.subscribepage.com/reganbarry